"Stop looking at me that way!" she demanded

"What way?" he asked, his brows rising slightly as if in innocence. But Stephen de Burgh was as far from innocent as anyone outside of hell itself could be.

"What is it, Brighid?" Stephen asked in a slumberous, sultry way that made her blood run sluggish and her body grow warm and languorous. But she shook her head, clearing it, and steeled herself against his allure.

"You know exactly what I mean, *my lord*." Brighid spat out the title. "The look you have used upon countless females. The look you no doubt practice before the glass while admiring yourself! The look which is wasted on me! I've told you before, I have no interest in your charms."

Stephen's dark brows rose again. "Oh, really?"

"Yes, *really*," Brighid answered, staring at him stonily.

"Then how do you explain...*the kiss?*"

Praise for Deborah Simmons's previous titles

THE GENTLEMAN THIEF
"…Ms. Simmons has a delightful flair for comedy."
—*Romantic Times Magazine*

ROBBER BRIDE
"…totally captivating, Simmons' powerful characters
do magical things with this excellent plot."
—*Affaire de Coeur*

THE DE BURGH BRIDE
"…wonderful and passionate characters…a thrilling
and dangerous story. 5★s"
—*Affaire de Coeur*

MY LORD DE BURGH
Harlequin Historical #533—October 2000

MY LORD DE BURGH

DEBORAH SIMMONS

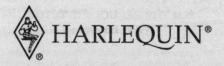

HARLEQUIN®

TORONTO • NEW YORK • LONDON
AMSTERDAM • PARIS • SYDNEY • HAMBURG
STOCKHOLM • ATHENS • TOKYO • MILAN • MADRID
PRAGUE • WARSAW • BUDAPEST • AUCKLAND

ISBN 0-373-29133-7

MY LORD DE BURGH

Copyright © 2000 by Deborah Siegenthal

**Available from Harlequin Historicals and
DEBORAH SIMMONS**

Please address questions and book requests to:
Harlequin Reader Service
U.S.: 3010 Walden Ave., P.O. Box 1325, Buffalo, NY 14269
Canadian: P.O. Box 609, Fort Erie, Ont. L2A 5X3

For my nephew Michael Robert Smith
and his wonderful bride Diana

Prologue

Sometimes destiny needed a little nudge.

Few knew that better than Armes l'Estrange, one of a long line of those well versed in the vagaries of fate. However, she had yet to convince her sister Cafell that their current situation called for such drastic measures. Armes understood Cafell's reluctance, for she, too, rarely used her special gifts, but in this instance what else could they do? Slanting a questioning glance toward Cafell, who was wringing her hands in distress, Armes decided that very little persuasion would be required.

"Surely, there is something we can do," Cafell moaned, her white curls bobbing wildly. "We must act ere Brighid does something rash."

Armes paused to eye her sister askance. "Brighid is never rash," she argued.

Cafell paused to reconsider. "Well, perhaps that is not the right word. Ill-advised then."

"Yes," Armes agreed, with a firm nod. She walked past her sister, effecting an ominous tone. "I fear for her. She is oblivious to danger, for she does not heed the warnings of her l'Estrange blood."

"Yes," Cafell echoed, her agitation growing. "I have

had a chill feeling ever since she received word of her father's death. Didn't I tell you that our dear brother's demise portended great changes?''

"I believe that it was *I* who told *you,*'' Armes said, giving her sister a stern look.

"Oh, let us not quibble,'' Cafell said, waving one small hand in an airy gesture. "I know only that I have suffered a cold in my bones, a premonition that—''

Armes interrupted her impatiently. "We must act,'' she said, her gaze sliding deliberately toward the small cupboard tucked under the round window of the solar.

Cafell followed the direction of Armes's glance, then turned toward her sister with wide blue eyes, her dismay evident. "Oh, no,'' she whispered. "We promised Brighid that we would not!''

"Brighid need never know. Tis for her own good!'' Armes said, frowning at Cafell's guilty expression. Her sister could be counted upon to worry and dither, without accomplishing anything. Already more than a week had passed since Brighid had learned of her father's death, and though the two had never been close, the young woman seemed determined to view her inheritance.

"If we don't do something, Brighid is liable to hire some unsavory companions and hie off for Wales herself,'' Armes warned.

"Oh, no!'' Cafell wailed.

"Oh, yes! She is so stubborn that she might do it,'' Armes said. Stubborn, practical, and single-minded, Brighid was everything her aunts were not. Normally, this sudden impulse to return to the place of her birth would have pleased Armes, but Brighid could hardly undertake such a journey alone, especially considering the troubling political situation that had been brewing in

Wales ever since Edward had marched through in 1277. Although nothing untoward had occurred recently, there were always rumors of dissent among the Welsh princes, and Armes had seen ill omens....

"Well, then, we simply must act," Cafell said, with no little reluctance.

"Very well, then. We are of like mind," Armes concurred, and as their gazes met, they both began to smile. It was in their blood, after all, though Brighid would have them deny their heritage.

Once in agreement, the two moved quickly. While Cafell headed out the door, Armes moved to kneel before the cupboard, unlocking it with a small key she wore on a loop of leather around her neck. From inside, she retrieved an old hand-beaten metal bowl. Reverently, she set it on the worn surface of the cupboard just as Cafell returned with a pail of water. While Armes bolted the door, Cafell poured the liquid into the vessel, nearly to the brim.

Both sisters stepped back as she placed the pail on the floor, and then they leaned forward, white curls and graying locks pressed close when they stared into the water. At first, the surface remained still, then slowly it shifted, sunlight mixing with shadow to take the shape of a reflection that was not their own.

Armes drew in a deep breath. "Who is it?"

"Tis a man!" Cafell answered, clapping her hands together gleefully.

"I can see that," Armes said, squinting at the surface of the liquid. Although her eyes were not as good as they used to be, she wasn't about to admit that to her sister. "But who?"

"Why, he is Brighid's savior, of course. Her knight,

her lord, her own true love!'' Cafell whispered, with a sigh of pleasure.

"Yes, yes," Armes said, impatiently. "But do you recognize him?"

"Oh. Well, let me see," Cafell said. She bent close to blink at the image, only to jerk back with a squeal of delight. "I don't know which one he is, exactly, but look at that hair and those eyes and that...fine form," she said, pointing to the wavering image of a tall, broad-shouldered young man, darkly handsome.

With sudden insight, Armes, too, noticed a familiarity in the features of the likeness that filled the bowl. With a gasp, she glanced toward her sister. Their gazes met, and both spoke at once, their voices rife with awe and excitement.

"Tis a de Burgh!"

Chapter One

Stephen de Burgh was bored.

Leaning back in a heavy, carved chair in Campion's great hall, he reached for a cup of wine, hoping the liquor would either deaden his sense of boredom or enliven the tedium of his existence. Instead, he felt only a sort of dazed warmth, a sensation with which he was usually contented. Lately, however, it was not enough to carry him through the unrelenting repetition of his days.

Turning his head slightly, Stephen surveyed his domain, or rather the domain of his father, the earl of Campion. Around him servants bustled busily through a luxurious hall that was the heart of the modern, well-appointed castle known throughout the land. No war or hunger or pestilence was to be found here, Stephen mused.

Only boredom.

There wasn't even anyone left at Campion on whom he could sharpen his wit—and his caustic tongue. Of his six brothers, all were living or visiting elsewhere, except for Reynold, who wasn't worth tormenting. Instead of rising to the bait as Simon always had, Reynold simply turned stiff-lipped and limped away, an opponent undeserving of his efforts. Which had left precious little to keep Stephen occupied ever since the rest of the family's brief visit at the dawning of the new year.

Ever since his father's marriage to Joy.

Stephen frowned at the memory. Joy had been interesting, at least for a while after her abrupt arrival on Christmas Eve. But then, though little older than himself, she had wed his father, and the two were so besotted that it made a sane man nauseous just to watch them.

A swift glance toward the head of the table verified his opinion, and Stephen told himself that he was both nauseated and bored, when in truth he was seized by an odd, unsettled feeling brought on by his father's nuptials. It was not that he wanted Joy for himself, for she was no more appealing than any other woman.

All right, so maybe he had been a bit insulted by her choice of de Burghs, Stephen admitted with a shrug, but he had gotten over it. Unfortunately, the memory of his rather sorry behavior at the time lingered like a bad taste in his mouth that no amount of liquor could wash away. It distanced him further from his father, while making him even more aware of his own discontent.

Yes, despite the prevailing euphoria at Campion, he was unsatisfied, Stephen acknowledged. In fact, he had been running from his own unhappiness for years, but it was gaining on him, and so he drank more to ward it off and bedded women and mocked his brothers, who had made something of their lives. Recently, however, he had the black feeling that there was nowhere left to go.

The thought snaked through him, forcing him to down the rest of his wine in a hurried motion that little resembled his usual grace. He was faltering; he had been ever since Christmastide. But he had no idea how to save himself from sinking deeper into the morass that was his existence.

So dark were his musings that he didn't even hear Reynold approach until his brother spoke. "Visitors, Father, those who are sworn to Campion and seek an audience with you."

Visitors. Just the thing to enliven a dreary winter afternoon, Stephen decided as he poured himself more wine. Leaning back in his seat, he watched the party enter, led by two older women, a couple of strange-looking characters who held no interest for him. He stifled a yawn, only to pause in awareness as another figure appeared behind them. As always, his senses immediately focused on the younger woman, though he could see little of the heavily cloaked female except a bit of unlined face.

"Welcome," Campion called, and the two approached, though the younger one held back, as if reluctant. *Hmm,* Stephen mused. That was interesting. Usually, the earl's people flocked toward him like fervent disciples. Was she so in awe of the great Campion that she was rooted to her place?

The taller of the two women stepped forward, while the shorter one flitted about in a giddy fashion. "Oh, my lord, my lady," she said breathlessly. "We knew you had wed, of course, my lord, but would tender our congratulations."

"Yours will be a long and fruitful marriage," the taller one intoned, as if possessed of some foresight, and Stephen heard a low murmur from the nearby servants. He caught the mention of mystical powers, but dismissed the whispers with a slight smile of amusement. Although most of the villeins were a superstitious lot, Stephen believed in nothing less tangible than good wine and a soft bed. Grinning at the thought, he refilled his cup and raised it in a silent salutation to both.

"Thank you, Mistress l'Estrange," Campion was saying.

"Armes, my lord," she said.

"Please take a seat and rest yourselves after your journey," Joy said, the sound of her welcome jarring to Stephen's ears. Would he ever grow used to her presence as lady of the castle? Campion's household had long been the province of men, and he was growing too old for such changes.

"Thank you, my lady," Armes said. "But my sister Cafell and I would speak to you, if we may, on a most pressing matter."

"Oh, my, yes! We simply cannot rest until they—that is, until *it* is settled," Cafell said. When she spoke, her gaze darted round the hall, as if in search of something, until it landed squarely on Stephen. Her rather anxious expression was replaced by an ecstatic smile that startled him. Although well used to admiring glances from females, he was not expecting such a warm version from a woman of this one's years. Now, if the younger lady would look his way…

"By all means, speak, mistress, and I will do all within my power to aid you," Campion said.

"Thank you, my lord," Armes said, with a grateful nod. "As you know, we have been living on a small holding at the edge of your lands for some time now."

"Oh, yes, years," Cafell agreed, happily. "Indeed, we have been there since our uncle died. You might remember him—"

Before Cafell could continue, Armes cut in. "No matter. We have been grateful for your protection as our liege lord and the peace that has always prevailed over our home.''

"Is someone threatening you?'' Campion asked, surprise evident in his tone, if not his calm countenance.

"Certainly not,'' Armes said.

"Oh, my, no. Tis a, uh, personal problem that besets us,'' Cafell said. Again, she slid a glance toward Stephen, and his boredom abruptly vanished. With a frown, he roused himself to alertness and began racking his brain for the identities of the women who had shared his favors of late. Surreptitiously, he studied the younger female again, but what little he could see of her face did nothing to jog his memory.

Stephen wasn't surprised, for his lovely partners tended to shift together in his mind, with few leaving a lasting impression. For the most part, they were so pleased by his attentions, they sought nothing more than the satisfaction to be had in his bed. However, this wouldn't be the first time some enterprising young woman had tried to ensnare him into vows.

Obviously, these daft old ladies didn't realize that he left the marrying to his brothers. Of course, his father didn't approve, but since none of his dalliances bore tangible fruit in the form of progeny, Stephen saw no reason to change his ways.

And he was not about to now, either, he swore as he eyed the cloaked young woman. Long ago, he had discovered that while he could pride himself on his amatory skills, he would add no heirs to the family through his efforts. The knowledge had stopped grating upon him years past and now gave him the freedom to enjoy himself fully. Let his brothers reproduce as they wont, he told himself, with their new wives and their homes and their families....

Lifting his cup, Stephen swallowed a deep draught of wine and dismissed such thoughts. He needed his wits about him, lest these silly females constitute a threat to his bachelor existence. Homes and families aside, the very notion of joining his more staid brothers in the state of matrimony made him shudder.

"Although the matter does not involve you directly—" Cafell began with a sly smile only to be cut off, once more, by a sharp glance from her more forceful sibling.

"Still," Armes said, "we would welcome any advice that you, in your great wisdom, could give us. Indeed, we came especially to seek your counsel."

"Go on," the earl said, while Stephen listened warily. If his nuptials were their goal, the two old ladies were wise to approach Campion rather than himself. His father, Stephen had long suspected, suffered from an excess of honor.

"'Tis our brother Drywsone," Armes said. "He has passed away, leaving his property in Wales to his daughter, our niece. Come forward, Brighid," she urged.

Stephen's attention returned to the young woman who moved but little. Was she slow, or did she think her show of trepidation would gain Campion's sympathy? Surely, she would not pretend to carry a child, or to foist another man's get upon him? he wondered, his hold upon his cup tightening.

"Naturally, Brighid would like to view her inheritance," Armes said, gesturing for the girl to join her.

"She was fostered to us early on and has not seen her birthplace in many years," Cafell confided.

"Although we understand Brighid's wishes, we are getting on in age and hesitate to attempt such a journey," Armes explained. "Yet we do not wish Brighid to go alone, especially when it was only five years ago that the king asserted his authority there,'' she said, using a rather mild expression for the war that had brought down a Welsh bid for independence.

But who was Stephen to dispute her words? He found himself grinning in reckless relief at the old woman's story. As interesting as a row over some forgotten dalliance might be, he was more than happy to learn that the ''personal'' matter in question had nothing to do with him after all. Pouring himself more wine, Stephen took a long, pleasurable drink and let his attention drift. Warmth coursed through him while he listened vaguely to his father's speech, his interest in the guests flagging.

''I can understand your concern,'' Campion said. ''Although Edward has his holdings firmly in hand, the marches can be dangerous. Perhaps, you would be more at ease if your niece had an escort.''

''Oh, that would be wonderful!'' the giddy one said, practically clapping her hands with glee, and Stephen nearly rolled his eyes at Reynold. These two had to be the silliest women in all of creation, and the sooner they hied off to Wales, or whatever godforsaken place they were headed, the better. He lounged in his chair, wondering when he could gracefully make his escape from their company.

''We would be very grateful, my lord,'' Armes said. ''I'm certain that the protection of the de Burgh name would assure my niece of a safe journey. But we can hardly expect *you* to perform such a great service for us.''

''Oh, no!'' Cafell exclaimed. ''Not with your recent marriage and all.''

Stephen stifled a snort. By faith, these two were daft, if they thought the earl himself would accompany them.

They'd be lucky to get a few outriders, and grateful they should be for their lord's largesse.

"No," Stephen heard Campion say. "But I can send someone in my stead who will do just as well for you. Indeed, a younger man would better undertake such a journey and provide more protection for you."

Stephen barely listened to the breathless protestations of Campion's subjects, eager to flatter their lord's vanity. He had heard all of it before, and nothing bored him more than a recitation of his father's noble qualities. He stifled a yawn and sank lower in his seat.

"Thank you, mistresses," Campion said. "But I am certain that you will be content with my choice, for surely you agree that there are no finer knights in my household than my own sons."

It took Stephen a full minute to grasp the implications of his father's words, and when he did, he nearly choked on his wine as he jerked upright. Campion couldn't be serious! Why would he send a de Burgh on an errand of such small significance? To impress a pair of witless old women and their equally witless ward? Let the girl and her idiot aunts be happy with a guard, freely given, and the provisions necessary to feed them!

Stephen's gaze swiveled toward his father in horror, but Campion was busily playing the omnipotent host, smiling and nodding at the two women while steadfastly ignoring his own progeny. That small slight sent a sense of unease creeping over Stephen, for he knew that of the earl's seven sons, only he and Reynold were available for such an unpleasant chore. And Campion would not send Reynold riding in winter because of his bad leg, though, personally, Stephen thought his brother as able as anyone else.

Stephen's dismay grew when Campion finally looked

at him, his eyes revealing nothing of his thoughts, but his mouth firmly set. The earl always had a reason for his actions, although the logic behind this assignment escaped Stephen. Was this punishment for his recent churlish behavior? Or did his father simply want to rid the castle of his annoying presence, the better to enjoy his new bride? Stephen forced his mouth into an accommodating smile even as he frantically sought a way to evade the task.

"Stephen?" Campion said.

"Aye?"

"You will act in my place." It was an order, couched in the earl's gentle voice, but an order nonetheless, and Stephen called upon all his guile to elude it.

"Yes, father," he said in a properly agreeable tone. "But perhaps twould be better if we wait until spring when the lady would find it more comfortable weather in which to travel," Stephen suggested. He flashed his best smile at the two aunts, who appeared to be thrown into confusion by his words. What had happened to their giddy grins and admiring glances?

"I would go as soon as possible." The unexpected declaration rang out in the brief silence, and Stephen swung toward the speaker in surprise. The mysterious Brighid had finally stepped from the shadows, her slight shoulders squared. *Now she decides to make herself known,* Stephen thought, with no little irritation. She threw back her hood to reveal a rather plain, tight-lipped creature, whose features were hardened by resolve.

Stephen shuddered. He, for one, liked biddable women—especially those who fell all over themselves to do *his* bidding. He had suffered his fill of the other kind with the wives of his brothers. Geoffrey was married to a termagant who would as soon slit your gullet as talk at you, while Simon's bride, though attractive enough, was some kind of sword-wielding amazon. Even Marion, a once mild, sisterly sort, had developed a bossy, stubborn streak since her marriage to Dunstan. The worst of their sex, Stephen thought, and from the look on this female's face, she was just as intractable as the rest of them.

"I appreciate your kind offer of escort, but I would prefer to go now rather than wait, especially since precious time has already been spent in our journey here," she said, making Stephen's brows inch upward. Did she actually refer to her trip to Campion as a waste of time? Stephen silently urged her to keep talking, for further speech like that would only alienate her proud benefactor, while relieving himself of an onerous duty.

Unfortunately, the aunts stepped in to smooth things over, blaming Brighid's rash tongue on her distress over her father's death. While they prattled on, Stephen studied the young woman with increasing distaste. Although he had been known to bestir himself for a comely female, she did not meet his discerning standards.

Besides her unyielding expression, Mistress Brighid wore her hair pulled up tightly in a wimple that completely covered it, while giving her face a pinched appearance. Her body, too, was well hidden, but from the looks of it, there was little enough there to entice a man. Stephen liked his women to be womanly—soft and well-rounded and as sweet-smelling as possible. From the shape of her cloak, nothing of the sort lingered beneath Mistress Brighid's gown.

Dismissing her with a glance, Stephen turned back to his father, who was calmly listening to the babbling of the two old women with his usual patience. Stephen decided it was time to assert himself. "But, Father, this has been the worst winter in living memory, and the roads…'' he began, only to shrug as if to admit that nature was beyond his control. ''Wouldn't it be wiser to wait awhile, at least?'' he asked in his most persuasive manner. *At least until Robin or Nicholas return. Or Brighid the rigid takes off on her own. Or I find some other business that carries me away from Campion until the whole party is gone.*

Stephen gazed at his father with innocent expectation, but Campion was not to be fooled. Obviously, his mind was made up, and Stephen could not sway him. It was just like the earl to send him away for his own good, but Stephen could see no advantage to this errand. Whether punishment or test, it was a loathsome duty he ill deserved.

''I have faith in your ability to manage the roads, which should be cold yet and hard packed with winter,'' Campion said mildly.

Or impassable with snow or washed out by early rains, Stephen thought. But he kept the observation to himself while his mind swiftly sought another excuse.

''Still, perhaps we should send for Dunstan. He fought with Edward in Wales and would know that country well, as I do not,'' Stephen explained, only to blink, startled, as a muffled shriek came from the one called Cafell.

''Oh, no! It must be him,'' she said, pointing a bony finger his way, and Stephen felt the hairs rise on the back of his neck. Suddenly, the whispers that had amused him earlier did not seem quite so funny, even though he didn't believe in any of that mystical nonsense.

''And Stephen it shall be,'' Campion said. Standing with a beneficent smile, he called for refreshments to be brought for the guests, thereby dismissing Stephen's protests, just as if he had never spoken. *Just as his father always dismissed him.*

Veering away from that painful train of thought, Stephen turned his head to glare at the source of his troubles only to pause in surprise, for she was glaring right back at him. Accounted the most handsome of all the de Burgh brothers, Stephen knew that there were few females of any age who did not appreciate his charms. What ailed this Brighid?

Stephen relaxed his stare as he realized that he had not really exerted himself on her behalf. With consummate skill, he conjured an impression of warmth in his gaze, while he flashed her one of his most devastating grins. Lifting his brows slightly, he raised his cup, as if to acknowledge her victory. Then he paused, waiting for the inevitable reaction: either the blush and stammer of shyness or the more eloquent response of a bolder woman.

Stephen saw neither. In fact, not a flicker of response did he note. If anything, Mistress Brighid stiffened further, as though in distaste, before she glanced away from him entirely. Stunned, Stephen slumped back in his seat. Her reaction certainly was not that of a grateful traveler to her escort. And he, for one, was utterly bewildered by her behavior.

Was she married? No, for then her husband would have saved him this onerous trip, and besides, Stephen had known many a married woman who was eager for a dalliance. Perhaps she was smitten with someone else. His predatory instincts rose to the fore, and he wondered just how hard it would be to eliminate a former lover from her memory.

Lounging casually in his chair, Stephen watched

Brighid in a manner that was long honed and most successful. Although Reynold had once likened it to a wolf stalking its prey, the comparison had not deterred Stephen. He focused himself solely upon Brighid, taking careful notice of every detail.

For her part, the object of his interest appeared as rigid as ever, her back straight as she took her place at the table. She kept her attention on her aunts, as if expecting one of them to sprout horns at any moment, a fear not as far-fetched as he once might of thought, Stephen mused, smiling at his own jest.

He studied her critically, his mouth curving into a frown as he drew his own conclusions. She was no prettier than he first thought her, nor any more charming, certainly, but part of her unattractiveness lay in the way she dressed. In contrast to her aunts' bright clothing, she wore drab gray that sucked the life from her face. As a result, she looked waxy and ashen, though what little skin he could see was unmarked. He wondered if she hid so much of herself for a reason, perhaps because of scars, or whether her staid demeanor was responsible. Oddly enough, Stephen found himself curious as to what lay beneath her gown and what could be done to relieve her of it.

And slowly, against all odds, he felt his sluggish blood stir at the challenge the grim young woman presented. She kept to herself, her gestures few, her manner off-putting, as though she wanted none to approach her, and though unappealing, her behavior was somehow intriguing. Stephen could think of few women, besides his stepmother, who had refused him, and that…well, that had been due to highly unusual circumstances. This apparent rebuff from Brighid l'Estrange, who seemed to distance herself from all comers, was something else entirely.

Was she really indifferent to him? Stephen itched to test her.

Not only would the effort entertain him, but should he woo her successfully, his reward would be more than a balm to his pride. Yes, indeed, for it would be easy to coax her into delaying her journey *or abandoning it entirely.* Releasing a low sigh of relief that came with a victory well-assured, Stephen smiled as he decided to put the full measure of his charms to work upon the visitor.

Poor Mistress Brighid had no idea what was in store for her.

Chapter Two

Brighid had no idea how she had ended up at elegant Campion Castle, trying to appear grateful for an offer of escort that only dismayed her. Somehow her plan to return to Wales had taken her here instead, complicating an already difficult matter. It was all her aunts' doing, of course. When they suggested seeking the earl's advice, Brighid had seen no reason to bother such a famous personage with her petty problems, but they had been adamant.

Too adamant. Although she could not prove it, Brighid suspected something besides simple concern for her safety lay behind this visit, and she watched Cafell and Armes with an anxious eye. Although through her efforts their household had taken on a most conventional aspect, the two women were still unpredictable. Who knew when they might suddenly act in a wholly inappropriate manner?

Such as foreseeing a long marriage for the earl, Brighid thought, nearly wincing at the memory. She had heard the whispers that followed that announcement, too, although she had resolutely ignored them. For years, she had worked to dispel the odd notions about her aunts, but the rumors stubbornly persisted, as if defying all her efforts.

Why should she be surprised? It seemed as though she had spent her entire life seeking some semblance of normalcy, while living down the questionable heritage of her family. Although Brighid loved her aunts and was grateful to have a home with them, often she had envied the burgher's daughter her ordinary existence. Sometimes, she had wished to exchange her place with anyone, even the poorer village women who went about their business without the wary looks that were cast at Brighid, for no other reason than that she was a l'Estrange.

It didn't matter that her aunts had agreed to give up the practices that had earned them their unique reputation. The gossip continued, and, obviously, it had traveled as far away as Campion. Brighid frowned. Although she heard no threats among the talk, she remained wary, for she knew that the same villeins who came begging for help one day could revile and accuse with their next breath.

It had been a mistake to come, Brighid realized, but she had thought to appease her aunts before leaving for Wales. She had never dreamed that the earl of Campion would take such an interest in women who were the most minor of landholders. She had expected him, at the most, to tender some comforting counsel of little real worth, but to give her an escort? And to send one of his sons along?

Everyone knew of them, of course, this family of knights, each one larger and stronger than the next. Tales abounded of their exploits, although Brighid suspected many had been so embellished that all measure of truth was lost in the telling. But whether man or myth, Brighid wanted no part of any of Campion's sons. A few name-less, faceless soldiers would suit her needs far better than a de Burgh, who would make their route known to all as they passed.

Indeed, the de Burghs were too big, too handsome, too famous to ever go unnoticed, and so any of them would serve her ill. But to be stuck with Stephen! Of the seven brothers, gossip ran most rampant about this one. Unlike his siblings, who won lands and fought wars and routed brigands, Stephen seemed to have garnered his reputation solely by separating pretty maidens from their innocence.

Oh, people spoke of his charm and his handsome vis-age, but Brighid had never been impressed with such spurious gifts. And, now she could see all too clearly that Stephen de Burgh was little more than a drunken sot, too lazy to do his father's bidding. He would be no use to her! Indeed, he would surely be a hindrance, for she needed to travel swift and sure, with no time for dalliances with comely maids or stops at alehouses.

It was as if fate were out to bespoil all her well-laid plans, Brighid mused with some annoyance. But she re-fused to let it. Schooling herself to ignore all such por-tents, she had wrested control of her life from a capri-cious providence, and she would not give it up now. Too much was at stake. The thought set her mind more firmly on her task, and she felt a new measure of resolve course through her.

She was going to Wales, and an escort would be wel-come, except for Stephen. If she could only think of some way in which to leave him behind…. Sending a considering glance toward her host, Brighid wondered if she could reason with the earl, should she dare speak with the great man.

"Mistress?" The whisper was spoken so close to her ear that Brighid felt it as a caress, warm and distracting, upon her neck, rather than heard it. The odd sensation made her whirl her head sharply to find its source, and she drew in a startled draught of air when she came face-to-face with Stephen de Burgh.

Brighid stared, and it was no wonder, for he was incredibly handsome when viewed this closely. *Unbelievably handsome.* He was like some kind of fallen angel, a dark dream of paradise come to earth in the guise of a mortal. And yet, beguiling as he was, Brighid recognized that this man had more in common with the devil than a higher being. Her dazed mind registered the fact that he was much too near, and she leaned back, away from him.

Immediately, she could breathe more freely, and she did so, even as she likened the force of his appeal to a spell he cast upon unsuspecting females. *What would her family have made of that?* she wondered, the absurd notion oddly sobering. Although she swiftly dismissed the idea of so potent an allure, her mistrust remained.

Ever practical, Brighid knew she was not the sort of woman to inspire the passionate hunger for which Stephen was famous, so either he had an alternative motive for his impromptu display or he practiced his skills on every woman he met, just to keep them honed and ready. Suspicion made her narrow her gaze. What was he up to?

Brighid had no time to form a guess as Stephen gracefully took a seat beside her on the bench, his hard thigh brushing against hers with a familiarity that both annoyed her and made her body heat and throb. *What manner of magic was this?*

"Mistress," Stephen murmured. His deep voice was

seductive, a rasping sound that made Brighid think of linen moving against linen, smooth yet abrading. She blinked, bemused by images of sheets and a bed, its coverings tousled, its pillows scattered. With a shake of her head, she dismissed them, as she did any unwelcome visions. No doubt, Stephen de Burgh made every woman with a heartbeat think of such things, Brighid concluded, pursing her lips in disgust. His reputation obviously was well earned.

And it was not just his voice. He was tall, as was his brother, his shoulders wide, his body muscular, but not overly so. Among a family of handsome knights, she could see why he was accounted the most attractive. His features were even and pleasing, his dark hair falling thick and sleek to his shoulders, and his eyes... Brighid's pulse skittered, for they were a rich, seductive brown, hinting of secrets unfolding in dim chambers, sinful and compelling, while his lips were sensually curved and inviting. All in all, Stephen de Burgh reeked of wicked delights.

Luckily, Brighid wasn't interested.

"Yes?" she said. "Is there something you wanted?"

At her last word, Stephen smiled, a slow, provocative process so obviously designed to entice that Brighid wondered if he practiced before a mirror. The mannered grin grated on her, for she had no time for this foolishness! She wanted to be rid of the man, not suffer his indulgent displays.

"I *wanted*," he began, and despite herself, Brighid felt a shiver of reaction. What was it about his speech that made her want to close her eyes and let each syllable he uttered wrap itself around her? "Rather, I *wished* only to introduce myself to you, Mistress Brighid, to greet you properly, since I am to be your *escort*."

Although the words were laced with all sorts of illicit meanings, Stephen de Burgh's guise was so patently false that Brighid told herself she was little affected. Were these the wiles for which he was so infamous? Yes, he possessed a handsome face and form, along with a distinctive voice and a certain, rather primitive, allure. But it was like a glossy, rich design that covered an empty coffer. Brighid could only conclude that the maidens who had earned him his reputation were either extremely gullible or blind to all but the most superficial enticements.

When he looked as though he would say more, Brighid pushed away from the table. "Don't bother," she advised him. For some strange reason, disappointment stung her, though she had known immediately that Stephen de Burgh would be of no use to her. He was no more or less than what he was, and how he, alone, of his brothers had come to nothing was certainly no concern of hers.

"What?" Stephen eyed her with genuine puzzlement, and Brighid thought, once again, how truly beautiful he would be, if he were not so busy playing himself. As it was, he was too smooth, too fraudulent and too filled with drink to disguise the fact that this beautifully wrapped gift held nothing inside.

"You needn't bother wasting your time on me," Brighid said in dismissal.

Watching her closely, Stephen rested one hand on his chin while he leisurely perused her form. "Oh, really?" he asked, and the low rasp of his words sent a nerve fluttering somewhere in Brighid's body. But the effect was ruined by the smoldering look he gave her under thick, lowered lashes—a look that, for all its heat, never reached the depths of his dark-brown eyes, glazed already this day with the effects of too much wine.

When he lifted his dark brows as if in wicked query, Brighid could no longer contain herself. Loosing a snort of disgust, she leaned close. "I do believe you've missed your calling," she observed. "You ought to have been a troubadour."

As Stephen stared at her blankly, Brighid began to rise. "Please, excuse me, but I have some business with your father."

"But—" Apparently, Stephen was not ready to let her go, for he surged to his feet at the same time that she moved forward, and her head made contact against his hard form.

"Oh, I beg your pardon," Brighid said, as she looked up at his startled expression. He was clutching his mouth in an odd fashion, his dark eyes glinting, but she refused to be distracted any further by Stephen de Burgh.

"I really must go," she said. Brushing past him, Brighid turned her thoughts toward his father. Ignoring Stephen, who was gaping after her, she decided she must ask the earl to keep his errant son at home, without managing to insult him in the bargain. It would require some finesse, a skill that she was often accused of lacking, but she was determined.

Something about Stephen de Burgh made Brighid uneasy, and it involved more than the liability he would represent on the road. Her wariness toward him ran deep and primal, an instinct perhaps, and though she usually ignored such signs, all her observations about him only supported her feeling that the sooner she was away from the man the better off she would be.

At the head of the high table, Armes was chatting volubly to both the lord and his lady, but Brighid managed to step close enough to the earl's chair to catch his attention. He was an imposing man when viewed this closely, and she drew in a deep breath to bolster her resolve.

It was not necessary. When the earl turned his gaze upon her, Brighid knew a jolt of awareness, an impression of rightness that flooded her entire being. The sensation surprised her, for she had long suppressed such unwelcome feelings, and immediately, she armed herself against them. Still, some trace must have lingered, for Brighid was at ease with this man, who seemed more like a father than a powerful lord, *more like a father than her own.* The notion sent her wandering thoughts abruptly back to the task at hand.

"If I may have a private word with you, my lord?" Brighid asked, glancing toward where her aunts were seated not far away. At Campion's nod, she stepped closer.

"My lord," Brighid began. "I am most grateful for your gracious generosity. Never had I expected that someone of your standing would take an interest in one such as I." She paused to note, with some surprise, that Campion's lips twitched slightly, as if he were amused by her display of gratitude.

"And yet?" he prompted.

"I beg your pardon?" Brighid asked.

"And yet," Campion repeated. "Something disturbs you about the arrangement. Please, speak freely."

His insight ought to have disturbed her, but the gentleness in his gaze was so reassuring that Brighid did not hesitate. Drawing a deep breath, she blurted out her misgivings.

"It's your son, my lord. Truly, I am most grateful for an escort, but I assure you that a few soldiers, some outriders, if you will, are entirely sufficient, indeed, more than sufficient for my needs. Your son doesn't have to come along,'' Brighid said.

Clasping her hands together, she waited expectantly, while Campion exchanged a swift, telling look with his young wife. When he turned back to Brighid, his expression was unreadable, but he smiled ruefully. ''I assure you, my dear, that you need not fear Stephen.''

''Oh, I'm not afraid of him,'' Brighid protested, for she could not imagine a less likely prospect than her cowering in terror from the drunken charmer. ''I am only concerned that he'll be more of a hindrance than a help.'' She stopped, wary of her own frankness, only to hear Lady Campion erupt into a sudden fit of coughing.

Alarmed, Brighid glanced toward the earl, expecting to face his anger, but instead he gave her a long, assessing look that made her shift her gaze away. Although she had disdained such abilities all her life, Brighid had the eerie feeling that this man saw far more than she wanted to reveal. Yet, surely it was absurd to imagine that this family of forthright knights might possess any unique senses. Dismissing the notion, Brighid lifted her chin once more to meet Campion's inquiry.

''As I'm certain you are aware, people are not always what they seem,'' the earl said, his words refuting her own thoughts so well that Brighid struggled to hide her surprise. And just as if he knew her reaction, he smiled gently. ''Stephen, too, is more than he appears.''

''I am sure you are right, my lord,'' Brighid hedged. ''But tis not really necessary for him to accompany me.''

''And yet, your aunts are most insistent upon Stephen.'' The words, though softly spoken, jarred Brighid from her sense of ease, and she stiffened.

''I don't know what you've heard about my aunts, my

lord, but I assure you they possess no abilities beyond that of any other women," Brighid replied.

Campion smiled, but said nothing, and in his silence, Brighid saw his wisdom. He would not argue with her, and since she had no wish to belabor the subject, she decided to try a different track. Despite his seeming agreement, Stephen's prevarication had made his reluctance to escort her obvious, at least to Brighid, and so she baldly stated the fact. "He does not want to go," she said.

Unfortunately, Campion was not ruffled by the truth of her statement. "Perhaps," he conceded, with an inclination of his head. "But Stephen does not always know what is best for him."

When Brighid would have seized upon his words to prove her point, Campion stayed her with a glance. "He needs to get away, to take on a task outside of his usual ventures, to face a new challenge." The earl leaned forward. "Indeed, I would thank you, mistress, for presenting him with this responsibility, which will suit him well. And I wish you both a most successful journey."

With that cryptic comment, Campion gestured her toward an empty chair, and Brighid knew that no matter how graciously it was couched, she had been dismissed, along with her protests about Stephen. Whatever his reasons, the earl would not relent, and she was to be saddled with his son.

Although Brighid tried to accept her defeat gracefully, the thought of suffering that useless rogue made her mouth tighten in annoyance. Yet she had done all that she could—unless she applied to Stephen himself. His reluctance, disguised as concern for the weather and other trivialities, had been readily apparent to her discerning eye. Perhaps, she could convince him to stay behind....

Unfortunately, when Brighid glanced toward where she had last seen him, Stephen was not there. And a quick perusal of the tables revealed his brother, but no sign of Stephen. Perhaps he had fled, rather than do his duty, Brighid mused. Although contemptuous of such a course, she found herself wishing that he would escape his father's dictate by whatever means necessary.

Perhaps he simply needed a little nudge.

Slipping from the hall, Stephen lifted a finger to gingerly test his split lip. It still stung like the devil, as did his recent encounter with the woman responsible. He shook his head slightly, only to halt as his mouth throbbed in painful counterpoint. He simply couldn't understand it. He had put forth all of his charm and his most artful manners, and she had fled like a frightened fawn.

Only she hadn't seemed frightened. On the contrary, Brighid l'Estrange appeared to possess the fortitude of a prize bull, along with a personality to match. But there was no denying that she had run off—straight to his father. And, still smarting from Joy's preference, Stephen had seen enough. Let her admire Campion all she will, it mattered not to him.

After all, it was not as though the wench really interested him, he told himself, even if her eyes were the most unusual shade of green he had ever beheld. Dunstan's eyes were green, marking him unique among the de Burgh brood, but his were a dark color, while Mistress Brighid's were a strange hue, like the shifting depths of the ocean.

Witch's eyes. The thought came to Stephen suddenly,

and he snorted. All those whispers about mystical powers had him imagining things, and he shrugged away the notion as he moved down the steps. Instead of wasting his charm on a plain, tight-lipped stranger enamored of Campion's power, Stephen planned to seek out the comfort of a more amenable woman.

He had been pursuing a certain widow, and he wondered if the news that he was leaving on the morrow might prompt an especially pleasing parting gift. Stephen smiled, but the movement only reminded him of his sore lip. Moving it tentatively, he decided he would have to be creative tonight. The stimulating thought spurred his steps, but the sound of a door opening behind him drew him up short. The wine had not dulled his senses so much that he would ignore a possible threat, and Stephen turned swiftly only to grunt in dismay at the sight of a small, plump woman he recognized as one of the l'Estranges. Was it Cafell?

"Oh! I'm so glad I caught you," she said, hurrying toward him before Stephen could disappear into the shadows gathering in the bailey. "It is *you*, isn't it?" she asked, pausing to squint up at him with an odd expression.

"That depends," Stephen muttered. *On what you want,* he did not add, cursing himself for lingering near the entrance to the hall.

"Oh, my, you are teasing me! It *is* you, of course! I saw it at once, but I just wanted to make sure after... How is your lip? Here, let me see," she chided, lifting her fingers to inspect his mouth, just as though he were a stallion she was considering for purchase. *Obviously, the whole family was insane.*

When Stephen jerked his head away, she made a clucking sound that reminded him of an old hen. "You should put some betony on it. That would help," she said. "Shall I fetch a bit for you? I believe I have some among my things, but you mustn't tell Brighid, for she frowns upon our practice of the healing arts."

Stephen shook his head emphatically, although it pained him, for the thought of this woman tending his wound inspired nothing except horror. "No, thank you. I'll just—"

"Of course, I'm certain Brighid did not intend to hurt you in any way," Cafell continued. Stephen opened his mouth to protest that he was definitely not *hurt,* but the woman did not give him a chance to speak. "You must forgive her, you see, for she has so very much on her mind of late! Why, she has no idea that you..." Cafell faltered, giving him a nervous smile that made her look oddly guilty. "But our dear Brighid is not normally clumsy. Indeed, she is one of the most graceful of women. Surely you have noticed?"

"Yes, I could see that smacking me with her head required great agility," Stephen muttered, but his caustic comment was lost on the aunt.

"Oh, my, such a wit you are!" she said, playfully striking him on the arm.

What was it with these l'Estrange women, some in-bred proclivity toward violence?

"Our Brighid is witty, too, a very clever girl. She learned to study the ancient texts at a young age and has much lore at her disposal, although she disdains to use it," Cafell said, with a sigh.

"She is a proud girl, you know, and has become so practical. Why, I don't know how we shall fend for ourselves in her absence, for she runs the household so well. Tis a model of decorum and efficiency, thanks to her efforts! You'll find she is eminently capable," Cafell said, smiling as though sharing some great confidence with him.

Before Stephen could protest, she went on and on…and on, extolling the so-called virtues possessed by her niece, until his eyes began to glaze over. And everything she said only confirmed his own impression that Mistress Brighid represented everything he disliked. Practical, responsible, and efficient were not descriptions that would win his favor, but could only foster his contempt—a response that the grim Brighid had already garnered on her own.

Finally, when the voluble Cafell paused to draw a breath, Stephen removed her hand from his arm. "I must go. You see, I have an engagement to keep with a woman who is neither sensible nor practical. And thank God for it," he muttered, pleased to see that he had finally stunned the old woman speechless.

"Oh, my, no! That won't do at all," she called after him, once she had recovered herself. But by that time Stephen was already moving at a decent pace toward the stables. "Go on, then, but you've no choice, you see. Tis your destiny." The eerily prophetic words came to him faintly from across the bailey, but Stephen shrugged them off.

His destiny, he thought sourly, was to put up with the likes of Cafell and her sister, and, worse yet, her niece.

Chapter Three

Brighid rushed out to the bailey, frantically seeking the tall figure of Stephen de Burgh among those preparing for the journey to Wales, but he was nowhere to be seen, and she didn't know whether to be relieved or worried. A quick glance toward Campion showed the earl perfectly at ease as he chose six outriders from among his soldiers, apparently unconcerned that the man who was to lead them was missing—and had been missing since yesterday eve.

Brighid knew all too well of his absence, for she had spent fruitless hours searching for him, in the hope of trying to convince him to stay behind. But how was she to reason with him when he could not be found? Last night everyone she questioned regarding his whereabouts either winked or coughed or turned red in the face, so she assumed he was dallying with some maid, but he had to return at some point, didn't he?

Brighid had waited up long past the time she usually sought her rest, kicking her heels in the hall until the servants took their beds, to no avail. Her hours awake had made her sleep late this morning, a further annoyance, for she made it her business always to be prompt.

Instead, she had hurriedly packed her chest and raced out of doors, certain that she would have a chance to speak with Stephen at last, only to face further frustration.

Scanning the assemblage intently, Brighid saw Campion nod approvingly at the servants who were loading the stores, then turn and head back into the hall, leaving Reynold to oversee the final work. She frowned, for normally she would have been the one to organize the trip. And although grateful for the escort, she nonetheless chafed at being relegated to the position of traveler, instead of leader. What if something important was forgotten? Brighid was not accustomed to the ways of men and had little faith in their ability to prepare. What if...

Her thoughts were broken off by the sound of her aunt Cafell's squeal of delight. "There you are, dear! Why, we were beginning to wonder what was keeping you," she said, giving Brighid a sly wink.

Having long ago learned to live with her aunts' often incomprehensible behavior, Brighid didn't even bother to interpret Cafell's odd gesture, for she had no time for such nonsense this morning. "Why didn't you wake me?" she asked, with no little exasperation.

Armes gave her sister a quelling glance and stepped forward. "We thought you could use the rest, my dear. After all, you have a long and tiresome journey ahead of you."

"And you must take care of yourself," Cafell added, grinning like the cat that had swallowed the cream.

Brighid's eyes narrowed. "What are you two up to?" she asked, for she could easily envision her aunts planning all manner of mischief in anticipation of her absence.

"Why, nothing," Cafell said, her expression guileless,

but she was not adept at dissimulating and Brighid had learned to read her well over the years. Her aunt was hiding something. Brighid frowned as she slid a glance toward the train. Time was pressing, and still she had yet to see Stephen. Although his lateness could signal his intention to abandon his task entirely, he might very well appear at any moment. She had no time to dally.

"Promise me that you will behave while I am away," Brighid said, reaching out to clasp Cafell's hands.

"Why, of course, dear," her aunt said, as if offended by the very suggestion.

"Promise me," Brighid repeated. "Nothing unusual, no predictions, no—" she lowered her voice to a hushed whisper "—bowls."

"We promise," Armes said. "Don't we, sister?"

"Of course. I promise, dear," Cafell said. "But, look! I have something for you, not that you need any aids, of course," she said, fumbling around in her cloak. "Ah, here it is!" Smiling happily, she pressed something hard into Brighid's hand.

Opening her fingers, Brighid looked down only to frown in dismay at the object in her palm. "Amethyst," she said. For a long moment, she stared at the stone before realizing its significance: it was a ward against drunkenness. Brighid's head jerked upward. "This is just the sort of thing you promised not to—"

Cafell cut her off as she leaned close. "Try to get him to wear it, dear," she advised, giving Brighid a pat on the arm.

"This *rock* is not going to help me!" Brighid protested, her voice rising with her exasperation.

"Now, now, Brighid. Everything is going to be fine," Armes said, giving Cafell a look that assured her silence. Brighid's fingers closed once more around the ame-

thyst as she eyed first one aunt and then the other. The
heightened color on Cafell's cheeks only increased her
suspicions. "What do you mean? What is it that will be
fine?" she asked, knowing that the simple assurance
could represent something else entirely when uttered by
her aunts. "What have you done? Has this something to
do with my father's death?"

"Oh, my, no!" Cafell said, her expression showing
genuine surprise, and Brighid loosed a low sigh of relief.
The last thing she needed was these two dear old ladies
meddling in dangerous matters.

"Certainly not," Armes echoed, with a sniff.

"Oh, look! There he is!" Cafell said, excitedly, and
Brighid followed her gaze to where Stephen de Burgh
was mounting a huge destrier. Here, at last, was the man
she had been awaiting, but for one long moment, Brighid
forgot why she was seeking him out and simply stared.

He was magnificent. Whatever he had been doing the
night before, he appeared no worse for it, with the morning sun gleaming off his dark hair, his heavy cloak swirling about his broad shoulders and his strength evident
in the way he handled the massive beast. Brighid had
caught her breath, and suddenly aware of her own failure
to take in air, coughed and sputtered, aghast at herself
for gaping in blind admiration of a physical form that
boasted no real substance.

Squaring her shoulders, she filled her lungs with the
cool of the morning, a welcome draught to clear her
head. Then she stepped forward only to halt and glance
back at her aunts, who were both smiling benignly. Despite their innocent expressions, they were up to something, but Brighid didn't have time to find out what. She
only hoped it involved a harmless delusion on their part,

some silliness they attributed to their nonexistent magic, as was usually the case.

"Goodbye, dear," Armes said, and Brighid was soon enveloped in warm hugs, smelling faintly of mint and lavender. The scent of her aunts would go with her, and she blinked, surprised at a sudden surge of emotion.

"Behave while I am gone," she admonished.

"Of course!" Cafell said, looking affronted. "Take care of yourself," she added, and Brighid stepped back, turning toward where Stephen loomed on his huge horse. She was already moving when she heard Cafell call from behind her, "And him, too! Don't forget to use the *stone!*"

"Humph," she heard Armes mutter. "As for him being her savior, I have my doubts. I think *she's* the one who will have to rescue *him.*"

Although, as usual, Brighid couldn't make much sense of her aunts' words, she suspected that she was making her way toward the object of their discussion. And she had no intention of rescuing anyone, especially Stephen de Burgh.

Brighid's mouth tightened in disapproval, for no matter how dashing he might look, she knew what this man was, and he was *not* the sort who could be counted upon to provide a decent escort. Instead, he would probably fall into the first ditch they passed, insensate from drink, and lie there until spring arrived. His thoughtlessness was evident even now, for he had let others organize the train, while he appeared at the last moment.

Obviously, he had no interest in the journey. Now, if only she could convince him to abandon all pretense and stay at Campion... Although she had little enough time in which to do it, Brighid was determined to try. Marching across the bailey, dodging servants and dogs and last-minute well-wishers, she stopped beside his mount.

"Hello?" Brighid called upward, only to be ignored. *"Hello?"* she repeated, impatient.

Finally, Stephen's handsome face swung toward her, and although she had thought herself armed against his appeal, Brighid felt it wash over her again, like the swell of a spell. Like *magic*. And, for a moment, he almost made her believe again.

It was sinful for a man to be this beautiful, Brighid thought, as one dark lock of hair fell forward and she had to stifle an impulse to reach up to put it in its place. Unfortunately, Stephen seemed well aware of her reaction, for he lifted his brows slightly. Then he smiled, an artful movement so calculated that Brighid was jarred from her besotted state and the breath she had been unaware of holding was released in a rush.

"Mistress Brighid," he said, his deep, rasping voice drifting over her like a caress. But Brighid was aware of him now, and she told herself that the tone that so affected her was due to his consumption of alcohol. Too much drinking and late nights, she thought righteously, even as a shiver snaked down her back at the sound.

"None of that," she said, dismissively. "I want to talk to you. Seriously."

Stephen's brows inched upward again, but his smile fled. "The last time I tried to speak with you, I received a split lip for my trouble, so you'll pardon my reluctance to carry on a conversation while on a restive destrier," he said.

The horse was stamping and straining at the bit, but Stephen's powerful thighs and hands seemed capable of keeping the animal under control. *More than capable,* Brighid thought, swallowing hard. She forced her gaze back up to his face. "You're afraid of being thrown?" she asked, a bit incredulous.

He snorted. "I'm concerned that you, graceful and nimble though you are, might do something to provoke Hades. And I don't have the time or energy to play the hero."

"Hades?" Brighid asked. His horse was named after the god of the underworld? "Are you planning on riding into hell?"

His expression abruptly closed, the charming rogue disappearing behind a hard look. "Perhaps." Then he shrugged, a careless movement that seemed oddly forced. "From the looks of it, this journey might very well qualify."

Brighid seized on his complaint, her momentary distraction forgotten. "That's what I wanted to discuss," she said.

His dark brows rose, and that fantastic mouth curved upward. "You want to assure my enjoyment of this trip?" he asked, his voice humming along her nerves.

"In a way, yes," she answered. He had just begun to smile smugly when she continued. "I think you would rather stay home."

"Certainly," he purred. "Have you changed your mind about going?"

"No, but I believe you should."

"What?" His brows drew together.

Brighid took a deep breath and forced herself to look into his eyes, past the glint of his displeasure, to reach the man inside. "Although I must travel to Wales, you are not so obliged."

"How do you figure that?" he asked, dryly. He was no longer making an effort to bedazzle her, and Brighid found she preferred this sarcastic, cynical man to the arrogant charmer. Perhaps she could even reason with him.

"Twould be simple, really, if only you would remain here. I need no escort beyond the men-at-arms."

Stephen stared at her for a long moment, as if she had spoken in some incomprehensible foreign tongue. "You want me to defy my father?" he asked. He made the question sound so ludicrous that Brighid nearly winced. Instead, she nodded firmly.

After another long moment spent pinning her with his gaze, Stephen threw back his head and laughed, as if she had just told a witty tale worthy of his amusement. When his roar of humor died to a low rumble, he snorted, his expression turning surly. "Believe me, mistress, there is little I would like better than to see you lose yourself in the countryside, but no one defies Campion. Not even me."

"But—" Brighid's protest was cut off as he swung the mighty steed around.

"Get you to your mount, Mistress l'Estrange," he ordered, and without another glance, he sent the horse moving toward the head of the train.

Brighid could only stare helplessly after him as the carts began to roll forward. Someone, one of Campion's innumerable servants, brought her palfrey and urged her up. Disappointment, hot and acute, swamped her, along with an odd, anxious feeling at the thought of joining Stephen de Burgh on the road. It was nothing, she told herself, just a trick of nerves that had been jangling ever since she had received her father's summons, followed far too swiftly by the news of his death.

Brighid suppressed the sensation out of long habit as she took her place among the travelers. It was too late to do anything else. Neither Campion nor his son would heed her, and now she must hurry onward, at the mercy of someone else's errant leadership. It was a feeling she little liked and weighed upon her ill, until Brighid felt as though she was not in control of her life, but was hurtling toward some dark destiny.

Brighid's sense of foreboding continued as the day went from bad to worse. Well accustomed to running the l'Estrange household, to a routine of quiet, capable efficiency, Brighid now seemed little more than a helpless pawn on her own journey. And she did not like it one bit.

It had not taken her long to lose all patience with her so-called escort. Stephen had behaved much as she had anticipated, his progress leisurely, his attitude careless. They had barely left his home before he stopped for a lengthy midmorning meal, during which he ate little and drank far too much.

When they resumed their ride, Brighid wondered how he could stay in his saddle, let alone control the massive beast he rode, but he did, chatting amiably with the soldiers and causing much ribald laughter. The sound grated on Brighid's already strained nerves, and she kept to herself, chafing at the snail's pace that marked their progress.

When he ordered a halt long before sunset, Brighid made her displeasure known, to no avail. In any conversation with her, Stephen either played the charmer or dismissed her summarily. Brighid grew so impatient with his nonsense, that she felt like tossing his ever present wine into his handsome face. Alarmed by such violent tendencies, Brighid soon gave up all speech with him and retired to a tiny chamber of the abbey where they had taken shelter.

There, she sank into an ill mood such as she had not known in years. Although accustomed to a certain amount of isolation, Brighid missed the cheering company of her aunts with unexpected intensity. Eda, an older servant sent along to attend her, tried to soothe her spirits, but Brighid could not be placated.

"We would be better off had we never gone to Campion," Brighid grumbled. "Indeed, we traveled far faster with only those from the manor."

"Ah, but I fear that I'm not as brave as you are, my dear," Eda said. "I must admit I'm glad to have my lord de Burgh and the soldiers out there, instead of Tom and Will and their cousins. They are naught more than cottagers and could have done little to protect us."

Brighid scoffed. "Thus far I have seen nothing more threatening than the weather. Nor would I care to put these so-called soldiers to a test, with de Burgh as their leader. I think the only sword he's capable of wielding is the one between his legs."

Eda choked back a gurgle of laughter, and then sighed. "Ah, but what a fine one it is." She grinned wickedly at Brighid. "Or so I've heard, mind you."

Brighid simply ignored the comment, only the most recent in a long litany of admiration for their escort that the servant spouted. Eda's constant sighing over the man was enough to drive Brighid mad. Was there no one except herself who could see Stephen de Burgh for the lout he was?

"You're just used to being in charge, Brighid, but a woman must relinquish her place to a man sooner or later," Eda noted, unaware of the incendiary effect of her words.

"I have no intention of ever submitting to a man, let alone one of Stephen de Burgh's incompetence,"

Brighid said, glaring at the servant. "The arrogant, thickheaded drunk sees nothing beyond his own cup of wine!"

Eda clucked in dismay. "Brighid l'Estrange! Why, I've never heard you talk this way or behave in so mean a fashion."

Brighid frowned at the rebuke, but she knew that Eda was right. For years she had cultivated a reserved demeanor that was as far removed from the passionate follies of the l'Estranges as she could manage. But Stephen de Burgh seemed able to destroy her hard-won restraint with one look, rousing a temper long subdued. Brighid pursed her lips. Such an excess of sensibility was not good, and she struggled against the unwelcome emotions, straining for the calm that had once come so easily to her. *Before Stephen's arrival.*

"Perhaps you might ease your concerns about this trip and Lord de Burgh's abilities by looking to the future," Eda said, startling Brighid from her grim thoughts. Alarmed, she eyed the servant severely, only to be gifted with a wide smile of encouragement. And Eda blithely continued, just as if they were discussing something as innocuous as the weather, "Your aunts swear that you do not even need the bowl to divine, but can see into any water," she remarked.

Brighid drew in a harsh breath. "Hush, Eda! Do not speak of such nonsense," she scolded, glancing warily toward the narrow doorway of their small room. But she knew no one could hear through the thick stone walls. Releasing the air in her lungs with a sigh, she swung her gaze toward the shuttered window.

"You want me to predict our fate?" she asked in a somber tone. "My best guess is that we'll end up frozen to death in a ditch while the head of our company drinks himself into a stupor." But even as she voiced the words, Brighid knew they were wrong. There would be no ditch and no dead bodies, yet there would be water. Something to do with *water, rushing and boiling.* It drew her, and Brighid closed her eyes against the pull of it, shaking her head to dispatch the foolish notion.

An illusion, that's all it was, an illusion brought on by Eda's superstitious rambling and the mention of that ridiculous bowl her aunts regarded as some sort of divination aid. With a low sound of dismissal, Brighid prepared for bed, determined to forget her annoying escort for a few hours. But it seemed that she had barely closed her eyes when he drifted into her awareness once more.

"Brighid." *She blinked in confusion as her name was whispered in the darkness, but she readily recognized the voice. Deep pitched and gravelly, it sent shivers up her spine at the same time that the rest of her was seized by a liquid heat too powerful to ignore.*

"Brighid." *Again she heard her name. Softly, it came to her, like a moan or a plea that held none of the usual arrogance she associated with the man who spoke. She turned and he was there, taking her in his arms, and she was drowning in a rush of warmth and sensation as his hard body touched her, naked and welcoming. Limbs, slick with sweat, slid together, entwined, and then separated as she urged him to her. Finally, he loomed over her, his dark eyes so intent they stole her breath, and she knew that all the magic, all the mysteries of the universe were within her grasp.*

With a gasp, Brighid awoke, sitting bolt upright. Her heart pounding frantically, she glanced around the dark chamber, half expecting to find Stephen de Burgh beside her, his muscles gleaming as he reached for her. She drew in a deep draught of air, terrified by the thought, but even in the darkness, she knew that only Eda's small form shared her bed.

Releasing her breath in a shaky sigh, Brighid felt her panic ease. Of course, he was not here. Even a rogue like Stephen de Burgh would not sneak into her room and force himself upon an unwilling woman. *Force? Unwilling?* In the utter stillness, she seemed to hear his mocking voice, taunting her choice of words, and she slipped from her bed as if to escape it. Despite the chill of the night, Brighid was hot in the clothes she had slept in, and she felt edgy within the confines of the strange walls.

Moving toward the door, she opened it silently and stepped into the abbey gallery, seeking a relief from the stifling atmosphere in her tiny chamber. Immediately, she felt the caress of cool air drifting from the narrow window slits set high in the vaulted chamber. It revived her, and she stood still, drawing deep breaths as she tried to dispel lingering thoughts of the dream.

Yet, unbidden they came, one more insidious than any other: was it just a dream or was it a *vision?* Brighid shook her head, unwilling to entertain even the possibility. All that chatter about prophecies had left her susceptible to Eda's suggestion. *That's all,* she told herself firmly, except she couldn't ever recall dreaming so vividly, not even as a child when she still believed. No, this was something entirely differently, and Brighid shivered at the memory. It had all seemed so *real.* Worse yet, so *familiar, so glorious, so…*

A small sound echoed in the gallery, and Brighid peered out over the long space, lit only by the firelight from the hearth. Undoubtedly, some servant was stirring on his pallet, she thought, though her heart had returned to its earlier, erratic rhythm and she continued to stare into the darkness, as if seeking she knew not what.

Finally, she saw him. He was sitting on the floor, leaning against the wall, his head back, his eyes closed. He was probably too drunk to take to his bed, Brighid decided scornfully, but then, as if he sensed her attention upon him, his thick lashes lifted. He seemed to look right at her, deep into her soul, seeing all, including the images that had so disturbed her rest.

For a long moment, Brighid returned his gaze, feeling something pulse and flow between them across the night until all her perceptions of Stephen de Burgh seemed in error. He was the man of her dream, not this thoughtless knave, and she felt a nearly irresistible urge to go to him. *He needed her, even more than she needed him.* The strange thought alarmed her, and she blinked in astonishment. *What manner of spell was this?*

Severing whatever link she had imagined between them, Brighid turned toward the door to her tiny room and slipped inside, where she sank back upon her bed, trembling and determined not to dream.

Chapter Four

Uneasy about what fancies might plague her, Brighid spent a restless night and woke early. Although soon ready to depart, she found her plans thwarted by her escort, who was still abed. Indeed, from what she could gather, he had stayed up half the night imbibing for the sole purpose of sleeping the morning away.

As for her own disturbing encounter with the man, Brighid dismissed it as naught but a fevered dream. After all, he was asleep in some chamber this morn, not seated among the rushes that scattered the tiles. She must have imagined waking up and rising from her bed to look upon the gallery, let alone the conjuring of some bond between them.

No matter what delusions she had suffered during the night, Brighid was certain that the only thing she had in common with Stephen de Burgh was this journey, and the only emotion he inspired in her was disgust. It grew by the minute as Brighid watched the sun disappear behind gathering clouds, the new day slipping through her fingers. Although she refused to listen to any unwelcome promptings, Brighid knew a sense of urgency for her mission that would not be denied. Each delay stirred the temper she had thought well subdued over the years, and who could blame her when faced with Stephen de Burgh's continued, deliberate contempt for his responsibilities?

Her hands tied by his mockery of leadership, Brighid could only grumble and rage to Eda, who clucked over her impatience with annoying serenity—a serenity Brighid had once claimed. Now that calm existence seemed beyond her reach, as well as oddly stifling. "Well, if you're in such a hurry for him to rise, why don't you march into his room and drag him out?" the servant suggested with a chuckle.

So desperate was she that Brighid actually considered the notion. With special pleasure she contemplated separating the arrogant oaf forcibly from his cozy berth, and she might have done it, too, if she thought she could budge him. Unfortunately, he was too big, too heavy, too…Brighid closed her eyes against the image of Stephen de Burgh among tousled sheets, for it brought back unwelcome snippets of her dream. *His hands upon her. His mouth. The brush of his dark hair.*

Her heart pounding, Brighid firmly dismissed the memories. They were naught but phantoms, unreal, untrue, and never would they occur, she told herself. She could not see the future, nor could any of the l'Estranges, no matter what her aunts believed. She was a normal young woman, average and plain in every way, she told herself in a litany long recited.

Unfortunately, she was faced with a quest that few of her peers could claim, and it pressed upon her. Glancing at the now hazy horizon, Brighid was beginning to wonder how far they had come and if she could return to Campion Castle on her own when the object of her derision finally entered the gallery, looking fresh and handsome and infernally at ease.

And the simple sight of him wrought havoc upon her senses. Suddenly, Brighid was much too aware of the night before and the vivid vision in which this man had done things to her that she had never deemed possible. She, who had no knowledge of men, who had never been wooed or kissed, now felt her cheeks flame as she recalled the touch of his lips, his hands, his body upon her own.

Brighid blinked as that man, whom she knew was tender, fierce and loving, a being both vulnerable and strong, dissolved into this arrogant rogue. And despite her avowed distaste for her dream, Brighid felt a piercing sense of loss. That man did not exist. He was a phantom, conjured by an imagination too well suppressed, while Stephen de Burgh was a drunk who had wasted the precious morning hours sleeping off his swilling.

Her pounding heart slowing apace, Brighid straightened her shoulders and headed toward her escort, determined to forget her disturbing night and move on as quickly as possible. "At last," she muttered when she reached him, her lips pursed, and a scowl of disapproval upon her face.

"Did you say something?" Stephen asked, lifting his dark brows, and Brighid was annoyed to realize that his voice still managed to affect her. Too bad her aunts had not given her something that might stop his speech or spur his lackadaisical leadership, she thought. A little magic would be quite useful right now, if only to ward off his own power—that of a handsome face and a seductive drawl.

But Brighid didn't believe in talismans or spells or even Stephen de Burgh's potent allure. "Can we just get going? It looks like rain,'' she snapped, barely glancing toward him. With a shrug, Stephen seemed to assent, but she had begun to realize that despite his apparent agreement, the man would do just what he wished. It was maddening, and Brighid could only bite her tongue while he took his time preparing to leave.

And even once upon the road, he managed to dally. Cursing the precious time lost while he lay abed, Brighid tried to hurry them onward, but Stephen kept to his aggravating speed. ''Why do you ride that great beast when, at this rate, a pony would do just as well?'' she asked him after they had gone a short way.

Stephen let out a low rumble of laughter that danced up her spine, despite Brighid's efforts to steel herself against it. ''Why, mistress, haven't you heard that a slow, easy pace makes for the better ride?'' The words, drawled in an infernally sly tone and accompanied by the slight lift of his dark brows, made Brighid frown in response.

''I would sacrifice comfort for speed,'' she replied.

''Would you now?'' he asked, his brows rising higher. ''Interesting. But I prefer to take my time. And, as for the quality, well, that goes without saying.'' A soft burst of laughter from the nearby soldiers told Brighid that Stephen de Burgh was talking about something entirely different than road travel, and she urged her palfrey as far away from the wretched man as was possible.

It was a position she maintained until, all too soon, they halted for a lengthy meal. Too furious to eat, Brighid stood at the edge of the camp, disdaining even Eda's company as her ill mood continued. She kept telling herself that the trip would soon improve, that even someone of Stephen de Burgh's limited intelligence would soon realize that the more he delayed, the longer his journey would last. But still, they made little progress.

And then the snow started. A wet, blustering flurry, it threatened to freeze them all and slowed their pace even further. Pulling her hood closer about her face, Brighid ducked her head and told herself that at least they were moving forward. But it was not to last.

Concentrating on guiding her mount through the mire, Brighid had paid little heed to the shouts and commands that echoed around her and was simply following the horse ahead until the animal halted altogether. Glancing up finally, she was dismayed to see a small manor house. Already, youths from the stables were coming forward to claim the mounts, while she heard a booming welcome from a portly man who rushed forward to greet them.

"Where are we?" Brighid asked, as she was helped to the ground and urged toward the doors. *And why are we here?* she wondered silently.

"Glenerron, mistress. Tis one of the manors owned by his lordship, the earl of Campion," the portly fellow said, and Brighid stumbled on the threshold. Her lack of sleep, along with the foul weather, threatened to plunge her into despair as she grasped the full import of his words. They had not even left de Burgh lands yet. How would they ever reach her father's home in a timely manner?

Slowly, Brighid made her way toward the fire, stretching out her hands to its warmth, while behind her she heard servants bustling about, calling out effusive greetings to her indolent escort. She turned to see them gather around him, just as though he walked on water, and Brighid could not contain a snort of disdain.

Obviously, these retainers were blinded by their devotion to the family, else they would see the true nature of the tall, handsome man who strode forward easily. With a frown, Brighid watched him approach the table, all lordly manners laced with de Burgh charm, and for a moment, even she was taken in by his sheer presence. She shook her head as he took his seat at one of the hastily assembled trestle tables. Already, someone was placing a cup before him, and Brighid groaned aloud. She could see where this would lead, and she threw back her cloak as she marched forward, determined to stop it.

Outriders moved past her, sliding onto the benches at the table, and the odors of cooking meat and savory spices warned her that a repast was imminent. Brighid could easily envision these men eating and drinking the rest of the day away as she stopped before Stephen, her mouth a firm line. Her escort, by contrast, was leaning back against an elaborately carved chair, his tall, muscular form at ease and a beguiling smile on his handsome face.

Brighid was reminded of the snake that sidled into the Garden of Eden, bringing temptation in all of its guises and the downfall of man. "What is the meaning of this delay?" she asked.

"Why, I thought that would be obvious, even to you, Mistress Brighid," Stephen said with a sly smile. "Or don't you know enough to come in out of the wet?"

Ignoring the muffled snort from some nearby listener, Brighid remained focused upon the man she was coming to view as her nemesis. "May I remind you, my lord de Burgh, that your father entrusted you with the task of guiding me home?"

At the mention of Campion, Stephen's genial grin faded, and Brighid knew a moment's triumph before his casual demeanor returned. "I believe that is exactly what I'm doing, mistress," he drawled.

"No. So far you seem more interested in stopping to eat and *drink* than in leading us anywhere," Brighid answered in a cool tone.

Stephen's expression darkened briefly, as if in annoyance, before becoming unreadable. Then, he made a great show of sinking deeper in his seat and propping one long leg on the nearest bench. Brighid's gaze followed his movement, her attention drifting to the muscular calf encased in the dripping boot, and she wondered about the foot residing within before catching herself.

When she hastily glanced back at Stephen's face, she saw his lips curve slightly. Had he noticed her wandering eyes? Brighid hoped not, for she did not want him practicing his spurious charm upon her, nor did she care to contribute to his inflated vision of himself. She scowled, but he only seemed amused by her irritation.

"We're not going to get anywhere in this snow, so why not sit down and enjoy yourself? You do know how, don't you?" he purred, his brows lifting slightly in question.

That dratted voice of his again conjured up provocative visions that made Brighid grit her teeth. Now she even fought against an image of his naked foot before dismissing it. *The devil probably had perfect toes.* "Just how long do you intend to tarry here?" she demanded.

Stephen shrugged carelessly. "As long as it takes."

"It takes to do what?" Brighid asked, although she well suspected the answer. *As long as it takes to get stinking drunk.* Without waiting for his reply, she went on. "If we intend to wait out the weather, we could be here until midsummer."

Again, Stephen shrugged, and Brighid felt her patience run out. The man was a menace, with his sultry voice and sulky mouth and honeyed lies with which he thought to placate her. Did he think her an idiot who would eagerly swallow his sly words? She glared at him, incensed.

"Pardon me, but I was just wondering why Campion saw fit to provide me with such a noble train, when it seems to me that I would have made better progress with my aunts and our own small party," Brighid said.

Stephen's lips turned downward as he flicked a glance toward her. "Well, I suppose that he thought you might live to see your destination with a guard of real soldiers, instead of some ragtag band of your aunts' choosing."

Brighid met his scorning look with one of her own. "We made it to Campion without any trouble."

Stephen grunted. "And who, pray, would dare to attack you on de Burgh lands?" he asked. "You were traveling through areas that are known to be under my father's protection, if not within his demesne."

Brighid realized that, for once, Stephen might speak the truth, but still she was sorely tempted to return to Campion. If only she could do so without insulting the earl... Stephen must have seen her skepticism, for he blew out a low breath.

"You are truly witless, if you think to pass unaccosted elsewhere. Outside of Campion's realm, the roads are worse, often impassable, and even the most wary of travelers are prey to brigands and thieves and all manner of threats. My own brother Simon was attacked in the south and his entire train captured," he said, as if he relished the telling. Was he trying to scare her?

At her silence, Stephen leaned back and lifted one foot from the floor to cross it over the ankle that rested on the bench, as if to settle himself even more comfortably. "But, if you feel you can manage alone, by all means, take your palfrey and go." He uttered the challenge in a smug tone, while eyeing her from under thick, dark lashes that probably made most maidens swoon.

Even in her state of temper, Brighid could not deny a certain shivery awareness of the man. But she was no ordinary maiden to be lulled into acquiescence by a masculine spell, however potent. Nor was she stupid. She smiled slightly before tendering her reply. "Ah, but then what would you tell your father?"

Stephen reached for his wine, whether to quench his thirst or to divert her from the brief, telltale tightening of his jaw, Brighid could not tell. He took a long sip, and she found herself noticing the hand that held his cup, the fingers long and lean and perfectly formed. The wine swirled in the vessel, and suddenly, against her will, Brighid saw those hands on her, stroking her skin, dissolving her will, inciting passion she had never known. The image became a dream, a memory, *a premonition....*

Brighid swayed, caught up for a moment in an illusion so strong she had to struggle to banish it. It was naught but the phantom plaguing her again, she told herself, though the vision had been subtly different. Brighid swallowed sharply, returning her attention to Stephen's face, only to find his expression curious.

"Are you unwell?" he asked, those deep-brown eyes studying her more closely than usual.

"No," Brighid snapped, in firm control of herself once more.

"Good," Stephen replied, and whatever concern he pretended was gone as quickly as it had come. "Then, it appears we are stuck with each other, mistress. I would advise you to sit back and try to enjoy the de Burgh hospitality,'' he added, with a wry twist of his lips. Then he paused to fix her with his dark gaze, and Brighid had the uneasy sensation that he saw more than she would expect from his lazy demeanor. *Perhaps there was a little of his father in him after all.*

"Unless, of course, you are in an especial hurry to claim your inheritance?'' he asked, lifting his brows slightly at the query while raising his cup.

It was a casual question, tossed off carelessly, and Brighid told herself he knew *nothing.* Indeed, he probably meant the question as a barb, aimed at a greedy wretch he thought anxious for her father's money. But Brighid knew there was no coin waiting for her in Wales; that was not to be her legacy.

"No. There is no hurry,'' Brighid replied. Although her every instinct pressed her onward, she denied the need for haste, her innate caution far greater. Besides, she knew Stephen de Burgh well enough to suspect that such an admission would only prompt him to move even more slowly, for the man seemed to take pleasure in deliberately thwarting her.

Nodding as though he well expected her answer, Stephen gestured expansively for her to take a seat beside him, but Brighid only shook her head, drawing his laughter. As she watched that handsome face swing toward his men in apparent dismissal of her presence, Brighid knew an unsettling urge to put him in his place.

Fingering the stone that still rested in her pocket, she eyed him with slow consideration. If only she still believed in magic....

Stephen listened to Glenerron's bailiff, Waltheof, who hovered close, but his eyes followed Mistress Brighid as she marched away, her slender form straight, her small shoulders squared. Watching her proud carriage, her air of supreme competence, he felt oddly uncertain.

She was a strange slip of a thing. Stephen had received many responses from females over the years, most of them enthusiastic, a few of them less so, but none of them quite like that of Brighid l'Estrange. She seemed oddly immune to his charms, yet, sometimes, Stephen could swear that he sensed her interest. But, if so, why would she spurn him, as she repeatedly did, and with such vehemence?

Stephen shook his head in puzzlement even as he tried to quell his annoyance, for it was not as though he actually *wanted* the woman. She was far too boyish for his taste, and irritating besides, with her grim demeanor and constant nagging. Why, she was everything he decried! He frowned. All right, so maybe he had been tempted to woo Mistress Brighid to his frame of mind, but how far he would have gone for the sake of escaping this trip, Stephen wasn't sure.

Now, things weren't so simple. For instance, there was the delightful little lecture he had received from his father before leaving. Campion, in all seriousness, had actually warned him to keep his hands off the stripling, which was enough to send him chasing after her, had she been more to his liking.

Stephen's lip curled at the notion of his father advising him to mind his manners around the wench, a memory that still rankled. Whether it had been Campion's intention or not, Stephen had been offended at this sudden interest in his amorous inclinations, seeing it as outright question of whatever honor he had left.

At the same time, he was aware of the subtle challenge of Campion's words, and his own perverse wish to defy his father. After all, shouldn't he continue to live down to the earl's diminished expectations of him? His mouth twisted at the thought, for he had been doing just that for years, in contrast to his more saintly brothers. *Every family needed a black sheep, didn't it?* Stephen lifted his cup in silent toast to his accepted position within the scheme of things.

And seducing the prickly Mistress Brighid would surely earn him new censure, he thought, flicking a glance toward where she took a seat on a stool by the fire. Unfortunately, he wasn't too enthusiastic about the prospect. In addition to her lack of womanly charms and her surfeit of annoying habits, Brighid l'Estrange was simply too unsettling, with those witch's eyes of hers. Although Stephen would never admit to harboring any superstitions, he shifted in his seat, uncomfortable with an unnamed something about Brighid l'Estrange.

Of course, the way she looked at him alone was enough to put him off. Already, Stephen was heartily sick of seeing the thin line of her mouth, lips pursed, as she glared at him with a blatant scorn none had dared show him before. What made her think she was so superior? Stephen reached for his cup, found it empty and thumped the vessel for more.

He felt restless, as if he were strung as tight as a bow, and he scanned the familiar hall, seeking distraction only to see Mistress Brighid leaning toward the fire. Obviously, she was cold, yet she had complained about stopping! Stephen grunted. The woman had no sense whatsoever and not enough meat on her bones to keep her from freezing. As he watched her, she glanced his way, sending him a chilly, accusing glare that made his own eyes narrow.

Ungrateful wretch! Deliberately, Stephen looked

away, determined, now more than ever, to enjoy every moment at Glenerron. He deserved a respite from the hideous journey that had been forced upon him, and suffering Mistress Brighid's condemning glower definitely was not his idea of enjoyment.

Indeed, if his luck ran as it usually did, he might find something a lot more to his liking, he thought, as his gaze swept the room once more. Of course, Glenerron did not boast a large number of residents, but... *There.* Stephen focused on a figure hovering near the stairway. A dark-haired woman with the lush figure that Brighid lacked eyed him from under lowered lashes. Stephen smiled slowly.

"Who is she?" he asked Waltheof, who had taken a seat beside him.

A short, hearty sort, Waltheof followed the direction of his nod and sighed. "Gaenor. My nephew's widow. He was taken by a fever last year, leaving her with a young son. I brought her to the manor, and she has proven an asset, for she is well skilled with a needle." He paused to hold out his sleeve as if to demonstrate the woman's talents. "She has taken charge of our looms as well."

"Very nice," Stephen said, flicking his gaze toward the man's tunic only to return it, full force, to Gaenor. A lovely young widow might be just what he needed to wash the cursed taste of this journey out of his mouth. Stephen studied her lips, full and red, and he was certain of it. He noted Waltheof's sigh, but kept his attention on the widow, whose cheeks flushed a becoming hue.

"Please, invite her to join us," Stephen said, and Waltheof made no real protest, but rose, with another sigh, to do his bidding. And soon Gaenor approached, hesitantly, as if shy, although her dark, inviting eyes told

another story. Stephen knew his women, and despite her
show of reluctance, her admiration was evident. *Now,
this is more like it,* he thought, relaxing in his seat, as
he prepared for the adoration he had come to see as his
due.

Indeed, after several more cups of wine and a decent
supper, Stephen began to feel more in charity with the
world and everyone in it, with the possible exception of
Mistress Brighid. As he had several times this evening,
he let his gaze roam the hall only to find her scowling
at him in disapproval.

Flashing her an unrepentant grin, Stephen knew a
heady sense of triumph, for he was in his element, not
stuck on muddy roads, but charming his way into a
woman's bed. Perhaps the rigid Mistress Brighid regretted her treatment of him, now that she clearly saw what
she was missing, he thought, with smug satisfaction.
Watching her under lowered lashes, he reached out to
toy with a black lock of Gaenor's hair.

To his immense gratification, he saw Brighid's gaze
follow his fingers until she jerked her attention away and
abruptly turned her head. Stephen smiled, and as he idly
stroked Gaenor's tresses, he wondered what color hair
Brighid hid beneath her wimple. Curiosity pumped
through him with alarming speed, and he dropped the
strands in his grasp to reach for his cup.

Perhaps she had nothing at all beneath that wretched
headdress, but shaved herself like some monk, Stephen
mused, taking a deep drink. She certainly behaved like
one, with her stern demeanor and her disapproval of
wine and leisure and all manner of comfort. While he
studied her, she turned her back to him, as if deliberately
scorning him, and Stephen felt a surge of something disagreeable in his gut. In an effort to ignore it, he em-

braced righteous indignation. Who was she to judge the widow and himself for snatching a few hours of passion? *Not a monk, but a nun, no doubt.* She knew nothing of pleasure, being nothing but a big pain in the…

Her rebuff was a challenge of sorts, and Stephen reached out to tug the far more lively Gaenor onto his lap. Although the widow's willing form did little to ease him, her shrieks of delight had the desired effect. Brighid whirled toward him, and Stephen enjoyed wrapping his arms around the squirming woman he held, more to scandalize Mistress Brighid than to sample his companion's charms.

Unfortunately, Brighid's reaction was not what he had hoped. Instead of shock, an expression of disgust crossed her face, a variation of the look she always gave him, only so much worse that it managed to churn that disagreeable something to life once more. Frustrated, Stephen felt Gaenor's warm breath against his neck and tugged her closer, egging her on, while staring at Brighid in mute defiance.

Finally, she moved, surging to her feet so abruptly that her stool teetered precariously. She stood, hands fisted, as if to charge forward to berate him, and Stephen grinned, his blood stirring. At last, he had gotten a rise out of the wench! Aware of her attention upon him, he slowly lowered his head to kiss the pale flesh swelling above Gaenor's bodice. Excitement surged through him, a welcome ancillary to his little display. Although Stephen had never been one to engage in public sport, this was different. This was a sorely needed balm to his much abused pride, as well as a punishment for the woman who had spurned him.

But when Stephen lifted his lips from Gaenor's plump curves, he realized that his diversion was all for naught.

Brighid's back was to him, and he watched in stunned surprise as she headed toward the stairs. Surely, she was not retiring so early? Or was she fleeing like a coward?

Suddenly, Stephen's game with Gaenor lost its appeal, and he lurched upward, nearly dumping her on the floor in his haste. *To do what? Follow Brighid? And just what did he intend to do, apologize?* Stephen sank back down in his seat, hard. *Not likely.* He felt a moment's confusion, then Gaenor's rough hands on his face as she tried to urge him back toward her magnificent bosom. Yes, the young widow was eager, and perversely, it was that same eagerness that annoyed Stephen. The admiration that had been so welcome now began to grate as he heard her breathy little noises and felt her fingers digging into his neck.

She was too pushy, Stephen decided, for he was not a man to rush his wooing. He glanced about to see even Waltheof wearing a pained expression, and he wondered if the wench was too free with her favors. She was attractive, but her forward manner was not to his taste. He was a discerning man and did not take kindly to sharing his women.

His jaw tightening, Stephen slowly began to disentangle the widow. She pouted, but he managed to put her from him without too much protest. Calling for more wine, he told her to behave herself and winked, as though promising later delights, even as he had the sinking feeling that he would feel no more inclined to sample her wares at the close of the evening.

Unfortunately, he suspected that his appetite was ruined, and he blamed Brighid. It was not as though he wanted that sour-faced female. Far from it! But that disagreeable something in his gut that she somehow engendered had gained sway over the rest of him. Why, for a moment, he had felt no more than a boy, chastened over a minor infraction.

Stephen took a long drink as he wondered just what it was about Brighid's disapproving manner that had robbed him of the pleasure he would normally have enjoyed with the dark-eyed widow. If he didn't know better, he might even think that the whispers about the l'Estranges were true and that they really did possess unearthly powers. Stephen had heard of men who claimed that a witch's curse had caused their nether parts to shrivel up, but he'd never believed them. Still, he shifted in his chair until reasonably certain that his own prodigious part remained intact.

A lot of nonsense, he muttered, as he lifted his cup. He had deceived his own brothers too often with outlandish tales to start believing them himself. The only thing witchy about Mistress Brighid was her disposition, and that was something he was going to try to forget with the help of the fine wine before him.

Chapter Five

It was late when Stephen rose from the table at last, his world sufficiently hazy and his body numb from the wine that he had consumed. His men had retired below or sat slumped on the benches, snoring, while the servants lay bedded down in the corners of the hall, lit by the fire in the hearth and one remaining candelabra that stood near the head of the table. Even the lovely Gaenor was nearly nodding beside him, and Stephen was tempted to leave her be, but she stirred when he rose.

Giving him a sultry look from under her heavy lashes, she stretched, the movement deliberately pulling taut her bodice to display her generous breasts. She was awake and willing, and Stephen fell easily into his role. Taking her hand, he drew her into the shadowed alcove under the stairs that led up to his chamber.

She giggled as he rested his hands on the wall behind her, trapping her between his arms and leaning forward. Her dark hair gleamed, as did the swell of her bosom, and Stephen dipped his head to place a kiss against the soft flesh. Yet, despite Gaenor's obvious charms, he felt no answering warmth in his blood, the usual enjoyment eluding him.

With a twinge of annoyance, Stephen speared his fingers into her hair and brought her mouth to his with practiced grace. She made a small sound and clutched his shoulders, opening eagerly beneath his lips, and he answered her plea. His tongue danced inside, and he waited for the slow heat to envelop him, obliterating all else with its sweetness.

But it didn't come. Although the woman who pressed against him was young and ardent, the kiss was sadly flat. Stephen tried again, using all of his skill and all of her passion, but the encounter remained oddly unsatisfying. Just like everything else in his life.

Drawing back, he knew a wave of desperation so intense that he shuddered. Never before had a lovely woman failed to move him, to remove him from himself, yet now he stood here, empty and longing even as he held her. What would he do when there was nothing to make him feel alive or real, to take the edge off the emptiness that was eating him up inside?

Gaenor looked up at him with wide eyes simmering with desire, and Stephen closed his own, unable to face the anticipation there. This woman had not had an easy life and would never know a carefree existence. She would have to rise early on the morrow, yet she had stayed up late, eager for what excitement he could give her. And he felt the rogue for not really wanting her, for not being stirred by her kiss and for not giving her what she so craved.

But he could not. And if he tried to explain, she wouldn't understand. How could she, with her simple ways? She would find his complaints incomprehensible, since he had been born to privilege, luxury, and a family that, if not loving, at least put up with him. He couldn't tell her that he'd always been different from the rest of them, that he felt kinship only to Reynold, although he had no bad leg to excuse his moodiness.

Pushing away from the wall, Stephen turned his head. "Go on, back to your son," he murmured, without bothering to tender any reasons for his dismissal. After all, her disappointment could be no worse than his own, for now he would have to face the night alone.

The next day dawned wet and dreary, giving Stephen an excuse to linger at Glenerron, but the once-inviting prospect now seemed less to his liking. At the mid-morning meal, he sensed Gaenor's dark eyes upon him, and for once, he felt oddly uncomfortable under a woman's speculative gaze.

Stephen was not quite certain exactly what had transpired the night before, but he knew a vague sort of guilt for not living up to his reputation. Had he drunk too much wine? Stephen shook his head, for liquor never affected his performance. His eyes narrowed as they lit upon Brighid, glaring out the window and champing at the bit to leave, despite the weather. Had she done something to him? Surreptitiously, Stephen adjusted himself under his tunic, but all seemed to be in working order.

Perhaps it was her glower that had put him off his game. Yes, that might well be it, Stephen thought, for the other possibility was too grim to contemplate. Already, he felt the darkness gnawing at him, taunting him that his usual comforts of wine and women would not serve him any longer. Rising hurriedly as if to escape that death knell, he headed toward the kitchens. Perhaps some ale would hold the bleakness at bay for now.

Once supplied with a hefty cup, he found a corner away from the blazing heat of the fires, where no feminine eyes watched him with either malicious or lascivious intent. There he sipped the pleasant brew in peace until Waltheof stumbled upon him.

"There you are, my lord! Mistress l'Estrange has been asking for you," he said.

"I'll bet she has," Stephen muttered.

Waltheof looked decidedly perplexed to see his lord perched on a low stool, tucked away by the buttery, but the bailiff could be no more puzzled than Stephen himself. "Who do you see before you?" Stephen asked, as he crouched over his cup.

Waltheof blinked as he moved a barrel and sat down upon it with a grunt. "Why, my lord de Burgh, of course."

"Really?" Stephen asked, reaching up to find his lock of familiar hair and the same jaw he had shaved earlier this morning. "I was wondering, for I don't feel quite myself." He paused to sip the ale.

"What is it, my lord?" Waltheof said, leaning forward with an expression of concern.

"I'm not sure, but I think this is the first time in my life I've actually hidden myself away from women," he said, ruefully. "A most unusual occurrence."

Waltheof threw back his white-haired head and laughed heartily. "Well, if the one with the wimple has sent you scurrying into the corners, I don't blame you one bit. She looks quite the frightening sort, with her constant scowling."

"Not frightening, exactly," Stephen began only to halt when he realized he was tempted to defend Brighid to the bailiff. He took a drink. "*Annoying* is more the word for her."

Nodding sagely, Waltheof called for more ale and settled himself against the wall.

"Mind you, there are few women whom I can say that about," Stephen noted.

"Well, if you're not an expert on the ladies, then I don't know who is," Waltheof replied, reaching for the drink a servant handed him.

"Thank you," Stephen said, accepting the compliment as his due. There wasn't much that he took pride in anymore, but his reputation was inarguable. "I've often thought that I was born with my appreciation of the fairer sex," he said, leaning his head against the rough wall behind him.

He had always been fascinated by women in all their guises, and thanks to a lovely pilgrim passing by Campion, he had been initiated into the joys of their company at a relatively young age. Although, perhaps due to that initial encounter, he preferred a certain voluptuousness in his partners, that didn't mean he was exclusive or that he couldn't admire other women. He did.

Indeed, he had long held them in esteem, wanting and needing them, not only for the pleasure they gave, but for their softness, the tenderness that could not be found in male companions. Although Stephen would never admit it, that was part of their appeal to him. Frowning, he considered Brighid l'Estrange and decided that she didn't have a tender bone in her body. No wonder he sought her not.

"Your brother Robin claims that you never met a woman you didn't like," Waltheof recalled with a grin.

"Well, I'm not sure about that," Stephen said. After all, he did have his standards, and some women, including the rigid Brighid, did not meet them. He kept seeing her straight back, her lifted chin, her blessed *dignity,* and he wanted to destroy it, to wipe that look of disapproval from her face and stop her mouth, with its incessant nagging. "She gives me a headache," he muttered before downing a gulp of ale.

"Who?"

"That l'Estrange woman, the boyish-looking thing with the scowl and the wimple. What do you suppose she's got under there?" Stephen asked.

Waltheof chuckled. "I expect if anyone could find the answer to that, twould be you, my lord."

Stephen shuddered. "I don't want to find out," he said, even though he knew his words to be a lie. *All right,* so maybe he was curious about her hair. That didn't mean that he wanted to engage in any kind of sport with the sour-faced wench.

"Well, if you're wanting to take your mind off the ladies, I have a little something that might distract you," Waltheof said. Opening the small bag at his waist, he tossed a pair of dice upon the tiles at their feet. Stephen grinned and forgot all about his troubling charge—for the moment, at least.

By late afternoon, the play had turned into a rousing affair with several knights joining in and a good amount of coin changing hands. As always, Stephen was doing well, his success in games of all kinds well-known. In fact, for the first time since embarking on this wretched journey, he was in his element, totally at ease and enjoying himself—until Brighid appeared.

"There you are!" she exclaimed, giving him a dour look that made him feel like an errant boy called before his father. The sensation was most unwelcome, for he was long past the age for embracing guilt of any kind. By faith, he was an adult and a de Burgh, and would not be brought low by this slip of a female! Armored by ale and flushed with success, Stephen fixed her with a hard look.

"Are you speaking to me?" he asked. His dark brows lifted in arch query, and the tone of his voice brought all nearby conversation to a halt. The dice rolled loudly in the sudden quiet as all eyes watched their lord and the woman he escorted.

"Of course!" Brighid snapped into the hushed silence, staring down her nose at where he was crouched low to the ground. There was something about the way she looked at him that stirred Stephen's dormant temper, and with slow deliberation, he rose, unbending his tall body until he towered over this woman who dared speak to him so boldly.

"You'll understand my confusion," he murmured. "You see, I didn't hear my title. Surely, you know the one, the sign of deference due me? But perhaps I should remind you. It's *my lord,*" he said evenly. Never before had he demanded such submission, but never before had a woman dared scold him like a callow youth. Sometimes a lady might turn too possessive of him, or want too much from him, but even those he scorned dared not treat him this way.

Just who did Brighid l'Estrange think she was?

Stephen waited, his attention focused intently on her green eyes, which were flashing angrily at him. For a moment, he was nearly enthralled by the shifting hues, like the depths of the sea. Wild and untamed, they reflected little of the staid woman before him, he thought, before catching himself. No one had changeable eyes. It was only a trick of the light, he decided, with a frown.

"*My lord,*" she said through gritted teeth.

"Yes?" Stephen said. He kept his expression neutral, though he felt a heady triumph at this small capitulation.

There was something strangely gratifying about nettling her, even if she rarely responded to his barbs. He wondered just what he would have to do to rouse a real reaction from her, to shake her from her stiff stance, and he knew a sudden sharp desire for her total submission.

"I would ask you if you intend to leave today or waste the precious daylight hours gambling?" The scorn in her voice was palpable, and Stephen felt again the force of it. What was it about this unattractive woman that had the power to affect him, when so little else did? *Too bad the effect was an unpleasant one.*

"Judging from the state of the weather, I would say the latter," Stephen answered, with a shrug.

"But tis hardly even snowing," Brighid said.

At least it *was* snowing, Stephen noted. He had been too absorbed in dicing to notice, his task as escort long forgotten. He felt a small prick of guilt that was easily dismissed when he saw her outraged expression.

"You cannot mean to tarry here until spring!" she protested.

"Didn't we have this discussion yesterday?" Stephen asked, effecting a yawn as his men, having lost interest in the conversation, returned to their game. He paused to fix her with a direct gaze. "I could have sworn you told me then that you had no real need to hurry."

To his delight, Brighid blanched a little at the taunt, confirming his suspicions that she was in some haste to reach Wales. What, beyond her nasty temperament, drove her? A lover? Surely not, for she would never relinquish control to another. More likely, she wanted to count her new coins, Stephen decided. Well, she could just wait to do so.

She made no answer, and as her silence continued, he lifted his dark brows in query. She seemed to be grinding her teeth, he thought, with no little satisfaction. Then she looked away. To compose herself? When she glanced back toward Stephen, her lips were pursed in that infernal manner of hers. "Nevertheless I would like to arrive before some brigand takes over my lands."

"Ah, so that is what worries you," Stephen said, though he still felt there was something more behind her hurry. "Well, I can assure you that we shall rout any and all pretenders to your inheritance." He gave her a placating smile, delighted to note that she appeared to be gritting her teeth again.

"You can hardly do so, if we never arrive, can you?" she asked.

"We'll get there, Mistress. There are some things that you just can't rush," he added, his voice dropping to a low purr that hinted at other meanings.

"Indeed," she muttered. "And you seem to be one of them." She turned on her heel and walked away, back stiff, slender shoulders straight, as some of the men began snickering. Stephen whirled around, stopping the sound with a stare. No matter what he might think of this woman, his soldiers would tender respect to her.

He felt a bit of grudging respect himself, which he dismissed with a careless shrug of his shoulders. He had won the point, hadn't he? Then why did he feel so vaguely unsatisfied by the encounter?

By evening, Stephen nearly wished he was on the road instead of ensconced in Glenerron's warm hall. The dice game had lost its appeal soon after Brighid's interruption, and his enjoyment of supper had been tempered by Gaenor's dark gaze, which lingered upon him throughout the meal and afterward.

He should have just swept her off her feet and up to

his room and had done with it, but he didn't like the sensation of doing someone else's bidding; it reminded him too much of his relationship with his father. This whole journey had been forced upon him, and between Brighid's nagging and the weight of his responsibilities, Stephen began to feel tense and put-upon. The careless attitude he had long embraced became more and more difficult to assume, and he drank his wine with a new desperation.

Finally, he escaped to the stables, where the dicing resumed, but his game was off, and he soon withdrew to a corner to watch and drink. But the longing for female companionship, for the blissful forgetfulness that came as he joined with them, crept over him, and frustration increased his ill mood.

Surely, there was someone else here, some other maiden who might stir him as Gaenor did not? Stephen rose to his feet and walked through the gathering twilight in the bailey. The snow had stopped, and he was surprised that Brighid was not dogging him to leave. Maybe she had given up looking for him, he decided, but the glee he ought to be feeling didn't come. It was not as though he *wanted* her to pester him. God forbid. He was sick to death of her and her righteous attitude.

He desired a woman who was not an ice maiden, someone soft and warm and welcoming, not some shrew who passed judgment on him. Aimlessly, Stephen wandered through the muddy yard and around the various buildings crowded within the walls. A dairymaid perhaps? But no one lingered in the chill wooden structure that held the cattle, except for a young lad, nodding at his watch.

Inside the manor, he saw only a few older women, little more than villeins, who probably helped in the kitchen or laundry. Glenerron was simply too small to boast many residents, let alone the kind of attractive females Stephen preferred. After all, he had his standards, and a reputation to uphold that had badly slipped last night.

With grim determination, he strode into the hall and stopped in the shadows near the door, only to find his gaze drawn immediately to the one woman who seemed oblivious to his charms. Interest surged to life, and he frowned at his errant blood, telling himself that it was the challenge she represented—and nothing more—that stirred him. *It wasn't as though he wanted her.*

Turning his back upon Brighid, Stephen prowled the rooms of the old building, absently noting how well kept it was and anything else he might report. His father would expect no less of him. Thoughts of the earl depressed him further, for if Brighid returned to Campion with her complaints, his disgrace would be complete. Was that what he really wanted? He wondered, not for the first time, if he should even return home.

But where would he go? And what would he do? He was ill equipped for anything but a life of leisure, yet had little money of his own. A fine de Burgh, he was. No lands. No wealth. No power. And he had not the heart to earn his living by killing others, as a hired knight or one of the king's men, as Dunstan had done. The bleak thoughts fed the blackness around him, forcing him back to the kitchens for more wine.

When he finally returned to the hall, neither Gaenor nor Brighid was in sight, and he sank into his chair, feeling as though he were old beyond his years. He was cold, despite the fire, and leaning his head back, he closed his eyes against the onset of another night spent alone.

* * *

And that is how Brighid found him.

Escaping another night of restless sleep, she wandered down to the hall, only to stop short when she came upon an unmistakable figure seated at the head of the table, presumably insensate from drink. Yet when she looked at him, his reason for sleeping there was hard to remember, for his beauty nearly stole her wits.

Lush dark hair fell back from his face, its handsome planes lit only by the faint glow of firelight. One thick lock lay across his forehead, atop his mobile brows and nearly touching the thick, black lashes now in repose. Yet, it was not his looks that drew her, but something greater, some mysterious force beyond her control. Surely, here was the man of her dreams, not the Stephen de Burgh she knew, and Brighid fought an overwhelming urge to reach out and touch him.

"Shouldn't you be in bed?" His low voice caught Brighid by surprise, for his eyes remained closed. How had he known she was here? she wondered, suppressing a shiver. He had heard her footsteps, Brighid told herself, and could not know who stood before him. Suddenly, she was seized by the urge to turn and flee, lest she be tempted to stay.

"Well, mistress?" he asked, and Brighid thought perhaps he caught her scent, though she disdained perfumes. "What are you doing up in the middle of the night?"

Brighid simply stared at him, confused by a tumult of emotions. Why was she here? She hardly understood it herself, and she certainly did not intend to admit that she had been driven from her chamber by the sensation of someone in pain, a feeling so strong that it overcame her natural reluctance to obey such prompting. And, still she felt it, a great wash of despair that seemed to emanate from the man before her.

A fancy, nothing more. She was as deluded as her aunts, for no one was in pain here. There was only a drunk slumped over his wine. The knowledge roused Brighid to anger, which she easily directed at the man before her. "What are *you* doing? We need to leave early on the morrow," she asked, sharply.

"Actually, I was thinking about you, mistress," he answered.

Brighid felt a moment's startlement, her heart racing at his words. Had he drawn her here? Nay, he only played with her, for hadn't she just sworn that no one possessed such power? Twas a trick of chance that brought them together. Or, more likely, a trick of his tongue, for why should he be thinking of her?

As if sensing her skepticism, he continued, his hoarse voice even more enticing in the darkness, and Brighid steeled herself against its allure. "In fact, I was wondering why you are unaffected by my legendary charms. Would you care to enlighten me? Believe it or not, most women find me irresistible."

He lifted his head slightly, his thick, dark lashes slowly rising to pierce her with his moody gaze, and Brighid felt heat wash over her until she felt limp and languid, yet curiously alive. And he thought her *unaffected?* It was a misconception she would take pains to foster. "Well?" he asked.

But Brighid had no intention of discussing his appeal, real or false. Already, this man thought too highly of himself. She shook her head and stepped back, surveying him with a jaundiced eye. "You're drunk."

"I'm never drunk," he answered easily.

There was no point wasting her time arguing when

the dawn would come all too quickly, Brighid thought, and the realization made her even angrier with him. "Go to bed," she said.

"Is that an invitation?" he asked, his lids lifting lazily, and she felt the intensity of his attention, despite his casual demeanor.

"No. You can sleep on the table, then, if you prefer, like some sot. I have no need of a bed partner, but an escort," Brighid replied, denying everything inside her that might gainsay her words.

"Ah, we're back to the momentous trip," he said, closing his eyes once more, as if to dismiss her.

"Yes, and if you truly want to know, one of the reasons I dislike you is that you don't consider anything important except your own selfish wants. Look at you," Brighid said. Warming to her subject, she flung out an arm to encompass his casual pose and the cup before him. She drew on her anger, desperate to avoid the appeal she so vehemently rejected.

"You've had everything, a proud name, a wonderful home, a good family, and what have you done? Squandered it all on drink." She lashed out, the words her only weapon against the unwelcome feelings he roused. "You're a failure."

Even that harsh accusation, which left Brighid trembling, seemed unable to rouse a response. "Ah, you've been talking to my father. Did he put you up to this?" Stephen asked, lifting his lashes to slant her a glance.

His casual demeanor astonished and disappointed Brighid. Couldn't he bestir himself enough to defend himself? Didn't he care at all about what she said? Didn't he care about *anything?* Brighid shook her head as she stared at him, no longer seeing the man of her dreams, nor even any sort of man.

"I can't believe you're a de Burgh," she said. Then, she turned on her heel and strode away, not stopping when she heard his low reply, for once in assent.

"Neither can I. Neither can I."

Chapter Six

Stephen heard her footsteps receding, but he didn't call her back even though the night closed in upon him as soon as she left. What more was there to say? Brighid had said it all quite succinctly. Her seeming revelations were no news to him, but Stephen had to admit that she was the first person to ever voice them aloud. And even though he was very much aware of his own failings, he was surprised at how much it pained him to hear her catalogue them.

Only the last, weak vestiges of his control kept the despair at bay. That and a simmering resentment for Mistress Brighid. What made her so perfect, with her drab clothes and grim manner and mysterious hair? She was hiding something else, too, he suspected, but right now he couldn't summon up a whit of curiosity about it.

Leaning his head back, Stephen loosed a low sigh. He just wanted to sink into blissful sleep, though he wasn't sure if that was possible now. Panic nudged at the edges of his awareness, but he suppressed it. Deliberately relaxing himself, he forced his thoughts away from Brighid and toward a warm bed where they belonged, and gradually he felt the tension that had seized him ease to a bearable level.

Stephen sat up slowly. He could have stayed where he was, sleeping the night away in the hard chair, and it would certainly not have been the first time he had done so. Yet, somehow he shied away from the thought of her finding him there slumped over the table in the morning, like the hopeless wreck she thought him. Although she had made it quite plain that he was beyond redemption in her eyes, he didn't want to prove it to her.

With a grunt of annoyance, he rose to his feet. It shouldn't matter to him what she thought, especially after the way the wench dared speak to him, and yet Stephen felt a churning in his gut that rebelled against her words. Despite the truth of them, he would love to throw her accusations back in her face, to find some way to show her to be wrong.

But how? Even should he miraculously become one of his driven brothers and spur the train on to Wales at top speed, Stephen sensed that her opinion of him was unalterable. It would be too little, too late, and God knew that he could not change himself now. Grunting against a sudden ache at that knowledge, he headed toward the stairs.

His gait only slightly unsteady, Stephen climbed the steps to his small chamber and swung open the door. Closing it behind him, he leaned his back to the worn wood and shut his eyes against the darkness that awaited him. But even in his less than sharp state, Stephen immediately sensed that he was not alone. Although he remained where he stood, he lifted his lashes, his body taut and ready as he scanned the room by the dim glow of the firelight. Then, just as swiftly as he had tensed, he relaxed.

A woman was in his bed.

Such an occurrence was not unusual enough to surprise him, but here, tonight, after what had happened, it was astonishing. Despite everything, his heart thundered a welcome, his blood running fast and hot until he caught a glimpse of black hair tumbling about a pale face. Gaenor. Stephen let out his breath in a harsh sound, his momentary excitement washing away just as swiftly as it had come, leaving him cold and empty.

Pushing off the door behind him, Stephen stepped forward as Gaenor smiled provocatively, yet his response was only a hard disappointment that he didn't even want to identify, let alone examine. But he had spent a lifetime perfecting the art of ignoring that which he didn't want to see, and Stephen swept it all aside, down into the abyss, as he approached his bed.

Although the sight of Gaenor clad in nothing except a strategically placed blanket provided a distraction, it did little to rouse his senses. Oh, she was pretty in her way, and well-rounded, but Stephen had lost interest in a game too easily won. And her presence here, after he had already refused her, smacked too much of manipulation for his taste. The bedchamber was one of the few venues where he was in control, and he did not care to cede his reign to a demanding widow, no matter how lush her figure.

Indeed, Gaenor's appearance made him feel vaguely like a stallion required to perform on demand. Not that he couldn't, of course. But he did have his standards. Stephen sauntered closer, his gaze upon her ripe form. "I think you're in the wrong bed," he observed.

"Surely not," she answered. Her tongue snaked out to lick her lips in the manner of a cat eyeing some cream, and for once, Stephen felt oddly uncomfortable with his mantle. Did she think he serviced every wench like some animal at stud? He might have little choice in most areas of his life, but he still would decide just who was the lucky recipient of his skills.

"Ah. But I fear so," he said, eyeing her directly.

Gaenor sputtered, her cheeks flushing with anger, as she sat up against the heavy headboard. And, suddenly, the quiet widow was replaced by a hard-faced viper. "Think you're too good for the likes of me, do you? Well, if you imagine you'll find sport elsewhere, you are sadly mistaken. Even I can see that!" she said, all traces of her submissive demeanor gone.

Stephen lifted his brows in some surprise at the change in the woman who had once appealed to him. His instincts had served him well about this one, at least, for the last thing he wanted was a shrew in his bed. If that was his desire, he could have pursued Brighid. At least she was honest. She had behaved foully from the beginning and continued to do so, without resorting to any subterfuge. But, then she wasn't out to win his favor, either, Stephen mused, with a disagreeable feeling that he told himself was *not* disappointment.

"I don't think to find it elsewhere, but thank you for your advice," he said.

Gaenor snorted. "Do you think I'm stupid?" she asked, a question which Stephen politely refrained from answering. "I've seen the way your eyes follow her, but you are a fool to lust after that one. You will find more pleasure here, with me, than you would ever know with that witch."

She was speaking of *Brighid*. Stephen swung slowly toward her in disbelief. How dare this wench insinuate that he was drooling over *Brighid*, of all people? What would this lowly female know of what he wanted or how he felt? She knew nothing about him. Nothing! Nor could she comprehend him, even if she did.

And how dare she disparage the woman he was escorting? Although it made no sense, Stephen again knew a sudden, fierce desire to defend Brighid. He shook his head in disbelief. What was it about her that made him constantly come to her defense, when she had done nothing to deserve his loyalty? Quite the opposite, in fact, for she deliberately courted his contempt.

Stephen shook his head again before returning his attention to Gaenor. "You are mistaken," he said quietly. "Tis late, so I suggest you seek your own bed."

She rose with an indignant scowl, dragging the blanket with her and wrapping it close, and Stephen realized that she had no clothes. Had she come to his chamber draped only in that? Although his reputation had been built on such, he felt oddly uncomfortable with the notion that she might be seen sneaking about in this fashion. It would give a false impression, he told himself.

At the door, she turned. "Very well. I leave you to your l'Estrange hag. Obviously, she has cast a spell upon you that you cannot see her true form!"

With that, she slammed the heavy wood behind her, rousing anyone within hearing distance, Stephen thought, wincing. Then he grunted in disgust at her accusations. Brighid was a witch all right, but she possessed no special powers beyond the sharpest tongue in Christendom. That he could see quite clearly, thank you, he thought with a frown.

The problem was that he still seemed to want her, despite everything.

Brighid heard the whispers as soon as she entered the hall. She had always made it her business to know what others were saying, for her own protection, but this time the talk wasn't about her. It concerned her escort and his late-night tryst with a certain resident of Glenerron.

Brighid told herself she wasn't surprised, for such behavior fell well in keeping with her opinion of Stephen de Burgh. And yet, somehow the knowledge of his bedding the woman disturbed her, as if it rang with some wrongness that went beyond the questionable morality. Had he gone to her after Brighid's confrontation with him, or was he fresh from the woman's bed when they spoke? Brighid felt sick at the thought, although she had treated him ill enough during their brief conversation. He deserved it—and more—she told herself.

Yet the odd sensation persisted, as if the timing of his behavior made it far worse than it normally would be. The notion was ridiculous, of course, and she dismissed it firmly. Such feelings were better kept at bay, and Brighid was well skilled at that task, for by maintaining a certain detachment she protected herself from insights she deemed useless and troublesome. Unfortunately, she was finding it increasingly difficult to maintain her stoic reserve.

Whether stimulated by her father's death or something else, the promptings she tried to ignore were growing stronger and more frequent. And just a glance at Stephen seemed to conjure a host of them, though why *he* should spur them, she had no idea.

The mind was a tricky thing, as Brighid well knew, and this unpleasant journey was taking its toll upon hers. Obviously, she must arm herself more fully or manage to accept her situation, lest she lose all the composure she had fought so hard to win.

As if putting her vow to the test, Brighid's nemesis appeared just at that moment, striding across the tiles with an ease and arrogance that bespoke nothing of his late hours, his drink or his nightly activities. If anything, he looked even more handsome, and Brighid was hard-pressed not to shiver at the sight of him. She was staring, she knew it, yet she could not seem to tear her eyes away from the man until she remembered the rumors. And her stomach churned.

"Ah, I see my lord de Burgh looks none the worse for wear this morning," Eda said, with a low chuckle.

"What?" Brighid swung toward her, bringing the woman into focus with some effort only to face the servant's intent scrutiny.

"What is it, child?" Eda asked, her tone gentle.

"Nothing," Brighid said. If Stephen de Burgh was naught but a vile seducer, it was none of her business. "I was thinking."

"Ah. About *him,* were you?" the servant asked with another chuckle. "Now, that's a good sign. But I hear that a lovely young widow was the lucky recipient of his attentions." She clucked her tongue. "Seems like a waste, doesn't it?"

Brighid tried to manage one of Stephen's careless shrugs, but it felt more like a painful twitch. "Stephen de Burgh's entire life seems like a waste to me," she said, her lips pursing. "He's just as lacking in honor as I suspected, but as long as it doesn't affect our journey, I could care less what he does."

"Really, mistress?" Eda asked, her tone oddly inquisitive.

Brighid's eyes narrowed in speculation. "Do you know something I don't?" she asked.

Eda clucked again. "I am merely a lowly servant, mistress, and cannot boast of any foreknowledge, but if you opened yourself to your l'Estrange powers, instead of closing the door upon them, you would know far more than I.''

"Hush! I will not listen," Brighid said, turning away from the servant in disgust, but Eda grasped her arm to detain her.

"You're denying your heritage, your blood, your very self," the servant said, her expression serious. "Tis unhealthy and unwise. Heed your heart, Brighid."

Brighid felt a moment's panic, before she regained her composure once more. "No," she said, extricating herself from Eda's hold. "Tis unwise to put one's faith in a lot of gibberish." Her grim look stopped Eda from responding, and the servant only shook her head, while mumbling something about destiny willing out.

Brighid scowled. If she had a destiny of any sort, it was to return to her home to find some explanation for her father's summons and precipitous death. And, to do that, she had to convince Stephen de Burgh to leave his gambling and wenching and return to the road. She could use a bit of magic to manage that feat, she thought sourly, like the ability to turn him into an ass and ride him all the way home.

The seemingly innocent thought led to shocking imagery, and Brighid drew in a sharp breath. Swiftly, she amended her wish to something simpler. *If only she could bring him to do her bidding.* The notion made her suddenly giddy, and Brighid smiled in spite of herself at the thought of the arrogant oaf brought low.

It was simply too bad that she had not the power to do so.

Stephen looked out over the rounded hills, deep valleys and woodlands, and wished he were back at Glenerron, sitting in front of the fire, his feet up and a cup firmly in hand. He was keenly aware that while there, he had felt oddly unsatisfied by his familiar habits, little enjoying the excellent Normandy wine and delicacies prepared by good cooks. And considering his monkish behavior, he had been a bit startled to learn that the whole manor was buzzing with gossip about Gaenor and himself.

Normally, Stephen thrived on such talk, but the lie had made him uncomfortable, and not only because it wasn't true. Oddly enough, he felt as if the whispers reflected ill upon him, though bedding the wench certainly had been his original intention. Still, a man had a right to change his mind, didn't he?

The troubling sensation plagued him until Stephen was tempted to announce to all and sundry that he had not been with Gaenor, and, in fact, suspected that she had dallied with one of his knights instead. But the remnants of whatever honor he possessed prevented him from publicly humiliating a woman who had offered herself to him. And so he left Glenerron, with none the wiser to Gaenor's tricks, and told himself that he didn't care what anyone thought, including Brighid. *Especially* Brighid, he thought mutinously.

She, with her constant nagging to hurry, was the reason he was back out on the road, and well did Stephen rue it. The snow was already melting, miring the track in a mushy layer of half-frozen ground that necessitated repeated stops to pull the wagons out of ruts. Never before had he seen such loathsome conditions, and all he wanted to do was walk away from the entire business.

Although Stephen had traveled many times, he had done so with his brothers, leaving the decisions to those who liked to make them, while he drank and watched the scenery and deigned to complain when any difficulties arose. Now he could complain to no one, for he was in charge, and it was not a mantle Stephen assumed with enthusiasm. He had spent his life sparing as little effort as possible for any endeavor, preferring to oversee others, if that. He did not like having to think about what to do next, which road to take, whether to stop or go on and where to find shelter.

Although his brother Geoffrey probably had committed every map he had ever viewed to memory, Stephen had paid little attention to such. And while he suspected that Dunstan and Simon could sniff their way to a destination, he could not. Nor could he manage to gather his bearings from the moss and lichen on trees or the stars that never shone through the clouds. And so he could only stop and look and wonder whenever a fork appeared in the road, the direction unmarked.

Finally, *she* had informed him that if he didn't know his way, he ought to inquire in the next village, lest they waste their time traveling elsewhere. Grunting his displeasure at her suggestion, nonetheless, Stephen had been forced to acquiesce. And so he had faced the ultimate humiliation: asking for directions. It was bad enough that he did not feel up to his task, worse yet to display his ignorance to a passel of idiots and his own men besides.

Not that he cared what *she* thought. Stephen's jaw tightened. He hated the unwanted assignment that had been thrust upon him. He hated the cold, the damp and the mud. But, most of all, he hated the look on Brighid's face. No matter what he did, whether it be to the good or ill, she wore the same disapproving expression. Whenever he glanced her way, she was watching him with that hideous smirk that told him he was living down to her expectations of him.

His resentment simmered until Stephen felt like a pot that had been heated too long and might readily explode. Very rarely did he let anyone or anything rouse his temper, but now he was seized by but one desire: to wipe that smirk off of her face. And he knew just how he would prefer to do it, too. *With the wench flat on her back beneath him.*

Yes, Stephen had come to the bizarre conclusion that although Brighid l'Estrange had nothing whatsoever to recommend her to him, he felt a certain…stirring in connection with her. He could have laughed at the irony— that a man of his reputation should be stricken with a case of unrequited lust. And if he believed in destiny, which he didn't, he might have even thought it fitting. But Stephen was not amused. Nor did he placidly accept a situation that he found absurd, frustrating and utterly maddening.

Why Brighid, of all the women in the world? She was not voluptuous or tender or soft or any of the things he sought in a woman. She was cold and heartless and rigid. Utterly baffled by the peculiar bent of his heretofore discerning nether regions, Stephen finally decided it was a question of dominance. By swiving the wench, he could gain the power over her that he craved—and satisfaction besides. Consequently, his greatest wish was to have her panting and writhing in a manner wholly unlike her usual stiff demeanor and *begging him for it.*

The very notion brought a smile to Stephen's lips. Unfortunately, he had about as much chance of that happening as he did of sprouting wings and flying to Wales, another fantasy that grew stronger by the minute. So he ignored her as best he could and drank as much as he could, yet every day he felt wound tighter than a knotted rope. He would have just drunk himself into a stupor during the hours of traveling as well, if the trip were not so difficult. As it was, he needed his wits about him.

His wits and his strength, Stephen thought, as he shoved the beleaguered wagon up a hill, the horses straining ahead. But even the addition of his muscles to that of his men could do little to budge the cart, and with a groan of frustration, they fell back, the animals dancing in place, the vehicle slipping, inch by inch, over a slick patch of ground.

With a low oath, Stephen shook his head. "Enough," he said. "I saw the remains of an old castle about a mile back. We'll make camp there for the night. Maybe by morning this muck will have dried out enough to make better progress." Heaving loud sighs of relief, his men began to lead the horses off the road, and Stephen surveyed the scene with approval. It was still early, so he could crack open a cask of wine before supper, sit by the fire and...

His gaze, which was sweeping the area, landed squarely on the one figure that stood rigid and unmoving. At the same time, a familiar prickling sensation climbed up the back of his spine. "Don't...give... me...that...look," Stephen warned her as he swung slowly around. But he was too late. In one swift glance, he took in the pursed lips, along with the startling disdain in those infernal green eyes.

"Do you have something to say?" Stephen asked, his jaw tight, his body tense. For a long moment, he thought she would deny it, but finally she spoke in an even, measured tone, as if he were a dolt unable to comprehend the simplest discourse.

"I realize that you did not want to escort me, but the sooner we get there, the sooner your task is done. Yet it seems to me that you make every excuse to delay us," she said. Then she proceeded to stand there, expectantly, as though waiting for his answer.

Of course, he was delaying them! He could barely stand to spend any time on the road. But he was not about to admit anything to Brighid, especially when he felt that gut-churning sensation that came with her disapproval, as if she were unmanning him. Singlehandedly. "And just what do you suggest I do?" he asked, spreading an arm to encompass the cart that stood at the bottom of the track.

Mistress Brighid waved her hand in a gesture of impatience. "Go around!" she said.

"Go around?" Stephen echoed. "You want us to leave our course and wander about in a terrain that is probably worse, losing ourselves in some bog?"

"Scout ahead, then," she said.

Stephen stared at her in silence. Of course, he could send a scout ahead, but why bother? The land was probably as bad as the narrow path that passed for a road, if not worse. Why make more trouble for himself? Yet he knew a nagging suspicion that, had his brother Dunstan been escorting the train, the man would have gone forward himself, found the right way, and mapped out another trail back to the road. *All with his hands tied behind his back and two enemies chasing him.*

Stephen, however, was not one of his brothers, and he would never be, so why expend the effort, especially for this stripling of a female? He shrugged, ready to dismiss her pleas in exchange for a warm fire and a full cup, but that churning in his gut stopped him. Before he knew what he was about, he had opened his mouth.

"Fine," Stephen said, throwing up his hands. "We'll go around." He had no intention of trotting off to do her bidding by himself, so over his shoulder he called to his men. Their low grumbling was audible and perversely pleasing to his ears, but if he expected effuse thanks, or, indeed, any sign of gratitude from Brighid, he was to be disappointed. Only a firm nod, as if his largess was her due, acknowledged his decision.

Although hardly much better, at least it wasn't the look, Stephen thought, with a scowl. But why should he expect anything else from his unwelcome charge?

Two hours later, Stephen began to wonder just how lost they were. He had tried to veer back toward their original route, but the ground had given way, leading them higher and farther from their goal. Now, they were mired in shocks of browned grass and uneven ground, amid groves of mossy-limbed oaks, with little hope of improved landscape ahead. He was cold and tired and sore, his usual equanimity having deserted him about two miles back.

He should have never left the road. Roads led to villages and inns and alehouses. Roads drew other travelers, who could advise them of said havens—or at least what direction they were going. Now they were stuck in the middle of nowhere, with little hope of progress.

And it was all her fault, Stephen thought, with a harsh glance toward Brighid. Without moving his gaze from her, as if daring her to give him her customary look of disdain, he called a halt. "Let's make camp here, if you can find a dry spot," he said, yanking off his gauntlets, while his men murmured gratefully.

Of course, Brighid, who seemed to have a constitution beyond that of the most hardened soldier, showed no such appreciation. Instead, she actually turned her back on him, her slender shoulders squared, her head, in that ridiculous wimple, held high.

Why did she keep her entire head covered? Had she some disease of the scalp or a bald pate? Stephen had known his share of women in his lifetime, but he had never known one as secretive as this one. He told himself he didn't care in the least about whatever mysteries were going on behind that expressionless face of hers, but he would certainly relish the opportunity to do something—anything—to rattle her maddening reserve.

As she stalked past him, Stephen was seized with the childish impulse to trip her, to see her flat on her face in the mud, or perhaps flat on her back.... No, he didn't even want to think of that now. He might be forced by his nether parts into some kind of perverted *desire* for the woman, but he heartily resented it, just as he resented everything to do with her.

He wouldn't trip her, Stephen decided swiftly. That would be ungentlemanly in the extreme. But if he couldn't wipe that smirk off her face, exactly, then at least he could disturb her infernal dignity a little. And so, just as she had nearly moved past him, he reached out and snatched the hideous wimple from her head.

She didn't shriek, much to Stephen's disappointment, but she whirled around with a look of astonishment on her normally forbidding countenance that was a pleasure to see. She lurched toward him, in a vain effort to reclaim her garment, but Stephen held it crushed in one fist as he stood staring at the hair that spilled forth, his own expression gradually coming to mirror hers.

He had expected shorn locks or, at the most, dull, nondescript hair to match Brighid's personality. Instead, he found himself gaping as long tresses, streaked with every shade of blond, fell over her shoulders in a rippling sheen. Strands so pale they were white were mixed in with those of gold and shimmering sunshine, until they dropped to her waist like a river of light, leaving him dumbfounded.

Abruptly, all of Stephen's aches and chills and weariness disappeared, to be replaced by a rush of lust so strong it startled him. He had been numb for so long, going through the motions even longer, that he never expected to feel the heady surge of hot blood that swept through him.

"Are you satisfied?" she asked him, her carefully neutral mask back in place, though her green eyes flickered with indignation.

Faith, no. He wasn't satisfied. Stephen wondered uneasily, if he would ever be satisfied again. Stunned, he simply stared at the slender young woman who transformed before his very eyes from a plain, unappealing thing to the world's most beautiful woman. He wanted her, not with the vague, undirected ardor that had been plaguing him for days, but with a sudden, immediate fierceness that stole his breath and made him dizzy. It didn't matter that her expression, as she faced him, was one of outrage and loathing. In fact, he had a swift, sudden suspicion that her contempt made her even more desirable.

Yes. Lifting a hand, he reached for that magnificent hair just as she made a lunge for her wimple, and the next thing Stephen knew, they were both falling backward. He braced himself, taking the force of the impact, before rolling to the side. And then, against all odds, he had Brighid right where he wanted her. *Beneath his own body.*

And it was even better than he had imagined. With an ease born of long experience, he settled himself between her slightly parted thighs and grunted at the feeling that washed over him. It was nearly overwhelming, and he had to struggle against the urge to thrust himself against her to ease himself. But he was no untried boy, and he rallied his wits enough to look into her face and what he saw there was even more shocking than Brighid's hair.

Hunger. Those unusual green eyes were dark with it, like the raging sea, and without pausing to question his own sight, Stephen rested one hand to the side of her head and put the other to her cheek, holding her still as his mouth took hers.

It was no seductive kiss, meant to woo and pleasure, but a punishing one, to conquer her and test this strange attraction she had for him. And though only a moment before Stephen would have claimed his sexless charge could never move him, the minute his lips touched hers, he was afire. Perhaps it was his enmity that fueled the blaze, but it seemed to Stephen's stirring senses that no kiss had ever been quite so gratifying.

Brighid gasped under his onslaught, and Stephen took advantage of the movement to gain entrance with a sense of heady triumph. Finally, he had some measure of power over this infuriating woman, and the victory fed his passion. He slanted his mouth over hers to delve deeper, exploring every recess and stroking her with his tongue even as he felt her fists pressing against his chest as if to ward him off. He had never taken an unwilling woman before, but he paid no heed to her protest. Sliding his hand down to her buttocks, he cupped her, drawing her up tight against his groin.

Cursing the mail he wore on the road, Stephen wanted to feel her against him without any hindrance, to seek out the secrets she kept hidden beneath gown and cloak to see if the rest of her was as surprising as the hair that slid against his cheek. His body ached for her in a way that was nothing like his usual, careful lovemaking, and he could have easily rucked up her skirts and taken her here, on the cold ground, for once slaking his own passion without thought to her own.

Dimly aware of the presence of his men nearby, Stephen knew that he should not take this encounter too far, but he welcomed the sensations she had unleashed—sensations that proved he was not dead, not empty, but hard and hot and wanting. All the chivalrous notions fostered by his father died as Brighid tried to push him away, and he took an unholy delight in holding her fast.

And then, suddenly, her fists uncurled, sliding up his chest and over his shoulders, and she returned his kiss with a fervor that stunned him. As if she, too, had been dead, she abruptly came to life, pressing her mouth to his, her tongue dueling with his own. Stephen groaned aloud and, lost to the desires that drove them both, he might well have surrendered all semblance of reason, if not for his men.

The sound of a loud guffaw penetrated his awareness just as he felt Brighid stiffen beneath him. They had an audience, and Stephen never performed in public. With a grunt, he broke the kiss and tried to gather his wits about him. But they were slow in coming, especially when he looked at the face before him. Surely, this passionate beauty was not *Brighid?*

Winged brows rose over eyes the color of a sea storm, while her luminous skin wore the unmistakable blush of ardor. And lips that he had disdained as too thin now were plump and ripe and wet from his kiss. Stephen groaned. And all around him spread the most amazing hair. He lifted a lock in his fingers, and nearly groaned again at the luxurious feel of it.

"*Brighid?*" Stephen asked aloud, his fogged brain

still baffled. But, true to form, his companion swiftly removed all doubts about her identity. The dazed expression of pleasure on her face swiftly disappeared, to be replaced by one of outrage. Stormy eyes grew wide, and she pulled back her arm to deliver a stinging slap to his cheek.

Stephen released her, rolling onto his side with a grunt. He could count on one hand the number of times he'd been slapped, and surely no one, not even the woman who later became his stepmother, had given him such a vicious blow. Raising a palm to his face, he ruefully rubbed the spot, taking a certain satisfaction in her anger as she struggled to her feet and stalked away. He had managed to wipe that smirk off her face, finally, for a few moments at least.

And then Stephen smiled to himself, a slow, wicked grin that warmed him, despite Brighid's chill dismissal, for he had discovered a little secret about the rigid Mistress l'Estrange. For one delicious moment, he had felt her respond to him, her body pressing against his own, her mouth opening beneath his, her disdain replaced by a hunger that had stunned him.

Yes, indeed. Brighid might feign outrage after the fact, but now he knew better. Inside that proper, grim exterior was a passionate woman just waiting to get out. And who better to release her than Stephen de Burgh?

Chapter Seven

Stephen felt better than he had in days. Even though the morning had been spent struggling back to the road through difficult terrain, the dark sense of failure that had been oppressing him had lifted somewhat. And as for the lust that plagued him so fiercely, he had a feeling that it wasn't quite as unrequited as he thought.

Slanting his gaze toward where Brighid was stiffly seated upon her palfrey, her hideous wimple covering everything except her pinched face, Stephen shook his head. Why would a woman hide such glorious hair? And why did she cover her body under drab, shapeless garments? Though not voluptuous, she was soft in all the right places, far more than Stephen had ever imagined.

Just thinking about their encounter on the ground made him hard, and he tamped down his enthusiasm with some effort. He had spent long hours riding, and not upon Brighid, who had been studiously avoiding him ever since that passionate interlude. After slapping him, she had hurried to her tent, keeping her attendant close and refusing to speak with him. Stephen's eyes narrowed in contemplation as he studied her rigid stance.

Suddenly, as if somehow aware of his study, she

turned her head and flicked him a contemptuous glance, but the look no longer held the power that it once did. His gut didn't churn, and he didn't feel a clawing need to numb the bleak realities of his existence. Indeed, he felt rather invigorated, for he was in his element at last. *Just like nearly every other woman he had ever met, Brighid l'Estrange wanted him,* and Stephen relished his triumph. The situation that had mired him in frustration, acerbating his own desperate mood until it was nearly unbearable, was firmly back in his control.

Stephen hated to think how close he had been, teetering on the edge of the abyss, as if one push from Brighid could send him careening into the depths, but now he had the odd sensation that she had yanked him away from the precipice. For a while at least. The vaguely ominous thought shot through him before he relegated it to the place for those things better left unexamined. Instead, he turned his full attention on Brighid and smiled, a slow, knowing curve of his lips that made her turn away indignantly.

Her reaction had him nearly crowing with delight. Perhaps he could find some entertainment in this hellish trip after all. Indeed, he could think of nothing more enjoyable than putting Brighid l'Estrange firmly in her place. Excitement surged through him, out of all proportion, but he didn't care. He only knew that he felt *something,* and it was sorely welcome.

With anticipation firing his blood and his mind as well, Stephen called a halt for the first meal of the day. He relished Brighid's black look of disapproval, and sending her a hot glance of promise, he dismounted swiftly and strode to where her palfrey stood.

"Mistress Brighid, you look pained from your ride," he said, tongue firmly in cheek. "Please, let me help you.'' And, despite her hissed protest, Stephen reached up to lift her to the ground, taking the opportunity to slowly slide her along his body. It was a move he had made in the past with practiced ease, and yet, somehow it seemed wholly new and wildly arousing. *Perhaps because murder flashed in Brighid's green eyes as she threw off his hands.*

It was a different experience for him, a challenge Stephen met with a grin and a shrug that told her he knew the truth, no matter how she might object. And, as she stormed off, he remained where he stood, watching her with a pleasure that no longer inspired any twinges of unease. Her gait was stiff, without the slightest hint of a woman's sultry sway, and yet he was struck with a nearly overpowering urge to press himself against that straight back.

Sucking in a harsh breath, Stephen tried to get himself under control before shrugging his acceptance and following. He seized his chance when he saw Brighid reaching up into one of the wagons. Her hands were occupied, so it was easy to step behind her, trapping her there. Stephen lifted his arm, ostensibly to help her, but in the process, he managed to mold his body to hers in a way that left no doubt of his intent. She gasped, and he was glad of it, for it covered up the low grunt of pleasure that he could not contain. He cursed the mail that kept him from fully enjoying the softness he discovered even as he held himself still, reveling in his position.

Abruptly, Brighid turned her face toward him, and for once, she did not wear her usual grim expression. Indeed, she was fairly blazing with fury, and Stephen wondered how he had ever thought her cold. Certainly, her green eyes were deceiving. Cool as rain, they nevertheless churned with the force of a raging river, running deep and fierce, hiding secret currents and shoals. As if some prior blindness had been lifted, Stephen could see that beneath the scowls and the stoic demeanor she so carefully cultivated, churned a veritable host of emotions, and Stephen knew a deep, piercing yearning to tap them. To *possess* them.

For an instant, he let her see his desire, and they stared at one another, their gazes held as if by the sudden, surging attraction between them, a force so strong it seemed beyond their control. Shaken, Stephen blinked, only to see a mixture of dawning horror and something else he could not identify in those green depths before they were shuttered once more.

"If you don't mind?" she asked him. She spoke sharply, with her usual forcefulness, but they were too close for her to fool him. He could feel her heart pounding and see the shiver that stole through her. With an effort, he assumed his most innocent expression as he snagged the cloak that was just out of her reach.

Stepping back with reluctance, he handed it to her. "I was just trying to aid you, mistress."

"I'm sure," she muttered as she pushed away from him, and Stephen had to hold back a laugh. Her outrage only seemed to fuel his excitement. Faith, he felt good, better than he could remember in a long time, the darkness that plagued him seemingly at bay for the moment, at least.

As she stalked away from him, Stephen watched her again, this time with renewed appreciation, for he had discovered that her backside, though not ample, was delightfully supple and gently curved. Perhaps he had become tired and jaded with his usual fare, for his other women suddenly seemed too fleshy and round, while

Brighid was far more intriguing. He closed his eyes, imagining taking her from behind, subjugating the haughty wench to his will as he pounded between those firm cheeks, and the fantasy was so powerful that he shuddered.

Lifting his lashes, Stephen grinned wickedly and followed his prey, eager for a meal. The food didn't particularly draw him, though Oswin could do wonders with salted herring, hard cheese, and other potable supplies; it was the opportunity to tease and torment Mistress Brighid that he relished.

He waited until she was seated, with her meal before her on a slab of hard bread they had purchased during yesterday's travels, and then he stepped forward. Halting in front of her, he flashed one of his best grins at the elderly attendant beside her.

"Excuse me, Eda, is it?" Stephen asked, gratified by her immediate cluck of welcome. "I wonder if I might have a word with your mistress."

"Eda, no!" Brighid said, eyeing him warily.

But the woman was already moving to the other side of the fire. "Certainly, my lord," she said, with a smirk and a wink that left no doubt where her loyalties lay. Pleased, Stephen winked right back at her as he took her place on a fallen log next to Brighid.

"Ah, what have we here?" Stephen asked as his squire delivered a trencher into his hands. He took up a hunk of cheese and sliced a small portion with his knife.

"Have a taste," he urged, spearing it and presenting it to his companion. It was a game he had long played, and he had seduced many a maid over a meal, but Brighid, as usual, was uncooperative.

"No, thank you."

"No, thank you?" Stephen echoed, his brows lifting slightly.

"No, thank you. I have some of my own," Brighid snapped as she scooted toward the end of the log.

"Are you speaking to me?" Stephen asked, enjoying the scowl that descended as soon as she understood his question.

"No, thank you, *my lord*," she said, through gritted teeth, and Stephen wondered how she would manage to eat with her jaw muscles so tightly clenched. The thought sent his mind careening toward other muscles clenching and unclenching, and he sucked in a harsh breath. He would do well to remember the idea was to taunt Brighid, not himself.

Deliberately, Stephen paused, pretending to make a great study of his food before choosing a bit of herring. "Perhaps this one, then?" he asked, tendering it to Brighid.

"Nay, *my lord*. I have my own," she repeated, as if he were slow of wit. Stephen heard the attendant chuckle, and his eyes narrowed. He would like to stop her charge's haughty mouth, and not with food, either.

"See?" Brighid said, brandishing her own hunk of yellow cheese with a new spirit. Then, as if to prove her words, she lifted the food to her lips and took a large bite.

If she had hoped simply to silence him, she succeeded, for Stephen was struck speechless. However, if her intention had been to discourage him as well, Brighid failed miserably, for Stephen felt himself stir at the sight of her white teeth. He remembered that tongue dueling with his own as he tasted her, hot and passionate and tangy, and he could easily imagine her nipping his shoulder—or elsewhere. Stephen stifled a groan. Had she any idea what he was thinking? Perhaps he should enlighten her.

"Do it again," he whispered, leaning close.

Swaying away from him, Brighid chewed her food, while glaring at him. "What?" she asked. Her mouth full, she appeared totally oblivious to the blood that was running riot through his veins.

"Do it again," he repeated.

"Do *what* again?" she asked, eyeing him as if he were mad, and Stephen smiled. Perhaps he was.

His hand stealing toward her trencher, he lifted up the yellow cheese. "Take another *bite*," he said, his gaze leaving no doubt as to his desire.

Brighid's eyes grew wide with horror, and she made a choking sound even as she lurched to her feet, scattering the contents of her trencher onto the ground. She whirled toward him, and, for a moment, Stephen reveled in the picture of her, breasts heaving and fists clenched in outrage. It was as if, having hammered a chink in the stiff armor of her demeanor, he had let loose a maelstrom that she could no longer contain. And all he had to do was sit back and watch.

"I demand that you cease plaguing me at once, *my lord*," she said.

Stephen casually popped a bit of herring into his mouth. "Me? What have I done?" he asked, effecting his most innocent expression. "You were the one eating so provocatively." For a moment, he thought she might explode, but she appeared to master herself with some effort, much to Stephen's disappointment.

"Excuse me, *my lord*," she said, with her usual stiffness, before turning to stalk away from him.

Stephen grinned as he watched her go. Run, then, if you will, he thought smugly, but he knew there was no escaping each other, confined as they were to the small train on the road. And he was just beginning his campaign.

Brighid had reached the limit of her patience. Ever since that drunken dolt Stephen de Burgh had *forced himself* on her, he had been treating her to seductive, knowing smiles with that sulky mouth of his. Worse yet, he seemed to be taunting her, taking every excuse to touch her in some manner, usually in an intimate fashion that was most inappropriate. Insulting, even.

And that's what she suspected he intended. A man like Stephen de Burgh had no real interest in her. He simply was angry about having to serve as her escort, and so he sought to punish her in whatever way possible. The slow pace and the delays, while he ignored her protests, had been bad enough, but this unwanted attention was far worse.

Oblivious to her luxurious surroundings, Brighid stared at an elegant tapestry, seeing nothing except the face of her nemesis. They were spending the night with one of the marcher lords, the de Burgh name having insured them a grand welcome, and, for once, she had hoped that Stephen would be diverted by his usual pursuits of wine and women, but his eyes still seemed to follow only her. She didn't know whether he actually intended to try to seduce her or only to torment her, but either way Brighid was having none of it.

She had escaped to her chamber early, taking her evening meal with her, just to get away from him, for he seemed always to be close. *Too close!* Wherever she went, there he was, his presence radiating heat and seduction, his eyes dark and compelling, and that voice caressing her with its gravelly whisper until she felt as

if all her good sense and will would be torn from her
and she would end up as she had in the cold field, abandoning everything....

Brighid flinched, fleeing from that memory as if it
were the very devil itself. She would not think of that
dreadful moment of weakness. *Ever.* Drawing a deep
breath, she put aside her trencher, unable to stomach
another mouthful of food. Walking to the window, she
opened the shutters and welcomed the bracing chill of
the air. There was rain in the wind, and she dreaded
being trapped here for days, while Stephen drank and
wenched. *Or, worse yet, drank and pursued her.*

Brighid frowned. She had to do *something*. She felt
ready to panic at the mere thought of Stephen's attentions, a fear that had less to do with what he might do
than with how she might react. Although she had always
considered herself the sensible member of the family,
strong-willed and pragmatic, this man had the power to
unnerve her, to sidestep her defenses, to change her into
someone else.

Pushing aside the notion, Brighid tried to concentrate
on more serious matters. She still had a goal to accom-
plish, and she felt the urgency of her quest more than
ever, especially since they had reached the border. She
could probably travel to Rumenea, her father's manor,
in a few days, if the weather held, but not if Stephen
planned to linger here. Brighid shivered at the visions
that thought provoked. *Stephen crowding her against a
wall, leaning too close, running his hands along her
arms.*

Brighid shook her head. Such was nonsense, a bunch
of jumbled images brought on by her own unease. Yet
that same anxiety grew until she felt like fleeing her
room, this place, her very skin.... She drew a deep

breath to regain control. She could go on alone, of course. She was fairly certain she could find her way, but it would be dangerous, and she had already heard the rumors of political unrest swirling among the castle residents. She would prefer an escort. *If only it wasn't Stephen.*

Unfortunately, she could hire no one else, not with the de Burgh name attached to her train. She must travel with him or go alone. Brighid drew a deep breath. Either way, hiding in her chamber would do nothing to achieve her goal. Nor would it drive her escort away. As much as she might hope he would lose interest, Brighid suspected a man like Stephen would only pounce upon weakness. She needed to be firm and final with him.

Pushing aside any other notions of dealing with him, however tempting they might be, Brighid straightened her shoulders and drew on the strength at her center. With new resolve, she decided that if he would not take her home immediately and on her terms, then she would simply have to do it herself. It was a situation she had faced many times before, growing up as the only responsible person among those whose heads were in the clouds more often than not, and she knew her own capabilities.

Her mind set, Brighid retrieved her trencher, aware that the remains usually were given to the poor at the castle gates. She opened the door and hurried forward, only to run directly into the man who so plagued her thoughts. Startled, Brighid glanced up at his handsome face and was forced to catch her breath in order to forestall its effect.

His appeal was so strong that for a moment she again wondered if the de Burghs wielded any abilities beyond that of normal men. But the scent of him, of man, horses, leather and *wine,* made Stephen all too human. With a scowl, Brighid tried to shrug away the hands that had reached out to steady her. She didn't want him touching her now in the dimness of the torchlit tower. Or ever. It was too dangerous.

He was too dangerous. And he proved it by retaining his hold and ignoring her protest, as usual. Surely, he wouldn't attempt anything more intimate here, outside her chamber, would he? Fighting against the slow well of panic, Brighid glared up at him, trying her best to appear both possessed and resolute. But her attempt at composure was undone by the look on his handsome face. His full lips swept into a slow, sulky curve, his white teeth gleaming, while his dark eyes hinted of some secret, some knowledge about herself that Brighid knew to be false—and which she would deny to her death.

"Stop looking at me that way," she demanded.

"What way?" he asked, his brows rising slightly as if in innocence. But Stephen de Burgh was as far from innocent as anyone outside of hell itself could be. Yet, even knowing that, Brighid felt herself waver under the force of his gaze. It was naught but a glossy sheen, hiding emptiness, and yet...

"What is it, Brighid?" Stephen asked in a slumberous, sultry way that made her blood run sluggish and her body grow warm and languorous. But she shook her head, clearing it, and steeled herself against his allure. Whatever powers he might or might not possess, she had no intention of letting them sway her.

"You know exactly what I mean, *my lord.*" Brighid spit out the title, which she thought wholly unnecessary and undeserving. The earl of Campion was a mighty baron and a wise man deserving of respect; his son was not. "The look you have used upon countless females.

The look you no doubt practice before the mirror while admiring yourself! The look which is wasted on me! I've told you before, I have no interest in your charms."

Stephen's dark brows lifted again. "Oh, really?"

"Yes, *really.*" Brighid answered, staring at him stonily.

"Then how do you explain the kiss?"

Brighid deliberately kept her face impassive. "Is that what you called it? I call it attacking me, and I intend to tell your father how—"

Her words were cut off by the feel of his hands sliding slowly up her arms. "That's not the way I remember it. I remember you warm and welcoming and wanting more," he said, his breath a soft caress against her that set her pulse pounding.

Brighid betrayed not a sign of the riot of emotions invoked by the memory of an encounter she would like to forget. Instead, she spoke as coolly as possible. "I was pretending compliance in order to obtain my release, and if you—"

Her threat was lost in the low rumble of his laughter, replete with de Burgh arrogance. "Shall we put it to the test?" he asked.

"No," Brighid answered, trying to push by him. But his fingers tightened, holding her fast, and she felt her panic increase. Despite all his practiced lies and laziness, this man was a threat to her, and she had to get away from him. Forcing her lips into a grimace, she practically spat her reply in his face. "I don't want you!"

"I don't want you, either," he murmured, but his eyes darkened. For one long moment, Brighid feared she would be lost to him and to herself, but he had forgotten something, and so had she. When he pulled her close, the trencher, still clutched in her hands, upended and smashed into his chest, and Stephen jerked backward as the remains of the greasy meal clung to his fine tunic in great globs.

With one surprised glance at the mess, Brighid did not hesitate. When he loosened his hold upon her, she fled to her chamber, barring the door behind. Then, she leaned against it weakly, torn between relief and an urge to laugh at the look on his face as the handsome charmer realized his elegant attire was covered in food. There she waited, catching her breath, until she heard him stomp away.

So much for her determination to speak with him! But Brighid knew there would have been little talking between them this night. *Tomorrow,* she vowed. She would leave on the morn, either with him or without him, Brighid decided, not certain for which outcome to hope. Once on the road, they would soon reach her old home, and she would be free of the man forever. Brighid loosed a shaky breath at the thought.

Until then she would count up his thin veneer of civility and whatever remnants of de Burgh honor he might possess to keep Stephen at bay.

Chapter Eight

Although the skies had warned of rain, Stephen had not heeded them. Nor had he heeded his hosts' delicately couched warnings of travel farther into Wales, which was rife with whispers of discontent, complaints about English administrators and reports that Llewelyn nursed personal grievances against the crown. Stephen had ignored them all, leaving behind the good food, fine wine and ambiance of a large and comfortable castle, to take to the road. Why? He had no idea.

Instead of sitting by a fire, cup in hand, oblivious to anything but his own pleasure, he was shivering in a downpour. And the only reason he could think of was his absurd obsession with a certain witchy female. His hosts had warned him about her, too, all in a very oblique, enlightened manner, of course. They had scoffed at the old tales of the l'Estranges, who supposedly fled England for the wilds of Wales many generations ago to continue their strange practices among the remote hills. Mystics, seers, healers or worse? They had speculated, while Stephen snorted. Of course, he didn't believe a word of it.

But they were right about one thing: the rain. Appar-

ently, it had begun ahead of them, for the farther they
traveled, the more muddy the ground. It made the route
difficult to travel, but where were they to take shelter?
He could see nothing except cairns and standing stones
along the steep slopes, rising to snow-capped peaks in
the distance.

Jerking on the reins, he brought Hades to a halt and
waited until Brighid appeared. She was as wet as he, but
since she looked just as rigid as ever, Stephen wasted
no sympathy on her. Hadn't she pressed him to leave
this morn, with a grim determination worse than ever
before? As for his own agreement, Stephen blamed the
bizarre urgings of his increasingly indiscriminate nether
regions.

"Are you sure this is the right road?" he shouted.

At her nod, he shook his head, unconvinced. He had
little faith in the memory of a woman who had been
away from these hills since a young age. Narrowing his
eyes, Stephen peered through the dwindling drizzle.
"It's hardly more than a drover's track, probably used
to herd sheep to market," he muttered. Brighid, of
course, made no response. She had been avoiding him
as much as possible, even riding ahead, though he had
ordered her not to more than once.

Stephen had enough problems without having to chase
after her, and he cursed the weather that would not seem
to let up. If she was really the last in some long line of
sorcerers, the least she could do was improve the conditions for this trip. "Can't you make it stop?" he
taunted, swiping his face and lifting an arm to encompass the heavens.

He was rewarded by a startled expression, quickly
masked. "It rains more in Wales in winter than in

spring,'' she replied, her infernal composure back in place.

"Now you tell me," Stephen muttered even as he wondered if there was anything else of importance his charge had failed to divulge, beyond her family's bizarre reputation. He felt a nagging ominous feeling at the thought, but shrugged it off when he heard a cry from ahead. The carts were stuck. *Again.* Stephen swore under his breath even as he nudged Hades forward. He wanted nothing so much as a drink, but instead he dismounted, putting his horse before the others while he tried, once again, to roll the vehicles from the clutches of the black, sucking mud.

But it was no good. Although the rain seemed to slacken, the ground remained slippery beyond his feeble efforts. Stephen suspected that Dunstan would have hefted the vehicle with one hand, and he felt his own lack sharply, along with a powerful thirst. Finally, Stephen glared at the immobile wagon in a burst of frustration.

"Abandon it," he said, and, with a fierce shout, he ordered his men to move the essential supplies it carried. They quickly began adding rolled pallets and foodstuffs to the backs of the horses, for all in the train were eager to be rid of what had become a hindrance. *All, that is,* except Brighid. Although she accepted some items from one of the soldiers, she made no effort to hide her disapproval. As usual.

She even gave him that look, but Stephen only lifted his brows and raked her with a leer that left no doubt he approved of the way her damp cloak molded to her upper body. Shooting him an outraged glance, she urged her palfrey to a faster pace, as if to flee him. With no little annoyance, Stephen caught up with her easily, reaching out to grab her by the arm.

"Stop fondling me," she snapped, glaring at him.

"If I start to fondle you, you'll know it," Stephen answered, even as he fought a sudden surge to do so. The rain had stopped, but Brighid was still wet, and the sight of her gleaming skin and clinging garments had an abrupt effect upon him. He quelled it with some effort. "Now, keep back. I told you to stay close to the men."

"Since you refuse to send anyone to scout ahead, I'll do it myself," she said. Something flashed in her eyes. Fear? Panic? Stephen blinked. He couldn't imagine the grim Brighid being afraid of anything. Like his father, she appeared to be above such mortal failings. Indeed, the only thing that made her human was the passion he had discovered. Is that what sent her running? Or was it something else? Stephen still suspected there was a reason for her haste, but she held her secrets closely guarded. Too many of them.

Stephen's eyes narrowed at the thought. "You're not going anywhere," he said. "As much as I despise the task, my father ordered me to escort you, and that means making sure you arrive at your destination in one piece. After that you can traipse about the countryside as you wish, trying to get yourself killed."

She gave him that look, rife with contempt, as if scorning his abilities to lead the train or keep her safe, and Stephen felt his jaw tighten in response. "Scouts are well-trained to explore, to find a route and to keep themselves hidden from enemies." He paused to let his gaze leisurely survey her form again, ending at her face, which had blanched at his perusal. *So, perhaps it was him she feared.* All the better, he thought, his lips curving.

"I see no sword or mail over those drab garments you favor. How do you propose to kill a wild boar, should it attack?" Stephen asked. "And what of the rumors of unrest in the land? Men bent on mischief won't stop to ask your ancestry or your allegiance, especially if they be a band of brigands, intent upon thievery and murder. They might even recognize your sex, though I admit it's difficult to discern, and I doubt if you would find their wooing as pleasurable as mine."

At his words, Brighid tried to shake off his hold, but Stephen urged Hades closer. He was so intent upon her that he could see her breasts rising and falling with each breath, more rapidly now. Against all reason, he knew a potent urge to pull her onto his lap, remove that hideous wimple, free her hair, and take her, wet and slick and wanting.

Brighid must have seen something flicker in his eyes, for she threw off his hold with a harsh sound and sent her palfrey racing past him. Watching her go, Stephen drew in a deep, ragged breath and tried to gain control over the lust that seemed to come upon him in a most inconvenient and demanding fashion these days. It took him a few moments to subdue the urges of his body while Brighid raced away from him, and when he finally had mastered himself to his own satisfaction, she had disappeared over the rim of the hill.

Stephen swore under his breath. His men were still behind him, transferring the rest of the supplies, and he felt a weariness that seemed to weigh down his entire being. Suddenly, he wanted a drink so badly, he could taste it. He hesitated, looking longingly back to where his special flasks of wine were being moved. Perhaps he would snare one to nurse on the cold ride.

Turning his head once more toward the direction

Brighid had gone, Stephen frowned. He ought to let his recalcitrant charge see for herself just how dangerous it was; mayhap then she might think better of his efforts to escort her. Unfortunately, Stephen doubted if anything could redeem him in her eyes, while it would be just like Brighid to get herself killed. Then what would he tell his father? As maddening as he found her, Stephen really didn't want anything to happen to her. All right, so maybe he should qualify that: *nothing that he didn't do to her himself anyway.*

But the threats he had related to her were very real, as was the possibility that she might lame her mount charging off in this terrain. Vaguely, Stephen was aware of the sound of running water, and his concern doubled. It might simply be a river that he heard, but rains such as these sometimes washed out roads, and he had heard tales of men, horses and wagons carried away.

Although large stones often marked the way in desolate country like this, snow and floods were likely to close any road in winter when the track was difficult to discern. He had also heard stories of whole bridges breaking up in particularly hard winters, and so far this season had been the worst any man could recall. Abruptly seized by ominous thoughts, Stephen urged Hades forward.

And when he crested the hill, he saw that his anxiety had not been misplaced. A river that might be a gently meandering one come summer now filled its banks with chunks of ice and melt from snow. The raging flow, perhaps fed by runoff from the distant mountains, had snatched shrubs and debris from along its edges and was battering the bridge that spanned it with terrible force. Already, pieces of stone had been dislodged and followed the rest of the flotsam downstream in a torrent.

Where was Brighid? His eyes narrowing, Stephen swore again, louder, as he saw a lone figure hunched over a palfrey. Although the animal valiantly tried to make its way across the slippery surface of the bridge, it was being assailed on all sides by spray and worse. If the fool wench wasn't struck by debris, she might well be swept from the span by the wash that assailed it.

His heart pounding, Stephen lifted a hand to his mouth and shouted a warning, but he couldn't be heard over the roar of the water. He could only watch, stricken with horror, as a massive tree limb rose upward, heading straight for Brighid. A guttural sound broke from his throat when the wood surged higher only to suddenly drop and strike the arch of the bridge, where it broke apart with horrifying force.

The sight spurred Stephen to action, and with a bellow that resembled one of his brothers' battle cries, he sent Hades racing for the bridge. Apparently possessed of more sense than Brighid, the horse balked at the river, but finally obeyed, tossing his head in disagreement as he struggled against the water that splashed up to drench them. Still, Stephen pushed the animal onward, toward the palfrey that was sliding down the slope to the other bank.

And Hades was swift, his heavy hooves more sure than the smaller beast. Indeed, it seemed they flew over the slippery surface of the span in the blink of an eye, too quickly for Stephen to notice anything except his quarry—until he became aware of an ominous sound. Above the roar of the water, beyond the crash of wood and scrub against the bridge itself, came the terrifying rumble of stone separating from its moorings, along with the startling sensation of shaking, as if the very earth below were shifting. Shifting and *breaking apart*.

Fear clawing at his insides, Stephen urged Hades forward even as the animal scrambled for a footing. And in the flash of an instant, they were beside Brighid. Stephen reached out, caught her up with one arm and hauled her from her saddle onto his lap as the destrier charged down the last length of the slope and onto land. The speed of the animal kept them thundering across the muddy track, while the deafening roar behind them told Stephen that they had only barely escaped with their lives.

Finally, Hades slowed to a halt near a wooded copse. His chest heaving, Stephen turned to look back, and saw the palfrey, spurred to haste at the presence of the destrier, not far away. But, behind the palfrey was a scene that made him stare in horror. The bridge they had crossed was gone. *Completely gone.* Only the very edges on either bank appeared intact, while the remains of the massive stones tumbled in the raging flood, tossed like feathers upon the water.

Stephen shuddered as the full import of his narrow escape became clear. He had trained for battle in harsh and dangerous ways and even fought against his brothers' enemies, but his brothers jested that he always came away with nary a scratch upon his near perfect form. Never before had he come so close to losing his life, and suddenly that which had seemed dismal and bleak was very precious indeed.

As the realization dawned, Stephen swung his attention toward Brighid. Against all odds, he was alive, as was she. The stark terror that had seized him ebbed, to be replaced by a wild rush of relief that made him tear the wimple from her head. As she stared at him, wide-eyed and pale, he took her face in his hands and claimed her mouth in a fierce act of possession.

Stephen felt her startled gasp and then her response, hot and hungry and nearly as aggressive as his own. With a low groan, he welcomed it, and winding one arm around her, he pulled her fully against him. Although hampered by her skirts and her position across his lap, Stephen felt the press of her supple form against his hardness and wanted to cry out, to growl and bellow and shout with an excitement such as he had not known in years.

They might have remained entwined in a savage embrace, unable to do more, but unwilling to do any less, if not for Hades. The restive animal moved beneath them, and finally, they broke apart to stare, panting, into each other's eyes. Shouts rose up behind him, but Stephen heeded them not. He looked into those green depths and felt himself drowning as surely as if he had been carried off with the bridge. The life he knew seemed to slip away as he was sucked into the maelstrom, his world shattering, his very essence transformed into something new and frightening and yet...

Shaken, Stephen tore his gaze from hers when Hades danced away from two men, who ran toward them only to halt and gape at the lost bridge. Dressed in simple garb, they looked to be villeins or cottagers, and they murmured both prayers and imprecations at the river's fury. Following their gaze, Stephen saw anew the destruction, as well as his men at arms, who stood on the opposite bank shouting in vain, for nothing could be heard above the roar of the river.

Stephen sucked in a harsh breath as the full import of their situation struck him. His soldiers could not reach him, nor could he regain their company. He and Brighid were completely isolated, unless there was some other

way to cross the water. Glancing down at the two cottagers, he called to them. "You, there!"

The taller of the two cocked his head back, as if suddenly remembering the presence of strangers. "Yes,
sire? Are you all right?" he asked.

At the question, Stephen felt himself shudder anew,
and only great strength of will kept the telltale tremble
from taking over his whole body again, while the ever
critical Brighid was in his arms to feel it. "We are un-
hurt, but we've been separated from our train. Is there
another bridge where they can cross? We are headed in
the direction of Lampeter."

The fellow shook his head. "No, sire. Not near here.
Perhaps south at Llandeilo." His compatriot shrugged in
ignorance, while Stephen listened with startled disbelief.
Suddenly, he felt like laughing in the faces of the men
who stared up at him so earnestly.

Of course, there was no other bridge. He should have
expected as much from this hellish journey! For a moment, Stephen felt utterly at a loss, automatically turning
for guidance to the brothers who were not present. And
in their absence, he again felt his own lack. If only Dunstan were here, surely the famed warrior would sprout
wings and fly back to his men! A rumble of laughter
rose in his chest, and Stephen stifled it, for these simple
men would think him mad should he loose it. Then,
again, what did it matter? Perhaps he was going mad. *If
he didn't die of thirst first.*

The urgent need for a drink seized him so violently
that he jerked, and with sudden horror, he realized that
his store of wine was across the river with his men.
Hades carried a pallet and some food, along with some
of his personal belongings, but nothing to drink beyond

a flask of water. And a swift glance toward the barren countryside showed no signs of hospitality.

Fighting against a surge of panic, Stephen tried to concentrate on his next course of action. Keeping his massive destrier in line with an absent shift of his thighs, he could see no choices. "Well, I guess we will have to rendezvous at Llandeilo," he said, though he had no idea just how far south the town might be.

The words had barely left his mouth before he was confronted by the squirming, squalling woman on his lap. "You cannot mean to go back when we are so close!" Brighid protested.

"So close?" Stephen echoed. "I see naught here but wilderness. Just how many miles is it? Hours or days?"

She gave him that look, and Stephen's jaw tightened. "A day's journey, maybe more in this weather," she said. "But surely, even you can see how—"

"Careful," Stephen muttered, with a black scowl of warning. "Or I might forget that I just saved your hide."

Brighid blanched, her lips pursing tightly, and, for a moment he thought she might argue. All right, so maybe she could have made it across the bridge before it gave way without his help, but then she would have been stranded here, prey to these two fellows and far worse. The woman should be grateful, instead of churlish. Why, she ought to—

Stephen's thoughts were cut off by her sudden frown. She glanced away, as if gathering her composure, then, to his everlasting astonishment, her expression crumpled as she reached for his arm. "Please, Stephen. We are so close. I swear to you!"

Not *my lord,* but *Stephen.* And though he had long thought himself immune to the wiles of women, Stephen felt himself waver, for this was no haughty demand. Nor

was it a feigned entreaty. The grim and rigid Brighid
was practically begging him. All right, so maybe it
wasn't the sort of begging he had always envisioned her
doing, but it was certainly an improvement over her
usual behavior.

And, if they were as close as she claimed, there was
decent shelter ahead, with wine and food and a warm
bed... Stephen didn't let his thoughts tread too far in
that direction. Yet, if he rode all the way to Llandeilo
to meet his men, he would more than double the journey
to reach her home. And for what? Either way, they
would be traveling alone and unattended, for the most
part. Although Stephen had a healthy enough respect for
his own skin to shy from the dangers involved, he
couldn't deny a sudden surge of excitement at the
thought of Brighid dependent solely upon him.

"Very well," he told her, his lips curving. Then he
turned toward his men, who waited silently on the opposite shore. After a useless series of gesticulations, he
finally deposited Brighid on the ground, dismounted
himself and took up a piece of stone and a rock to mark
upon it.

"Go home," he wrote, despite the catch in his chest
he felt at the command. Although he could send them
on to await him at Llandeilo, Stephen had no idea how
long it would take him to deliver Brighid to her father's
manor. And there was always the possibility that he
might find another route back to Campion that would
not take him so far south. Of course, without them, he
would have to go home alone, a daunting prospect, but
he might be able to hire some men-at-arms to accompany him. In the meantime, there was no sense in making these fellows kick their heels on what might be a

wasted errand, especially if there was more flooding downstream.

Certain now, Stephen held up the stone, knowing that Oswin, at least, could read. When satisfied that they would do his bidding, he turned again to Brighid, who, for once, appeared satisfied with his decision. The familiar look of contempt was missing from her face. Instead, it appeared impassive, yet she seemed nervous and tense. *As well she should,* Stephen thought, with no little triumph. There would be no attendant to shield her and no men to interrupt them, should his taunting lead on to other, more enjoyable things. She was well and truly at his mercy, and Stephen tried to keep the smug smile from his lips.

But it soon became apparent that despite her outward strain, Brighid was not shaking in her slippers. She lifted her chin, shoulders straight, and met his gaze directly, holding it with her own as she spoke. "Thank you," she said, simply but sincerely. Although after what they had just been through, Stephen might have preferred a more effusive manner of gratitude, he would take what he could get.

He shrugged, suddenly all too aware of the ulterior motives that had influenced his decision. Although he did not care for this woman's disdain, neither did he court some misplaced sense of admiration from her. He was not one of his brothers, aglow with honor and glory. Whirling on his heel, he watched as his men and supplies disappeared over the crest of the hill across the raging river.

Then, reminded of his prodigious thirst, he turned toward the cottagers, who still stood close, gawking at them. "Is there an inn nearby?" he asked.

When the short one stared at him as though he were

speaking in tongues, Stephen bit back a growl of frustration. "An alehouse then?" he asked. But the two only eyed him blankly once more, and he felt panic rise from his vitals to grasp him about the throat. Surely, there must be a cup of wine to be had in this godforsaken country!

"Your lord. Where does he reside?" Stephen asked. They pointed to the track behind them, and Stephen blew out a harsh breath of relief as he envisioned a warm fire, a great hall, a gracious host and wine flowing generously. He would be all right, he thought, a smug smile beginning. If they could just reach the manor house owned by the lord of these lands, everything would be all right.

Chapter Nine

Nothing was right. Nor would anything ever be right again, Stephen swore as he stared at the sun that had begun to dip toward the horizon. Despite the cold air, he could feel the clammy cling of sweat upon his brow, and only the force of his will kept his fingers from shaking. He had the odd sensation that if he let go the reins, the trembling would take over his whole body until he was shuddering like one possessed by fits. *Or the devil.*

Right now, he was ready to believe in just about any possibility, including curses, witches and all manner of supernatural forces, for what had befallen him lately bore no relation to his previous charmed existence. Cut off from his home, his family, even his men, he was alone in the wilds of a strange country. No, not alone, he amended. Far better to be by himself, for then he would not have to maintain this pretense and could give in to the despair that made him long to sit by the side of the road and bawl like a babe at his fate.

Tis your destiny. Sliding a glance toward the woman beside him, Stephen wondered at the aunt's words. Perhaps Brighid was a witch, and all these trials were heaped upon him for not giving her respect. Even as he automatically dismissed the notion, Stephen remembered how those green eyes of hers had drawn him in until he felt as though he would be sucked away, his identity, for what it was worth, lost forever.

Stephen grunted at his own foolishness. Perhaps the mad dash over the bridge had done something to him. Reaching up to run a hand through his hair, he remembered that he was wearing no helm. Maybe he had been struck by flying debris and was too caught up in his life-or-death race to notice. How else to explain the way his mind careened wildly from one bizarre thought to another?

Stephen was not himself, of that he was sure. *He needed a drink.* His mouth felt dry, his throat tight with thirst, yet he disdained the flask of water that rested behind him. If only they could reach the manor belonging to the lord of these lands. Unfortunately, the men who directed him this way had gone on, following the bank of the river, though Stephen had seen no evidence of a path there. And Brighid was no help. She claimed she would know when they neared her old home, but appeared to be unfamiliar with other landmarks.

Stephen blew out a breath of frustration. Roads, he had learned, existed to connect towns, while other, less-traveled routes led from castle to castle, from manor to manor. If he had known this before, he paid no attention, for one of his brothers always led the party. Now, unfortunately, he was in charge, and all he had to direct him were a few words from a couple of doltish villeins, who seemed little better acquainted with the area than himself.

And now it was too late. The sun was going to set soon, and they couldn't be wandering around in the dark, losing the track entirely. He swore beneath his breath,

his jaw clamped shut, his chest tight, his throat con-
stricted, and threw all of his powerful charm, all the luck
that he had relied on without even thinking, into the hope
that something—anything—might appear over the crest
of the hill.

It did. Stephen drew in a sharp breath, laced with relief only to expel it swiftly as he realized that what he
saw ahead was only a croft, one of a handful along the
route he could hardly call a road. His eyes narrowing,
Stephen searched the landscape more thoroughly, but
nothing else lay in sight except the lowly huts, perhaps
that of freemen or cottagers such as the men they had
seen earlier.

The buildings were much the same here as at home:
two long timbers curved to meet at the top, the walls
were wattle and daub, and the floor, Stephen knew,
would be dirt. He groaned. As someone well accustomed
to his luxuries, the thought of bedding down in such a
place, where the family's precious cow or pig might well
join them, did not particularly appeal.

No doubt, Brighid would bear it all stoically, and why
not? This was all her fault. Hadn't he told her and her
daft aunts, aye, and even his own father, that it was too
early in the year to begin such a trip? If it were summer,
they could camp in the open beside a fire, but it was too
cold yet to do so, without the tents and shelter of the
carts. And why hadn't anyone thought to mention that
it rained more in winter in this godforsaken country?

Stephen licked his dry lips and wondered just what
they were going to do. Despite all his fine plans back at
the river, he felt totally unprepared to meet the future.
Already, the sinking sun was casting shadows on the
land, and Stephen felt the press of the night coming on
him. He took deep breaths to dispel the sensation and

with a jerk of the reins, turned Hades toward the nearest croft. It was time to beg for shelter.

The man who lived there eyed his visitors warily, but Stephen felt just as leery, especially when the stench of unwashed human bodies, animals and unsavory food rolled out of the door to meet him. He tried not to breathe as he spoke. "I am Lord de Burgh. I seek shelter for the night. Can you tell me how far it is to the manor?"

The man shook his grizzled head, not exactly the response Stephen was seeking. He felt himself shudder and firmly quelled it. "We were told that a manor lay this way," he said, lifting an arm to encompass the so-called road. When the fellow only eyed him blankly, Brighid urged her palfrey forward, as if she would usurp Stephen's position. Annoyed, he opened his mouth to put her in her place, only to shut it again, when she spoke in an unintelligible gibberish that he belatedly realized must be Welsh.

Great. The people here didn't even speak English. Scowling, Stephen watched the two speak rapidly even as he tried to remember his language lessons, but he had never been a good student. His brother Geoffrey, the scholar, could no doubt converse with anyone in any country, but Geoff wasn't here. He had warned Stephen often enough that someday he would wish he had paid more attention to his studies. Stephen grunted. Actually, his wishes right now were more along the lines of a warm fire and a cup of wine, preferably back at Campion, while someone else took over this hellish trip.

When at last Brighid nodded, apparently thanking the man, Stephen looked toward her expectantly. "Well?" he asked, his brows lifted. She urged her palfrey past him, away from the croft, as if to talk privately, which was not a good sign, Stephen decided. Did she think he would have a fit at any bad news? He very well might, he thought grimly.

"Tis too far for us to reach tonight," she said. Although she spoke evenly, without the slightest flicker of disappointment, Stephen felt himself shudder as despair leapt at the vestiges of his control. "But there's an empty croft farther down the road, where he said we can stay."

Stephen's eyes narrowed as he studied her bent head. "And just why is it empty? Did illness take the residents?" He wasn't sleeping in any hovel where the stench of death still lingered, ready to seize him next. He'd rather freeze.

"No. They didn't die. They just had business elsewhere. Why, it might even have been them we saw at the bridge!" Brighid said in a conversational tone that made Stephen eye her suspiciously. He wondered what sort of "business" those two might have leaving their homes in winter. Were they even freemen or were they bound to their lord for service?

"There! See? It lies just down this track," Brighid said, practically chattering as she pointed toward a hut much like the others. Stephen knew an ominous sense of dread, along with the feeling of oppression that came with the approaching night. His blood thundered, making his head hurt, and he felt a trickle of sweat inch down his neck.

The hovel ahead might provide rudimentary shelter, but it certainly wasn't going to give him the wine he needed, and the knowledge set his every nerve on edge. Stephen knew he wasn't dependent on drink. He knew it full well in his mind. Unfortunately, the rest of him was clamoring for that blissful escape, that wonderful haziness that would deaden his cold and exhaustion and all the ills that plagued him, *that would let him rest.*

Stephen sucked in a harsh breath as the full import of his lack settled over him. The long hours of the night lay ahead, stretching out before him with a starkness that made him flinch. That small motion turned into a shudder that wracked his entire body as he wondered helplessly how he was ever going to survive until dawn.

Seeing Stephen's scowl, Brighid tried to fill the brooding silence with speech, for she didn't want him to dwell upon her conversation with the cottager or ask her any pointed questions. In truth, she hadn't been quite honest with her escort.

Oh, she hadn't really lied. She simply hadn't disclosed all of the information she had received, like the fact that the manor wasn't too far away, but lay in the opposite direction. The sun was setting fast, so it was not as though they were assured of reaching the place before nightfall anyway, Brighid told herself. And who could blame her for not wanting to waste time searching for something out of their way, especially since Stephen, in his current surly mood, might want to dally there?

They were much better off taking the shelter that was at hand, Brighid decided. Even though the accommodations might not be up to de Burgh standards, she had been assured that the croft was clean and well-kept, having recently been vacated. That, too, gave her pause, but Brighid ignored it. Given Stephen's black expression, why should she tell him that the residents had been called by their local lord, anxious to arm against any incursions by the crown?

Besides, why should she feel compelled to share anything with Stephen, when he had been nothing except a useless, drunken rogue, taunting her with his practiced love play? But even as she lifted her chin in righteous defense, Brighid knew those thoughts no longer rang true, and she felt a strange sort of disloyalty for trying to cling to them.

Brighid sighed. Although she had not thought it so, everything had been so simple before they crossed the bridge. Stephen tormented her, she despised him for it and their roles were both clearly defined. Her goal was to reach her father's house, despite the company of the randy de Burgh, without succumbing to his wiles.

Her own infrequent lapses in such matters Brighid had dismissed as the natural reaction of a healthy woman unused to contact with men, especially one as handsome as Stephen de Burgh, and she studiously avoided any further contemplation of her response. Indeed, she refused to think of it, fleeing like a gutless coward from the temptation he presented.

But by letting that fear rule her, Brighid had disregarded every bit of good judgment she possessed, finally flinging herself headlong over a bridge that any fool could see was dangerous. At the time, she had thought of nothing except escaping Stephen, of freeing herself from that thick, hot, spell he wove around her that made her weak and vulnerable and witless.

Yet her single-minded flight had proven to be a mistake, all too quickly. Not only had she nearly gotten herself killed, but thanks to her own reckless actions, she was in an even worse position than before. Now, she was well and truly stuck with Stephen de Burgh. *Alone.* Although the whole situation fairly reeked of fate, Brighid dismissed such promptings as swiftly as she always did.

However, she couldn't dismiss the fact that Stephen

de Burgh had saved her life, an act of bravery that he appeared to shrug off with the careless ease of everything else. She didn't know whether to be angry or awed at his attitude, but she was faced with a new truth that rang out louder than any of her old perceptions about the man who was her escort.

Stephen de Burgh was not the useless creature she had thought him. Oh, she knew he was lazy and drank and didn't seem to care about much, but when the bridge began to collapse, he didn't pause to consider anything except the danger that threatened her. Certainly, he had no great reason to rescue her, a woman who had been at odds with him since their first meeting. Yet he had dashed forward, risking his own safety, for her.

He was a hero. Brighid had spent the hours since that realization contemplating this new version of Stephen de Burgh, and, uneasily, she began to wonder just what else she had misconstrued about the man beside her.

Already, he had proved her wrong again, by agreeing to take her home, when she expected him to go on to Llandeilo. And now, instead of throwing recriminations at her head, he seemed to accept her decision to take shelter in a croft. The thought of the arrogant de Burgh, pampered and elegant and demanding, spending the night in a freeman's hut was enough to make Brighid laugh. She might have, too, if the idea of being alone with him there wasn't so unsettling.

Suddenly, using the tiny structure because of its location didn't seem quite so clever, while the more distant manor with its separate chambers appeared far more appealing. As darkness settled around them, Brighid was acutely aware of the absence of Eda and the men who had served as chaperons by their very presence. There was no one else around and nowhere for her to run.

A shiver stole up her back, and Brighid promptly quelled it. She lifted her chin and straightened her shoulders, unwilling to let her anxiety cloud her judgment. Stephen was only a man, after all, she told herself, and one who had acted selflessly to save her life. That reminder would serve her well, for such a man would surely not importune her. At least Brighid hoped so, for if Stephen continued his taunting of her this night, she wasn't sure she would have the strength or wherewithal to refuse him.

Her heart beating wildly, Brighid stole a glance at her companion, but his expression was grim. No doubt, he was displeased with their shelter, but he said nothing as he dismounted and tethered the horses. Leaving him to care for the mounts, Brighid took some of her meager supplies and stepped toward the croft, opening the door with the hope that it would be livable.

It was. Brighid was pleasantly surprised, for, though small, it was clean inside. There was even a small supply of wood and by the time Stephen entered, she had a fire growing in the hearth. The heat was welcome and she rubbed her hands together over the blaze. Suddenly, she realized just how weary she was, and she wasted no time in laying out her pallet upon the dirt floor not far from the fire.

Not certain exactly what she carried with her, Brighid opened a sack and was pleased to find a load of small, dried apples. She offered one to Stephen, but he turned away with a snort, so she ate in silence. He was searching through his supplies and swearing, and for a long moment Brighid wondered what he could be seeking. And then it struck her: his wine.

In truth, her decision to stay here and not at the farther manor had nothing to do with his drink or lack of it. For all she knew, he kept a flask about his neck for constant imbibing. But now Brighid realized that he did not carry it with him, and she was caught between a cruel delight at his misfortune and a deeper, unwelcome concern for his plight.

With a loud oath, he tossed half a wheel of cheese upon the ground, startling Brighid, who snatched it up and dusted it off. Watching him warily, she cut off a piece and held it out for him, but he shook his head, his expression hard and bleak.

"Come. You must eat something," Brighid said. They had been riding hard since the morning meal, and a man of Stephen's proportions must surely take in plenty of food. But he only snarled at her, like a cornered animal.

"I'm going to sleep," he finally muttered, and gathering a blanket around himself, he lay down upon his pallet, his back to her. It was not exactly how Brighid had imagined the evening passing, and she stifled a burst of anxious laughter at the thought. Her fears, it appeared, had been unwarranted, and she felt both relief and a kind of unbidden dismay at the realization that Stephen de Burgh had no intention of tormenting her.

Silently, Brighid ate a large wedge of cheese and another apple before drinking the water she carried with her. She considered offering some to Stephen, then thought better of it and put the flask away. Eyeing him warily, she slipped outside to take care of her personal needs. When she returned, Stephen gave no sign that he had noticed her, but lay still on his side, facing away from her.

Emboldened, Brighid dragged in a pail of rainwater and placed it on the hearth, then found a clean gown among her things. Hanging her cloak as a makeshift curtain, she swiftly washed as best she could and donned the dry garments. For the first time since the rain began this morning, she felt warm, and she put her damp garments by the fire.

Briefly, Brighid considered offering Stephen the heated water, but the thought of him bathing with it made her feel faint. He would hide behind nothing, flaunting his naked body, tall and muscled and tempting... Shutting her eyes tightly against the image, Brighid told herself that the rain and floodwaters had kept him clean enough, while a man such as he wouldn't be bothered by a little dampness in his clothes.

Settling on her pallet, Brighid tried in vain to put some sort of order to her unruly hair. She had lost her last remaining wimple in the bridge disaster, and she was not skilled at braiding. Finally, she dragged it all over one shoulder into a thick mass and laid down, letting the night quiet wash over her. But the strange surroundings, coupled with a certain tension in the air, made it difficult to relax. She knew that, despite his prone form, Stephen was not asleep. He was lying there, wide-awake, unwilling even to talk to her.

Oddly enough, Brighid felt rather insulted, but hadn't she known all along that she held no real interest for him? His behavior this evening reminded her of his priorities, wine being most important to him. He might be a hero, but the man was still flawed, Brighid noted, and she would do well to keep that in mind.

Brighid awoke with a start, the sound of something ringing in her ears. A scream? A groan? Her heart pounding, she opened her eyes, recognizing immediately her lowly surroundings. *Stephen!* She sat up, certain that he had called to her, crying out in anguish. She glanced at his pallet, found it empty, and knew a sudden, heart-wrenching alarm.

"Stephen!" Brighid whispered his name into the stillness, just as she swung her gaze toward the door and finally saw him, stalking across the small confines of the croft. "Are you all right?" she asked.

She was rewarded with a dark glare that gave her his answer. "I can't sleep," he muttered.

Dumbfounded, Brighid lifted a hand to her loose hair and tried to adjust her thinking. Just like the other night she had been awakened by the promptings of a soul in pain, only to find Stephen de Burgh nursing a minor complaint. Yet this time he was not slouching over a cup, careless and seductive. Indeed, he was so strained that the very air seemed to resonate with tension, and though Brighid steeled herself against it, his distress washed over her in waves.

"How can you not rest after the day we've had?" she asked, studying him curiously.

Stephen just shook his head and continued to pace the area near the entrance, as though becoming more and more agitated. Brighid wondered if he had an abhorrence of small, contained spaces.

"I need a drink!" he finally snapped before swearing long and low, and at last, Brighid saw the truth. This was not the complaint of a pampered nobleman, but something else entirely. Did Stephen require wine like other men did water? Brighid remembered enough of healing to know that some potions enslaved a man, causing a constant craving if not fed. Perhaps, he was not the drunk she thought him, but a captive of his own needs.

The notion made Brighid shiver, sending her thoughts veering far away from wine until she reined them in resolutely. She took a deep breath. No matter what her personal feelings might be, this man had saved her life, and now he was in pain. If she had it within her power to aid him, then she must. But, then, that was the question, wasn't it? Had she any power?

"Come, sit down," she said, without pausing to consider how Stephen might interpret her words.

His dark brows rose. "Dare I hope that you wish to distract me?" he asked, his lips curving into a mocking smile.

Brighid shook her head. "Nay, but I know a little of healing. Perhaps I can help you," she said.

Stephen eyed her skeptically. "No, thank you. Your aunts already tried to work their arts on me, and they claimed that *you* wouldn't approve."

Brighid frowned. Leery of asking just what it was that her aunts had wanted to do to him, she simply motioned him to take a seat beside her. "Did they?" she asked as casually as possible. "They tell me that they no longer practice the healing arts, but I have suspected their lapses more than once."

To her surprise, Stephen sank down on the narrow pallet, but remained wary. He was strung taut as a bow, his muscles visibly tense, his jaw tightly clenched, and Brighid felt her heart go out to him. "Lie down," she said, drawing his head into her lap. He shuddered, his body trembling before becoming unnaturally stiff, as if to hide the shaking from her.

"Are you sure it's healing you have in mind, Brighid?" he asked, derision evident in his deep voice. "Because, as much as I'd love to pick up where we've left off before, I'm afraid I wouldn't perform up to my usual standards tonight. Perhaps it's the lingering scent of hogs in our luxurious surroundings."

"Hush. Close your eyes," Brighid whispered. After giving her a last glare of warning, he did so, and she smoothed the dark hair away from his brow, startled by the heat that shot through her. Even now, in repose, Stephen seemed to cast his spell upon her, but she tempered her touch, trying to work a different kind of magic, for his sake. His hair was beautiful, lustrous and smooth, and she stroked it gently from his face, deliberately making her caress that of a nurturer, a healer.

"I can see why you wouldn't want your aunts doing this," he muttered.

His wry comment startled a laugh from her. "Each healer must work in her own way, but I expect my aunts would proffer a potion…or perhaps something else," Brighid said, suddenly remembering the amethyst.

"And are they so bad at it that you forbid them to practice?" Stephen asked, in derision. "I can well imagine that."

"Nay," Brighid said, slipping her hand into her pocket, where the stone her aunts had given her remained. It was worthless, she knew, and yet she was desperate.

"Take this and hold on to it," she said, pressing the rock into Stephen's palm. Although he snorted, his fingers closed over it in a rather fierce grip, as if it were a lifeline he would cling to, and Brighid felt his anguish so strongly that she had to catch her breath. Stephen de Burgh was not a drunk. He was ill, and she must do her best to make him well. Loosing her air in a low rush, Brighid forced herself to calmness and resumed the stroking of his hair, searching his skull for certain points that were known to ease distress.

"Actually, my aunts are quite good at healing, but I have asked them not to practice for their own good,"

Brighid explained. "Too many wise women are accused of causing harm, if the ignorant people they seek to aid do not recover as those around them hope."

Stephen grunted at the press of her fingers. "They may be foolish, but I can hardly imagine anyone accusing them of causing harm."

"Perhaps, but it would not be the first time such a thing had happened in our family. You see, my own grandmother was drowned as a witch," Brighid said. Immediately, she felt the jerk of Stephen's body as he lifted his head and turned to look up at her with a shocked expression. Gently, but firmly, she drew his head back down into her lap. "Don't tell me that you haven't heard rumors about the l'Estranges," she murmured.

"Yes, but I had no idea your...that *anyone* was murdered in such a barbaric fashion. That's incredible! Unconscionable! Who's responsible?" he growled, just as though he would personally exact justice for the crime.

Quelling a tiny twinge of pleasure at this response, Brighid passed a hand over his eyes, closing them. "It happened a long time ago. People fear what they don't understand, and they are notoriously fickle," she said softly. "The same man who claims a wise woman healed his son from a fever may turn around and accuse her of putting a curse on him. My aunts mean well, but I would they watch after themselves and not others."

Although Brighid saw the frown that curved his lips, Stephen said no more. Gradually, she felt his body relax again and she realized that she, too, was at ease. There was something comforting about touching him, the rare contact with another person a balm after all her years of loneliness. She had her aunts, of course, but they were her family. This was different, and Brighid welcomed the weight and warmth of him in her lap, the scent of him weaving into her senses, the feel of his smooth hair and masculine skin.

Filled with a peace that transcended all else, Brighid leaned against the wall of the croft and let her eyelids drift shut. But she kept at her task, her fingers massaging Stephen's temples until she drifted off to sleep to the soft sound of his even breathing.

Chapter Ten

Stephen awoke slowly, to the pleasing realization that his head was cushioned in a female lap. It was not the first time he had found himself so cozily ensconced, and he nuzzled deeper into his nest, drawing in the scent of woman, along with some elusive, heady spice. As usual, the memory of the evening's encounter was rather vague, but the lady must be quite a lover, for he felt better than he had in years.

Indeed, the more he roused himself, the better Stephen felt. His body was refreshed and his mind clear, after having slept deeply and heavily the night through, a nearly impossible feat. And while he often despised the niceties required of him when he woke up in a lady's bed, Stephen found himself oddly lighthearted and eager to continue his dalliance.

With a yawn, he stretched his arms upward, stroking along thighs covered with some simple material. She was dressed? Stephen realized that he was, as well. They must have been in a hurry last night, but he knew no such haste today. He let his hands explore leisurely until they settled upon a firm set of buttocks. Smiling, he cupped them and squeezed lightly, only to hear a loud thump as his berth jerked and shifted.

Lifting his chin, Stephen saw his companion rubbing her head as if she had just conked it on the wall behind her, and it was only then, when he noticed the scowl on her face, that the evening's events returned to him, with the impact of a cudgel. All too well, without the haze of wine to dull his memories, he recalled his struggle to get through the night.

It had always been difficult, but he had learned to ease his way with drink and the warmth of womanly charms. Last evening, however, had been worse than ever before. Without the wine to dull his senses, the blackness had seemed to close in on him with a stultifying intensity. In desperation, he had begun pacing the tiny hut, but there was nowhere to go, no place to hide....

And then Brighid had called to him.

Closing his eyes against the harsh glare of the truth, Stephen realized that this woman, his least likeliest of paramours, had seen him at his most vulnerable. *Naked.* Not bare of body, but of the soul, and he felt the cold wash of shame, whatever brief victory he had known in the war that had raged between them gone.

Stephen could easily imagine the look she would give him now as far worse than any she had tendered before. Along with the continual contempt, he would see pity— or worse. At the unbearable thought, he felt like running from this place and this woman, from everything that was his life. But he could not. Nor could he pretend to ignore what had happened here in the darkness, when she had rocked him like a babe.

If only the rocking had been of a different sort! Sex made it different. *Sex made it all right.* The women who shared his bed never suspected that he was not at ease in every situation, and they were too satisfied come morning to give him any look but one of gratitude. Unfortunately, last night he had not even touched Brighid. Stephen had felt too wretched to seek that remedy, even if she had been willing, which he very much doubted. Indeed, he had only lain down beside her in an effort to stop the throbbing in his head.

But it wasn't too late, was it? Stephen could feel the tension in her body as she remained where she was, awake but silent. Was she feeling sorry for him, even now? The intolerable notion made Stephen flex his fingers against her even as he turned his head toward her thigh. He nuzzled her there, through the drab-colored gown, and drew his hands back down her legs to her knees and beyond, where, at last, he found the hem of the garment.

Stephen eased it up slowly, letting his fingers drift across the ridges of her ankles, enjoying the feel of them through the softness of her hose. Although Brighid stiffened, he continued upward, raising the skirt even as he skimmed the limbs beneath. Normally such play would qualify as rote preparations, but Stephen felt his breath hitch and his heart thunder.

Her scent, subtle yet enticing, invaded his senses until he felt as though with every breath he took her inside himself. And he was even more aware of her own breathing, though it was soft and erratic. Each telltale gasp echoed within him, loud and enthralling. And the feel of her! Even the texture of her simple garment was exciting, though he had yet to touch her skin. Never before had he been so consumed, so taken with a woman, as if every fiber of his being were alive and in tune with hers.

Without pausing to consider the absurdity of such

musings, Stephen dropped his head and pressed a kiss to her calf. She uttered a strangled cry and went rigid, but Stephen eased her with his caress, a gentle massage that went all the way up to her knees, where her garters lay against pale skin that drew him like a bee to honey.

Gradually, Stephen felt the tension leave her body, saw her hands lift into the air as if she were not certain what to do with them, and he smiled against her thigh. Unfortunately, his heady victory meant little, for, by this time his own sex was swollen and hard. And any thoughts of ending this play were dismissed, as it was no longer pretense that drove him, but his own burgeoning need.

Stephen drew his thumbs across her garters and leaned forward, unable to resist. Inhaling deeply, he felt suddenly dizzy, giddy with a surfeit of sensation, though he had barely touched her skin. He kissed her there, in the indentation that lay above her garter and then behind her knee, where the flesh was kitten soft and sweet.

Drawing up her errant skirts more impatiently now, he pushed them away as each inch of smooth skin was revealed. He discovered it with his mouth as well as his eyes, all of his senses seemingly engaged as never before, while the scent of her arousal drew him closer and closer to the hot center of her. He kissed the inside of her thigh, reveling in her subsequent shivers, in the heady mix of innocence and forbidden fruit that awaited him as his mouth moved higher and higher...until he was abruptly dislodged from his position.

A knee slammed upward to strike him in the side of the head, and while Stephen was still reeling from that blow, the entire lap in which he was nestled disengaged, dumping him face first onto the dirt floor of the croft. If possessed of his usual poise, he might have managed to recover his balance, but somewhere along the line his fingers had begun to tremble, his body thrumming with the force of his desire. Somehow, in his efforts to discompose Brighid, he had succeeded in discomfiting himself. Stephen wondered idly if she had broken his nose this time instead of his lip.

"What are you doing?" she shrieked in a voice that seemed far louder than normal, perhaps because she was standing while he was lying prone on the ground.

Pushing up into a squat, Stephen spit out some dirt and gingerly tested his features. "Just trying to finish what I started last night," he said. He was a master at maintaining a careless pose, and he did so now, for he was determined not to give away anything to this woman who had seen too much of him already.

"What are you talking about?" she asked, her face ashen.

"I apologize for falling asleep. I was not at my best, but I am rested now and more than ready to make up for my lack," Stephen said, with a casualness he did not feel. He gave her a wicked smile, and was rewarded by her shocked look of dismay. Something flickered in her eyes that had far more to do with pain than disdain.

"We must go," she said, turning away from him, her back rigid as she leaned over to gather up her things.

Rising, Stephen brushed off his braies, rubbed his nose, and reached for the supplies even as he watched Brighid's stiff movements with something akin to guilt. He had won this latest contest between them, for he had surely altered her perceptions of the night before. So why did he feel like a churl? Stephen tried to shrug away the sensation, as he had any unwanted feelings in the past, but it wouldn't go away. He was struck by the odd, lingering notion that he had taken something rare and precious and trod it into dust.

Stephen felt no better when he went outside to be met by a dazzling sun that hurt his eyes and seemed to sear into his very brain. Was Wales always so blessedly bright? As if prompted by the light, his head began to throb painfully once more. With a sudden yearning, he remembered the soothing touch that had sent him off into the most blissful sleep he had known in years, but he scowled and drove the memory way down deep.

Holding up a hand to shield his eyes, Stephen blinked against the harsh glare of the morning. Surely, he had never seen the like before! Even the sky seemed bluer, the trees blacker, all the colors of the landscape richer in hue. Stephen shook his head. Obviously, Wales was a bizarre place, well suited to this l'Estrange who claimed to be descended from witches.

With a snort, Stephen began strapping his meager belongings on Hades's back. It was a good thing he didn't believe in witchcraft or sorcery or he might be wary of retribution for his latest skirmish in the croft. But when he glanced over at Brighid, he knew no fear, only a host of other emotions, including a fair amount of shock.

Stephen gaped, arrested by her appearance, her *greatly changed* appearance. Had he been asleep or simply too drunk to notice? Or had she hidden herself so well that none could see? Whatever the reason for his former inattention, Stephen made up for it now by staring, transfixed, at his companion, for in this stark light, she was absolutely, utterly beautiful.

Her wimple had been lost, so that startling fall of hair danced about her face in a shimmering veil that seemed to glitter in the light before she tucked it beneath the hood of her heavy cloak. Stephen wished that he had wrapped a heavy length around his knuckles this morning and buried his face in it, though he couldn't really complain about the place where his face *had* been buried.

Still, her hair drew him, as but one of many mysteries that were Brighid. He sensed them, running deep and rife with complexities, but here, on the surface, she was scrubbed clean, her loveliness apparent as never before. Her face held none of the plumpness of other women, but was finely wrought in even lines, each feature—from her delicate brows to her stubborn chin—a work of art. And there, along the bridge of her nose, were sprinkled a few freckles.

The discovery affected his insides, and not the nether regions that the sight of Brighid so often stimulated, but somewhere higher, closer to his heart. Stephen was seized by the strangest sensation that he had never seen this woman before, and the notion was so compelling that it took him a moment to shrug it away. Turning toward Hades, he mounted the familiar animal only to feel as if his destrier, too, were unrecognizable.

Very strange indeed, he thought, automatically dismissing any lingering thoughts of paranormal powers. He wondered again if he had been struck upon the head yesterday when the bridge washed away. That would explain the ache above, if not below, he decided with a scowl. If only he could have a drink, he thought, and dizzy with the very possibility, he spurred Hades back onto the narrow road, following Brighid as she took a fork to the west.

The air was bracing and flowed into his lungs with a freshness that he found nearly unbearable. What was this place, and what magic had it wrought upon him? But Stephen had long since ceased to believe in anything except his wine, and gradually, as they rode along, he began to suspect that the absence of that beverage was responsible for his current condition.

The throbbing in his head faded, only to be replaced by a blinding clarity. He had used the drink, in increasingly large amounts, to deaden his senses for years, and now, without it, everything was too bright, too loud and too much for his heightened awareness to handle. Stephen closed his eyes on a groan as memory washed over him.

His father's second wife, Anne, had once told him that she worried about the boys, especially those from Campion's first marriage, because they possessed such passion. Dunstan and Simon kept it all contained, exploding in rages, while Geoffrey, alone, seemed able to temper his feelings. As for Stephen, she had reserved most of her concern for the child who simply felt too much, bleeding his emotions. Anne had told him that he must find a way to modulate them.

He had. And it had been due to Anne, for when she died, Stephen had opened a cask of wine and downed the contents until he collapsed, his head upon the table. And he had kept on drinking to deaden the pain of the loss, as well as the unbearable sight of his omnipotent father, lost and hurting. And even after everyone came out of mourning and Campion appeared to be himself again, Stephen continued to drink. He had grown accustomed to that hazy, warm numbing of the senses that the wine brought him.

But without it, everything was too much: the sounds, the smells, the colors and especially Brighid. The plain, mousy woman with the rigid demeanor and permanent scowl had turned into a vibrant creature, too alive, too intelligent, and way too alluring. Stephen had thought himself obsessed with her before, but now he had only to glance her way to find himself hard and aching.

If they would just come across an alehouse! Was there naught in this godforsaken place except sheep? As they followed a rough track for what seemed like hours, Stephen's need for drink grew even more fierce. He had long ago given up all hope of seeing the manor they had sought last night, but there had to be some signs of civilization. Yet, all he saw were sheep, and finally, more of the low stone crofts.

As they became more numerous, Stephen felt a new urgency. At last, they must be approaching a village, and there he would surely find a brewery of some kind, be it only a filthy hut. At this point, he didn't care, as long as he could finally drink something—anything—that would dull his screaming senses. He shuddered, and like a man who had been sleepwalking only to suddenly awake, shut his eyes against the newness of the world.

It was then that the brigands struck.

Brighid sensed a presence immediately. A wave of apprehension rolled over her that even she could not dismiss, and she warily eyed the stands of trees and shrubs along the road. But it was too little, too late. While she looked on, several men rose from the underbrush to leap toward the horses, brandishing daggers and cudgels. The palfrey danced away, skittish, and Brighid tried to maintain control of the animal as she turned to shout a warning behind her.

It was not necessary. If these ruffians thought they were catching a rich merchant unawares, they soon discovered their mistake, for Stephen de Burgh was not an average traveler. With a howl of fury that raised the flesh on Brighid's neck, he unsheathed his sword and cut down two ere they could unseat him.

Brighid had only a moment to admire his magnificence, for one of the ruffians had reached her mount and was pulling at her cloak. She held the reins with one hand and tried to fend him off with the other, but she was losing the battle and she knew it. Then, suddenly she drew herself up and called out to the man, her voice rising above the sound of battle behind her as she intoned an ancient Celtic curse.

The words came back to her easily, for Brighid had spent many a year studying arcane lore. Although she had never practiced the black arts, she knew enough of ignorant minds to draw upon the fears of men such as these. And, as she suspected, when her words rang out, the fellow blanched and fell back, as if uncertain. That moment was all Brighid needed in which to pull out her small dagger and bring it down upon his arm, sending him to the ground, screaming in pain.

Whirling around, Brighid saw the rest of the rabble fleeing their fallen companions, while Stephen de Burgh loomed over them, a massive warrior upon his mighty destrier, brandishing a bloody sword. Brighid watched him lower his weapon, though his dark eyes remained watchful. He wore no helm, and his hair was whipped about by a sudden wind, while his broad chest rose and fell with the force of his exertions. Brigid stared, her breath caught in her throat, for she had never seen the like in her life such as this knight.

Was this Stephen de Burgh?

Brighid felt a wash of confusion and amazement, followed by admiration and something else that pooled low in her belly and roused her entire body in a way that the earlier threat had not. It was a sensation altogether new to her, though she had known something similar before when in the throes of Stephen's kisses. In fact, just this morning when his lips and fingers had played upon her skin, she had lifted her fisted hands only to freeze, breathless, in place as he worked some sort of magic upon her.

Loath as she was to admit it, Brighid felt a burning lust for the man who had saved her life, not once now, but twice. At the realization, she only hoped she could conceal it from his mocking gaze. But when she finally glanced upward, Stephen wore no taunting expression, only a fierce, dangerous one that made her feel hot and weak.

"Are you all right?" he asked.

Unable to speak, Brighid could only nod at this strange man who had taken over Stephen de Burgh's body. He was totally different: alert, commanding, considerate—and deadly. She swallowed hard.

"Then, let us be off, in case they return in greater numbers," he said in a firm, decisive tone that little resembled his usual speech.

"Yes," Brighid said. Emerging from her daze, she pointed toward the slope on the other side of the road. "This way," she called as she swung the palfrey toward the low brush and beyond. And, for once, Stephen didn't argue.

Brighid sent her mount across an expanse of winter grasses that covered the rounded hills. She was close enough to home to recognize her surroundings, and she knew the area well enough to evade any pursuers, had they been foolish enough to follow. She rode hard and fast over the now familiar ground, heading away from the village at a speed that the brigands could never match on foot. Past a stand of oaks, she continued, marking it as she made her way into a deep hollow.

There, ahead, were the old standing stones she remembered, and Brighid rode toward them, certain that superstition would keep even the most dogged pursuer at bay. When she neared the towering spires of rock, Brighid reined in and slid from her palfrey, leading the animal into the shadowy recesses of the circle.

Stephen was lagging behind, and Brighid took the opportunity to study him curiously, as if seeking some sign of the man she knew. He looked the same, and yet he did not. He appeared to hold himself differently, straighter and taller somehow, though Brighid suspected her eyes were playing tricks on her. Perhaps she only saw what she wanted to see, she realized, with sudden insight.

And there was the rub, for hadn't she judged him on sight and tenaciously clung to those beliefs until recently? Yet Stephen de Burgh was not as simple as she would make him; he was a man of many complexities that she was just now beginning to discover. And despite her quarrels with him, Brighid found her gaze traveling over his form with the deep pleasure of an admirer.

Throughout that thrilling examination, it seemed to Brighid that he was more handsome, more broad-shouldered and more well made than ever before, and she caught her breath, unable to moderate her thoughts or the frantic beating of her heart—until she saw the blood staining his lower right leg.

"Why are we stopping here? Are we lost again?" Stephen asked. The query, laced with disgust, sounded more like the man she knew, but Brighid took little notice. She could only shake her head stupidly as she watched the dark mark spread before her eyes, proving that it was not the blood of one of the brigands, but Stephen's own.

"What is it?" Stephen asked. Following her gaze, he reached down to the source of her interest. He touched his calf gingerly, then his hand to stare, as if in amazement, at the spot left upon his gauntlet. His eyes, deep and dark as the night, found hers, and Brighid sensed his bewilderment.

"I've been wounded," he said.

Chapter Eleven

The look on Stephen's face might have been comical, if not for the cause of his dismay, and Brighid hastened to assure him. "I'll tend you. Can you dismount?" she asked, as she approached Hades. Brighid stood close by the huge destrier, though she had no idea what she was going to do with two hundred pounds of muscular male should Stephen put his weight upon her.

"You don't understand," he said, his tanned skin looking slightly pale. "I've never been wounded."

"I'm sure it's just a scratch," Brighid said, hoping she was right. "But the sooner I can look at it, the better you shall be."

To her relief Stephen managed to slide to the ground, though he grunted at the movement. He was in pain, and Brighid knew her duty, yet she shied away from reaching for him, wary of this man who had transformed before her very eyes from drunken layabout to magnificent warrior. She had always been leery of touching him, but now...

The decision was taken from her hands as he swayed toward her. He was tall and heavy, and Brighid staggered under his weight, yet somehow, against all logic, he felt warm and wonderful. She drank in his scent and his heat like one long denied as he slung his arm over her shoulder, and with unsteady steps she led him toward one of the fallen stones, where he lowered himself with another grunt.

Brighid sank onto her heels in front of him, pushing aside his hands in their rough gauntlets. While he removed them, she reached toward his leg and was alarmed to see his entire body shudder. Laying a steadying hand upon his knee, Brighid leaned closer and saw that he had a nasty gash through the thick muscle of his calf, below where the mail coat protected him.

Drawing her small dagger, she cut away the bloody material of his braies, then hurried to her palfrey to retrieve her water flask and the pouch of healing herbs she kept for her own use, should the dire need arise. Although she had never thought to treat Stephen de Burgh with them, Brighid she did not hesitate. And kneeling once more before her patient, she washed the wound as best she could, keeping a firm hold to staunch the blood even as Stephen jerked beneath her ministrations.

"What are you about? Gad, is there no wine? I need a drink!" he muttered furiously, and again, Brighid felt him shudder.

Drawing his leg back toward her, Brighid glanced upward, a reprimand on her lips, only to swallow it as she met his dark gaze, so stark and tortured that it stunned her into silence. With an effort, she kept her shock at bay, holding his gaze evenly with her own, as if she could calm him with it. "You don't need wine," she said softly.

Although he turned his head away, staring off into the distance and swearing under his breath, Stephen left his leg in place, and Brighid finished cleansing the wound.

She had some linen cloths in her pouch, and she reached up to hand him one. Taking his fingers in her own, she gently guided him toward the gash, suddenly intensely aware of her bare skin touching his. "Here, hold this," she murmured shakily. Then she bent her head to search through her pouch, mixing up a poultice as best she could.

"What are you doing? I thought you were against healing, witch woman," Stephen muttered, and Brighid froze at his harsh words. He would use her heritage against her? Of course, Brighid had only herself to blame for foolishly sharing such a secret with him. Last night, lulled by the quiet intimacy of the moment, she had revealed some of herself, only to find that in the morning, Stephen had returned to his usual hateful self, lashing out at her and...

With sudden, swift insight, Brighid realized that he did the same thing now—turning upon her with an anger that stemmed not from her, but from what? His pain? His need for drink? Brighid berated herself for not seeing his tactics before, but she had been too focused on her own problems, too busy dismissing Stephen as a rogue. Now, she saw through his guise, catching glimpses of the man within, and she knew he was more than he pretended.

"Well?" he prompted. Betraying nothing, Brighid slowly lifted his hand away and smoothed her healing concoction upon the torn flesh. Despite her best intentions, her fingers trembled at their task, and she felt a warmth that traveled from their tips throughout the rest of her as she was seized by an urge to know more of his muscled body.

Abruptly, Brighid saw him as he had been in battle, and she knew that as long as she lived she would never forget the sight of Stephen de Burgh rising up in knightly splendor to dispatch brigands with a single sweep of his heavy sword. He had taken on thrice his number without blinking, his visage hard and determined, his movements sure and swift and deadly. Twas not the act of a drunkard.

"I'm willing to make an exception for those who save my life," Brighid said casually as she finished wrapping her work in clean linen. Then she looked up at him in all seriousness. "You were magnificent."

His face swung toward her, surprise and denial clearly etched upon his features. "I did what I had to do," he muttered, glancing away once more.

Brighid sank back upon her heels. "Well, mayhap you are accustomed to such heroics, but I am not, and tis not the first time you have displayed them to me. I owe you an apology," she said, her gaze unflinching. "All those things I said about you back at Glenerron..." Brighid paused to draw a deep breath. "I was wrong. I misjudged you, and I—"

Stephen cut her off with a snarl, his palm raised as though to ward her off. "No! You were right! Everything you said was true." He waved his lifted hand in a restless gesture and brought it to his dark hair as if agitated beyond words.

"No, I—" Brighid began again only to trail off as he met her gaze with his own, brimming with a desperation she had never imagined.

"Don't you see? I was scared to death back there!" He glared at her, as if he expected her to laugh in derision, and Brighid was taken aback. Did he think so little of her? Had she treated him so poorly that he would anticipate nothing less? If so, she must prove him wrong.

Calmly, Brighid held his dark, disturbing gaze, so rife with turmoil. "And why wouldn't you be?"

Stephen gaped at her and snorted. "Because only cowards are afraid! Do you think any of my brothers would have felt even a twinge of unease back there?" he asked, his arm sweeping toward the way they had come.

It was Brighid's turn to snort. "I'm certain they would never admit to it, but yes, they too would have been afraid. Everyone feels fear when they are attacked, no matter what they might say afterward."

"Not Dunstan! Or Simon!" Stephen argued.

"Then they are surely not human," Brighid said, her comment eliciting a growl of laughter from her companion.

"You may be right. Sometimes I think I'm the only de Burgh who is human," Stephen muttered as he stared off into the distance.

Leaning backward, Brighid wrapped her arms around her knees and glanced up at this man who was so tall and strong and handsome—and vulnerable. "So everyone else in your family is perfect? No flaws whatsoever?"

With a grim expression, Stephen looked away, his answer implicit in his silence.

"Ah," Brighid nodded. "Then all the rumors I've heard about them are untrue?"

Stephen's dark head swung toward her once more. "What rumors?"

Brighid assumed a thoughtful expression. "Well, let's see…we only hear a little, being on the edge of the Campion lands, but they say that Simon has a terrible temper." She glanced up at Stephen from under lowered lashes.

He grunted. "Aye. He's easy to bait, but—"

"So he's not perfect?" Brighid asked.

"Well, not if you think—"

"I see. And how about Dunstan?" Brighid prompted.

Stephen frowned at her. "What about him?"

Pulling her cloak about her more closely, Brighid studied her booted toes. "Well, they say he is coarse, gruff and lacking in social skills, and not nearly as clever as his brothers."

Stephen half rose from his seat. "Now, wait just a minute!"

"And Geoffrey always has his nose in a book and someone—I forget who—is always pulling pranks, and, of course, Reynold is grim and bitter, despite all his—"

"Enough!" Stephen said, as he loomed tall above her.

Brighid bit back her smile as she, too, moved to stand and dusted off her skirts. "All are good men, honorable and true, as well as powerful knights, but they aren't perfect." She sought his dark gaze, now tinged with anger, and held it. "And you are just as good as any of them."

With no little surprise, Brighid realized that she meant what she said. She had only sought to reason with this man, gifted in many ways and flawed in others, but when she spoke the words, she knew the truth of them. Somehow, over the past few days, the man she had seen as a handsome shell, devoid of any substance, had turned into a fully fleshed-out person, with his own heartaches and trials and victories. Behind that handsome, careless exterior was a clever man, sharp-tongued and brave and considerate when the spirit moved him, who was so haunted by his own demons that he had lost all sense of himself.

And with that discovery came something else: the

powerful feeling of a bond forged between them, as if she alone recognized the real Stephen de Burgh, and he, in turn, might know her better than she did herself. Nonsense, Brighid told herself, dismissing the unwelcome sensation out of long habit.

But she could not easily dismiss a sudden, sharp longing for this man for whom she had felt only contempt. Knowing Stephen, it was a dangerous yearning, and one that he couldn't help, by his very nature, take advantage of. Indeed, as if aware of her thoughts, his eyes darkened, so deep and rich and brown that Brighid felt herself sinking into them. Suddenly, she had the uneasy sensation that should she hold his gaze one more moment, she would be lost forever.

With a formidable will born years ago, Brighid quickly moved away, turning her back on him. "That should take you as far as my father's manor, but once there, the wound will have to be cleansed more completely," she said, her voice even and firm, though she was trembling inside.

If Stephen stepped behind her or put his hands on her, Brighid knew she had little chance of resisting him, for now the temptation he presented to her was twofold. Not only was she drawn to him physically, sucked in by his powerful appeal, but through her knowledge of him, the real Stephen, she had forged an emotional tie to him that would surely be her undoing, if she let it.

Waiting, her breath held, Brighid heard him grunt behind her, and she loosed her pent-up air in a rush of relief as she turned her head. As if he, too, felt a need to escape the stifling intimacy of the moment, he scowled and rubbed his leg.

"See? This is what comes of traveling alone," he grumbled. "You go racing off without any idea of what dangers are out here—wild animals, rumors of strife and brigands such as the ones who attacked us. We're lucky they did not number more."

Brighid cleared her throat and looked down at her clasped hands. "They might not just have been simple brigands," she said, being careful not to look at Stephen. Their brief truce would surely be shattered irrevocably when she told him, but she could no longer hide the threat from him, not when it might endanger him, as well as herself.

And chances were that it would, for even if the men who attacked were nothing more than common thieves, Brighid had announced her return just as surely as if she had marched through the village with a banner. Although she regretted the ancient curses that had given her away, it was too late to change them. Word would spread that a l'Estrange was back in residence.

"What do you mean?" Stephen asked, his harsh voice rife with suspicion.

Brighid kept her head bowed. "I am not certain, but I suspect that my father may well have been murdered." Leery of his reaction, she remained where she was, while her pronouncement hung in the air like a foul stench.

Finally, she heard Stephen's snort of disbelief. "And what makes you think that?" he drawled, his usual arrogance back in place.

Brighid whirled toward him, shoulders squared. "My father was an alchemist," she said. When he made a low, scoffing sound, she lifted her chin. "Despite what you might think, alchemy is a revered and ancient art."

"More l'Estrange sorcery," Stephen muttered.

Brighid found herself stiffening and willed her body to relax. She wanted to reason with Stephen, not argue with him. "You may have heard of Roger Bacon or

Arnold of Villanova, just two of the famous men who have written important works on the subject. I realize that to some untutored minds,'' she said, giving him a pointed look, ''alchemy is linked with the black arts, but those two men and others before them, are prominent in the church. In fact, some trace the lineage of lore back to Adam, who was endowed with singular wisdom. Moses, who learned from the Egyptians, Socrates, Plato and Saint John the Evangelist are all said to have been practitioners.''

Brighid heard Stephen's grunt, whether in dispute of her claims or from discomfort as he once again took his seat, she did not know. But she found herself in the dubious position of having to defend the very practices that had driven her from her father, for if she could not make Stephen understand the possibilities, then he would never see the danger.

''As I said, these men are scientists familiar with Aristotle's four elements of fire, air, water and earth. They believe that any substance can be transformed into another by simply changing its elemental proportions through the processes of burning, calcination, solution, evaporation, distillation, sublimation and crystalization.'' To Brighid's surprise, the words came easily to her after all these years, and it seemed as if she were still a young apprentice at her father's side.

''In this manner, they search for a way to transmute base metals into silver or gold by freeing the crude materials from their impurities,'' she explained, warming to her topic. ''Some alchemists believe in the existence of a potent transmuting agent capable of promoting the change of one kind of material into another. It is known as the Philosopher's Stone.''

Pausing, Brighid glanced over at Stephen only to see

him staring at her with a mixture of astonishment and horror. "You really believe this, don't you?" he asked.

Brighid drew a deep breath. "Whether I believe it or not is immaterial—"

"You certainly sound knowledgeable. Do you plan to follow in your father's footsteps?" he demanded, his dark brows lowered.

The question hurt, even after all these years, but Brighid gave no sign of it. "No. An alchemist must possess the ability to attract and make use of spiritual ingredients. I'm afraid that I lack the divine spark necessary."

Without waiting for Stephen's next biting comment, Brighid continued. "Supposedly, those in possession of the Philosopher's Stone remain hidden from the rest of the world, appearing perhaps to train an apprentice and then disappear, for they have discovered the ultimate mystery of life, the secret of immortality."

Suddenly, Brighid felt the strain of it all, the return of memories and emotions better left buried, of this quest to face a past she had turned her back upon. Fear, panic, or *something* nudged just at the edge of her awareness, making her short of breath, but in that instant, she fixed upon Stephen's handsome face. He was so familiar to her now that she felt a steadying reassurance, as if he drew her inexorably back to the present—and his own brand of logic.

"If your father found the secret of immortality, then how is it that he's dead? Or is he simply invisible?" he asked, his tone rich with sarcasm. He was in his element again, feeling superior, and Brighid felt herself smile as affection for this man welled up in her, driving away all else.

"I didn't say that my father found the Philosopher's

Stone, or even that I believe in any of his work," Brighid said. Her smile fading, she looked down at her hands and spoke as evenly as she could. "I was not adept and so of little use to him. He fostered me out to my aunts years ago, and I had not heard from him since—"

"Now, wait just a moment!" Stephen growled, surging to his feet. "You mean to tell me that your father sent you away because you couldn't or wouldn't do any of that hokus-pokus?" He spread his arm as if to encompass and condemn all of alchemic study. "And then you never saw him again?"

Brighid knew a swift surge of warmth at his vehement response. Would he always surprise her? "Well, no. That's not exactly true. I heard from him not too long ago. He sent a message just before he died, in which he claimed to have found the secret of life—"

Stephen's low oath cut off her words, so Brighid began again. "I was a bit skeptical myself," she admitted. "He begged me to search my heart and return home, so that he might pass his legacy on to me. But I did nothing." Brighid felt the customary press of her guilt and frowned.

"I ignored his missive and did not share it with my aunts. Then, but a month later, we received word of his death." She drew in a deep breath to sustain her through the ache that still surprised her. "Because his message was so unusual and his demise followed so swiftly, I wanted to travel here as soon as possible, so that I might find out for myself what happened."

Stephen lifted his dark brows. "So you can take up where he left off?"

Brighid met his questioning gaze with her own steady one. "I wish only to learn the truth and right whatever wrongs may have been committed against my father. I, too, find it impossible to believe that he made so momentous a discovery, but he obviously thought he found *something,* and perhaps he was murdered for it.''

Stephen snorted. ''Well, I think it's all a cartload of nonsense. I don't believe in anything that I can't divine with my own senses, let alone some magic rock that will turn one object into another.'' He glared at her from his seat on the ancient stone, totally oblivious to his surroundings, and Brighid felt herself smile again.

''But it might have been nice if you would have let me in on all of this *before* we left Campion. If I had known that the country might erupt into war at any moment or that you thought some gang of killers might strike us, then I would have taken a few more soldiers and armed them accordingly!''

Brighid looked into his face, still handsome despite his frown, and she knew that he was feeling vulnerable again and lashing out at her because of some imagined weakness. So, instead of cowering in the face of his apparent anger, she simply nodded at him.

''Oh, I think you are doing just fine, Stephen de Burgh, all by yourself. In fact, I feel perfectly safe in your capable hands,'' Brighid said, in all seriousness.

He stared at her for a long moment as if in total disbelief, then snorted in exasperation as he stood. ''And your recommendation is supposed to hearten me? This from someone who races across a crumbling bridge and thinks she'll catch a murderer out of hand? Lord, save me from this woman and her bizarre family,'' he said aloud, lifting his arms to the skies, as if in supplication.

Again, Brighid felt that dangerous rush of feeling for him, a sensation that went beyond desire into unknown territory. She wanted to cast her arms around him and cling to him as hard as she could, to drag him out of his darkness into a light that she had yet to discover herself. But she was afraid.

Glancing at the sky, where clouds were gathering ominously, Brighid knew she must focus her attention on reaching her father's manor and solving the mystery of his death. All else, by necessity, must be put aside for now, she told herself, stilling the small voice that accused her of cowardice.

"Let us go on," she said, heading for her palfrey. "Can you ride?"

"Of course, I can ride," Stephen answered with a scowl, as he mounted Hades. "If you haven't gotten us hopelessly lost."

Brighid mounted her palfrey and urged it forward. "Oh, we're not lost," she said, eyeing the hills that rose before them. "In fact, we are nearly there." Unbidden, a hint of trepidation washed over her, an ill omen of the future. Yes, they were nearing Rumenea, at last, but what would they find there? Although Stephen might scoff at her concern, Brighid could not so easily dismiss the threat, especially when her senses were abuzz with warnings.

Keeping a wary eye on their surroundings, Brighid headed home, straight into the thick of danger so palpable she could taste it.

Stephen followed, hoping that his companion truly knew where she was going, for he certainly didn't. He doubted if he had ever been so unsure in his life. Something about the old hollow made him uneasy, and he was glad to leave it, yet the odd feeling persisted. It was probably all that talk about alchemy and magic stones, the strange hokus-pokus that seemed a hallmark of the l'Estranges.

A lot of lunatics, Stephen thought. *Dangerous lunatics.* With a scowl, he felt a renewed sense of outrage as he remembered Brighid's tale. When she said her father had sent her away because she couldn't or wouldn't practice his bizarre rituals, Stephen had wanted to give the man a good thrashing even though he was dead. Dead and buried. And his daughter seemed no worse for it. So why had Stephen felt like wrapping Brighid in his arms and holding her, not for his own sake, but for hers?

He shook his head, uneasy with the question, but slanted a curious glance toward his companion. Except for those unusual eyes of hers, she certainly didn't look anything like a witch, Stephen thought, becoming arrested by her appearance. Her glorious hair was windblown, her beautifully sculpted face so very lovely that he found his gaze lingering over every smooth contour. When he thought of the freckles across her nose, Stephen grew hard instantly. He would blame his overblown senses, which were still hammering him with their ceaseless input, but focusing on Brighid actually made all the distractions around him die down to a dull roar.

Unfortunately, the result was that he was becoming even more enamored of the woman. Stephen told himself that she was no more appealing than the next female, less so, in fact, but it did him no good. Plain, rigid Brighid had become the most attractive woman he had ever seen. Her hair, her face, her voice, her scent, were all intoxicating, enthralling, exciting even, and beneath that stiff exterior was the comfort he craved, a heady combination.

But there was more to it than that, Stephen acknowledged. *Oh, I think you are doing just fine, Stephen de*

Burgh. I feel perfectly safe in your capable hands. Faith, if any other woman had said those words, he would have taken it for an invitation to put those capable hands on her. But Brighid wasn't referring to his legendary skills.

No, she thought him hero material! All because he had frantically waved his sword in an effort to fend off his own death. He had been so scared, he was lucky that he hadn't run himself through, yet she thought he had done something admirable! Stephen knew he should laugh at this abrupt elevation in her estimation, but somehow he couldn't force out a sound.

All his life he had felt like a stranger, the anomaly in a family of superior beings, the runt of the litter that should have been tossed out to make room for more and better siblings as Campion took on a new wife and had new sons. Stephen shifted uncomfortably in the saddle as he realized that part of his dismay at his father's recent remarriage sprung from that old bugbear. He had even gone so far as to hint that Joy was barren, hoping that was true, so that there would be no more de Burghs to make him look worse than he already did.

No doubt, such babes in swaddling would prove themselves champions, while he sank even lower into his place as the black sheep of the brood. Even young Nicholas had more than once proved himself valuable, Stephen recalled with a bitterness he had long struggled against and which none of his brothers would understand.

How could they when they sailed through life without ever questioning themselves? Oh, Geoffrey was more introspective than the others, but Stephen felt no kinship with his scholarly brother, either. He had felt too much pain, too much fear, too much distress, to ever be a de Burgh, let alone perform the great deeds that came naturally to them. At least that was what he had always thought.

Everyone feels fear when they are attacked, no matter what they might say afterward. Brighid's words echoed in Stephen's mind, making him wonder if his brothers had ever known anything like the gut-clawing terror that had stricken him on the bridge and later when those brigands had rushed at him. With a snort, Stephen dismissed the very notion that the massive Dunstan was afraid of anything, but then he had a sudden memory of his eldest brother in a dark dungeon, groping blindly for the help of his siblings. The recollection was so sharp that Stephen drew a harsh breath that made him strangely dizzy.

Had he always been so lost in his own hazy world that he had not seen such things? Or was his mind so narrowly set that it couldn't accept any information that didn't fit in with all his preconceptions about his family and his place in it? Stephen shuddered with the force of his new awareness, of discoveries that threatened the very cornerstone of his existence.

You were magnificent.

Women had told him that before, but in very different circumstances. And somehow that simple declaration from Brighid, whose opinion of him was well-known, was far more important than all the praise of every woman in his past. She was as daft as her aunts, of course, which would explain why she had changed her mind about him. And yet, Stephen felt a slow, mounting warmth in his chest at her validation.

For the first time in his life, he was away from his siblings, alone, and yet he had managed to survive—and to protect his charge. And to impress her, too! Without one brother at his side, he had come out of a skirmish pretty well, despite his own terror.

All right, so maybe he had managed to receive his first wound, but his brothers had far worse marking their bodies. And with a cocksure attitude he did not really feel, Stephen told himself that women would love to admire his scar. Yet, even as he made the claim, he knew that he cared about the admiration of only one woman.

Sucking in a harsh breath, Stephen told himself he was getting way too obsessed with Brighid. Being all alone here with her, the two of them up against thieves and bad roads and rumors of war, had distorted his perceptions. He was getting sex mixed up with other things. Despite what had happened last night, perhaps even because of it, Stephen reminded himself his interest in Brighid was limited to the lower portions of her anatomy.

And yet, he could not deny that he felt things for Brighid that he had never known before. The admission spooked him, and he licked his parched lips. If only he had some wine. A good cup would go a long way to restoring his equilibrium. If they were nearing her father's manor, as Brighid claimed, then surely he would find some plain drink among the exotic potions and metals the alchemist had left behind.

Stephen's mouth quirked at his own wit, only to drop into a frown as he realized his task was nearly complete. The earl had said nothing of returning Brighid to Campion; Stephen had only to escort her to her inheritance. The knowledge sent air hissing through his teeth in a rush of surprise. He would leave Brighid at the manor, and then what?

Then, he would go home, back to his old life and the comforts to which he was accustomed. No more sleeping in hovels or going without a drink. He would be rid of these strange sensations, freed of his obsession with this unlikely woman, and return to the relative normalcy of his usual existence. So why didn't the prospect cheer him?

His jaw tight, Stephen rubbed his leg and told himself that any discomfort he might feel stemmed from the gash in his flesh—and nothing else.

Chapter Twelve

When Brighid finally halted, it took Stephen a moment to realize that they had reached their destination, and as he did, the ominous feeling that had been nagging him all the way from the hollow blossomed, full-blown, in his chest. Sitting atop a windswept knoll stood Brighid's legacy, a small building that rose, bleak and forlorn, above a walled enclosure that was cracked in spots, its stone crumbling from age or neglect.

Even as Stephen stared in dismay, the dark clouds that had been gathering rolled in overhead, casting deep shadows all around and making the structure appear black and forbidding. Stephen felt the hairs on the back of his neck rise, for this manor did not resemble any owned by members of his family. It seemed a desolate place, well befitting its preternatural heritage.

But the forbidding setting was not what bothered Stephen. He took a dim view of Brighid's tales of drowned witches and murdered alchemists, and he usually shrugged off anything he didn't understand. As Stephen stared at his destination, it was not what clung to the place, but what didn't, that made him suspicious.

Rumenea looked deserted. The sheep that had been so

prevalent since they crossed the marches were nowhere to be seen, and the normal hustle and bustle of those who served a manor such as this one was absent. Not a soul could be spotted in or about the bailey, and no light from torch or candle flickered through the tall, narrow windows.

Had Llewelyn called them all to his army? Or did they know something he didn't, and was Edward, even now, charging across the land, sending those ahead of him fleeing? Stephen shifted uneasily. There was always the chance that brigands had slain the entire household, or worse yet, that plague or pestilence had driven the residents away. Stephen's eyes narrowed as he searched for recent graves, but he saw none from this distance, and his heightened sense of smell couldn't detect the scent of death on the chill air.

Still, something wasn't right. Stephen felt it in his bones, and urging Hades forward, he laid a hand across Brighid's reins. "Stay here," he ordered. Sliding from his mount, he cautiously made his way toward the wall, clinging to the shadows and the gnarled shapes of trees until he reached an opening.

Heaving his body upward, Stephen climbed over fallen stones and dropped to his feet in the bailey only to lurch to one side as the wound in his leg protested the force of his landing. Swallowing a grunt of pain, he righted himself into a crouch even as his hand moved to the hilt of his sword. But the interior looked just as deserted, the remains of overgrown summer grasses, various plants and even small shrubs cluttering the area surrounding a small pond, its water black and foul looking.

A sound from behind him made Stephen turn swiftly, his fingers tightening around his weapon, but the sight of a familiar drab gown stayed his hand. He swore under his breath as Brighid stumbled down to the ground. "I told you to stay out there," he muttered, his jaw tight.

Brighid shook her head, offering no explanation, but Stephen was hardly surprised. When had she ever listened to him? Scowling at her, he circled toward the back of the building, avoiding the arched entrance to the hall. Making his way through a maze of undergrowth, he finally found a low door that he suspected led to the kitchens, but no noise or heat emanated from the cold stone.

Drawing his sword, Stephen motioned Brighid back and opened the door, slipping into the darkness, ready for anything. For a moment, he blinked, nearly blind in the dim interior, then he saw a small fire burning in one of the massive cooking hearths. Although not nearly large enough to serve the residents of a manor of this size, it signaled the presence of someone, as did a sudden noise ahead. Alert, Stephen inched forward, slipping out of the shadows just as a figure appeared ahead.

With a bloodcurdling shriek, the person threw up his arms, sending something up in the air that produced a thunderous noise. For one frightening instant, Stephen thought some mage was causing the skies to hail down upon him right here in the kitchens. He lifted an arm to protect his face even as he bellowed a warning to Brighid.

But when silence fell once more, Stephen frowned ruefully, for twas no otherworldly attack, only a spill. The mysterious person in front of him was simply a poorly dressed servant who had been carrying a load of wood. It had flown in all directions when he saw Stephen and now lay scattered about the tiles, while the servant visibly quailed.

"Have mercy, sire! I know nothing! I swear it," the man said, falling to his knees before Stephen.

"Put away your weapon. Tis only Cadwy," Brighid said from behind him.

At her words, the man's head bobbed up, and he stared at her for a long moment, his mouth working strangely. "Mistress l'Estrange?" he finally asked. "Is that you?"

At Brighid's nod, he rose to his feet. "Tis a bad business, mistress, a bad business," he said.

"What happened here?" she asked, inclining her head toward the dirty walls, empty ovens and general disarray.

"Oh, mistress, tis a bad business," Cadwy repeated, shaking his head.

"But why are the grounds so neglected? Where are the sheep and the villeins? Why are the kitchens so deserted and ill kept?" Brighid asked.

Cadwy shook his head again as he bent to gather the wood. "Your father was always so busy with his work that he never had much time left for the household. We missed you sorely after he sent you away, mistress."

As the servant spoke, Stephen moved slowly toward the buttery and the hall, just in case other, less welcoming inhabitants, awaited within. Sword at the ready, he stepped into the hall, where the faint glow of a fire and the dim slant of day from the high windows cast enough light for him to see that it held no threat.

But what Stephen did see made him draw a harsh breath. Although more particular than most of his brothers, dirt was something he could live with, and Campion had not been the cleanest place in years past. But even he turned up his nose at the mess here. New rushes piled onto old ones, forming a thick layer that moved when he walked. Oddly enough, it was flung up in piles in some places yet so thin in others that the tiles showed through.

Smells assailed him—of rotten food scraps and dogs long gone and dirt that accumulated. Yet the mess here went beyond poor housekeeping: benches were over-turned, tables upended, and an expensive cupboard lay on its sides, doors wrenched off their hinges. It looked as if a great wind had roared through the place, and Stephen felt the hair rise on the back of his neck. Was this some doing of the alchemist? Had he created a storm within his own walls?

Glancing warily at said walls, Stephen noticed strange marks in some places. Runes? He stepped closer and lifted a hand to one deep gouge. Nay. It looked, rather, as if someone had hacked away at the stones in certain spots. Had the tempest produced hail or rocks? Stephen shuddered even as he told himself that there was a rational explanation for the destruction.

Perhaps Brighid or the servant could shed some light on the mystery, Stephen thought, only to grunt in dismay at the thought of Brighid's reaction. Would that he could shield her from the sight of her old home, but it was too late. Already, he heard her approach from the kitchens, and he watched as she stepped inside, her assessing gaze taking it all in. Although she never changed expression, Stephen knew that she felt far more than what showed on her face, and he moved to stand beside her. After a brief hesitation, he even lifted a hand to rest upon her shoulder, though he felt helpless to ease her distress.

"I'm sorry, mistress, but I haven't had a chance to do much," said the servant, Cadwy.

"I'm sure you've done what you could," Brighid replied, surveying the wreckage. "But surely, it hasn't been like this since I left?"

Cadwy shook his head. "Oh, no, mistress. Most of this is recent, though we missed you sorely. The sheep, the villeins, the household, all slowly... Well, the bailiff left, complaining that your father wouldn't lift a hand to..." His words trailed off as his cheeks grew ruddy.

"And you know how hard it was for most to understand your father's work. Still and all, we were safe here and managed to stay out of the troubles back in '77. It was only after your father died that everything—" Cadwy's voice broke, and Brighid urged him toward an upright bench. He sat down gratefully, and she joined him, her slender shoulders slipping away from Stephen's touch.

"Tell me. Tell me what happened," she urged Cadwy. Her voice, low and intent, drew Stephen, and for a moment he was jealous of the servant who held her attention. Frowning, he glanced away. "My father was murdered, wasn't he?"

Stephen whirled toward them once more, swearing under his breath at the servant's relieved expression. "You know then?" he asked.

Brighid shook her head. "Tell me."

"A woman came here from the village, Addfwyn by name. We always needed help, with so many of our own leaving, whether because of...the state of things here or called upon by our liege lord with the troubles and all. Anyway, we took her on gladly, and soon, she grew close to your father."

Cadwy's face grew ruddy once more as he avoided Brighid's gaze. "Some say too close. Some say she's the one who killed him in a jealous rage. All we know is that he was most secretive that evening, even more so than usual, and told us all to leave him alone with his work. None saw him during the night, and when one of the servants sought him in the morning..." Cadwy paused, his expression bleak. "He was dead."

Stephen narrowed his eyes at the servant, who seemed to impute motives all too readily where no proof existed. "How do you know he didn't have some illness or an accident?" he asked.

Cadwy looked up at him in surprise. "Well, the dagger in his back did give us some indication that his death was not self-inflicted," he said, sending Brighid an apologetic glance.

Stephen grunted in displeasure, but the man ignored him. "The rest of the household fled to the village or beyond, their ignorant fears driving them," Cadwy said.

His eyes narrowing once more, Stephen studied the servant anew. "You mean not all of them thought the woman did it?" he asked.

Cadwy frowned. "Why, ah, yes, I suppose some of them..." He cleared his throat. "Those who mistakenly thought the master involved in the dark arts prattled on about divine retribution or harnessing of powers beyond his control. They feared that all who lingered here would meet some evil end." He shook his head. "Nonsense, of course."

"Aye, nonsense," Stephen muttered, just to let the old man know that he wasn't swallowing any of that hokuspokus. He swept an arm toward the littered hall. "But, what of this? Did the cowardly servants ransack the place when they left?"

Cadwy shook his head. "Nay. Twas a band of brigands, intent on stealing any and all things of value. Perhaps they came across the manor and thought it abandoned, or maybe they heard of our troubles and came to pick the bones of the once fair Rumenea."

Stephen didn't care for the fellow's choice of words.

"And just where were you when these fellows descended upon your master's house?" he asked, his brows lifting.

Cadwy eyed him with surprise. "I was in the old dairy, milking the cows. I heard a noise and peeked through the broken beams only to see a handful of men ride up, and from their behavior, they were not the sort I wished to welcome. Perhaps I should have tried to stop them, but—"

"Nay," said Brighid, giving Stephen a sharp look of admonishment. "Then, you, too, would be dead, and none left to tell the tale."

How convenient, Stephen thought. And all we have is this fellow's word for anything. "So no one else saw these brigands?" he asked.

"Nay," Cadwy said. "The others had gone, and, of course, the villagers keep to themselves, as distanced from us as possible."

Although Brighid nodded at his explanation, Stephen did not feel so sanguine. Of course, there were roving bands of thieves and such, as he could well attest. And Rumenea wouldn't be the first manor to be abandoned, either, for ruins of old buildings, especially the early motte and bailey castles, dotted the countryside. But there was something very odd about the destruction here. Why kick up the rushes? And those marks in the walls, what did they mean?

Stephen shook his head. Whatever the answers, he didn't plan on being here long enough to delve too deeply. It looked as though they were safe for the moment, but now that he knew the state of Brighid's legacy, he wanted to head back home as quickly as possible. Of course, he would be saddled with Brighid for the return trip, an unexpected addition, but somehow the thought of spending more time in her company wasn't as onerous at it once would have been.

Instead, Stephen felt a certain lightness of being, along with a surge of desire so strong it rocked him. When would this lust cease to plague him so violently? His jaw tightened in frustration while he willed his body to relax. He needed a drink. The thought lanced through him even as he realized that, at last, he was in a position to get one. Shuddering with relief, Stephen turned toward the servant.

"What of your stores? Have you any wine?" he asked, refusing to look at Brighid. He told himself he didn't care what she thought, that his habits were none of her business, though he felt a betraying lurch in his gut.

"Nay, sire. We have had no wine in a long time," Cadwy answered, and Stephen's brief sense of euphoria spun away, leaving him feeling wretched and wanting, while his leg throbbed painfully. Was there no proper drink to be had in all of Wales?

"Ale, then. We grow thirsty after our long journey," Stephen said. Deliberately avoiding Brighid's gaze, he righted one of the tables and then a bench. Taking a seat, he eyed the servant expectantly.

Cadwy rose, as did Brighid. "I'll come with you. I would like to see the stores. And we need food. Food more than ale," Brighid said in a censoring tone that was not lost on Stephen. Although he hadn't heard it in a while, he remembered all too well how much he disliked it, and he didn't care to find out if she wore the corresponding look on her face. He didn't think he could bear seeing that again, especially after he'd been called *magnificent*.

Stephen grunted as that familiar disagreeable churning

began in his belly. And even though he told himself he didn't need her approval, that she had no right to dictate to him, he found himself remembering her admiration and longing for it. *Needing* it. The knowledge irritated him further, and he vowed to drink anything and everything in the manor.

But he could not. As much as he yearned for the hazy oblivion that had once been his existence, Stephen knew he must keep his wits about him while they were here, with no guards, no servants and no protection of any kind. Ruffians seemed to plague the countryside, within and without, and he wasn't too sure about that Cadwy fellow, either, Stephen thought, his eyes narrowing.

Perhaps the lack of wine would serve him better than a store of it, for the moment. He would appease his thirst with a little ale, but remain alert to any and all dangers. And mayhap he would keep Brighid's goodwill for a while longer, too, although such a consideration had no affect on his decision, Stephen told himself.

Leaning his head back, he closed his eyes, shutting out the brightness of his world for a moment. If only he could close his nose as easily. He took a deep breath through his mouth and knew some relief, but his leg ached, and he propped it up on the table. Shifting, Stephen relaxed against the wall behind him and within moments, he slipped into a heavy sleep.

When Brighid returned to the hall, she stopped in her tracks. Amidst the scattered remains of her father's possessions, Stephen de Burgh, the most famous seducer in the kingdom, was leaning against the sooty wall of the hall, his elegant garb stained. One leg, wrapped in a bloody piece of linen, was propped up on the table, his usually perfect hair was tangled, and his handsome features were streaked with dirt. His eyes were closed and his mouth hung open, and Brighid thought she had never seen anything more beautiful in her life.

He was sleeping, this man who seemed never to rest of a night as most people did, and Brighid was glad to see it. As she stood there watching him, she felt a welling of tenderness such as she had never known. New feelings, strange and wonderful, coursed through her, more dangerous than any momentary desire. Brighid tried to dismiss them, but they lingered, warming her being in a way she had never thought possible even as they bound her to the man before her in a manner far stronger than duty or companionship.

The sensation begged to be examined and explored, but Brighid told herself she could not afford to be distracted right now, not when she needed to solve her father's murder and put right his legacy. Later she would have time to consider her feelings for Stephen de Burgh, as well as those for a father she had considered long forgotten. For beyond the beauty that was Stephen lay the destruction of her childhood home, reminding her of the danger that threatened.

Squaring her shoulders, Brighid began moving toward the table once more. To discover the secrets here, she needed all of her wits about her and all of Stephen's, as well. To that end, she must feed him and properly tend his wound and find a decent place for them to sleep.

At the thought Brighid slanted another glance toward Stephen, uncertain whether to wake him or not. Aware as she was of his need for rest, she wanted to leave him be, but she knew he was well used to his comforts. Although what she provided was not exotic, Brighid knew Stephen would prefer his food to be hot. The thought that would have made her purse her lips in disdain only days ago, now made her smile instead, and Brighid knew she was in deep. Perhaps too deep to ever extricate herself again.

She set the platters upon the table gently, but Cadwy, unaware of Stephen's slumber, bustled into the room, talking loudly. Stephen jerked upright, his hand upon his hilt in an instant, his eyes immediately open and alert, and Brighid wondered how she could have ever seen him as less than a warrior. Her heart pounding with a sudden, erratic rhythm, she turned toward the table as Cadwy laid out the trenchers.

"'Tis not an elaborate feast, but we must make do with what we have," Brighid said over her shoulder. The stores, though low for the manor, were still well enough stocked since none but Cadwy had been using them. She had found salted whiting, herring and eel, figs and dates, various nuts and cheeses, as well as a large amount of grains. Cadwy had killed a chicken, Brighid had fetched some eggs, and between the two of them, they managed what seemed to her like a fine repast after the spare meals of the past few days.

Stephen leaned forward, blinked as if unable to believe that he had drifted off, and reached toward the table. As Brighid suspected, his hand went, not to his trencher, but to the cup of ale that Cadwy set forth. She watched surreptitiously as he lifted the cup to his lips only to spew away the liquid with a snort.

"What the devil is this?" Stephen asked, his tone deadly even, but his dark brows lowered with menace.

"'Tis ale," Brighid answered calmly while a wide-eyed Cadwy retreated to the kitchens.

"Nay! Tis a wretched brew fit only for hogs!" He thumped his cup upon the table, sloshing its contents over the rim.

Biting back a smile, Brighid hid her face from his accusing glare. Truly, the ale had a rather sour flavor to begin with, and it had not been improved by the water she added. But Stephen would find no other. She had ordered Cadwy to water down every one of the casks. Better that the drink taste poorly than for Stephen to like it too well. Ignoring his continued glare, Brighid put dishes before him, ladling the hot food onto his trencher in an effort to tempt him to eat, and she succeeded, for soon he had drawn his knife and was spearing pieces of chicken and fish.

"You did this?" Stephen asked, inclining his head toward the dishes before him.

Brighid nodded. "I am accustomed to overseeing the cooking and am well versed in recipes. Growing up in a family of mystics, one is forced to mature quickly or go hungry," she said, surprised when the admission came easily, without its usual bitterness. "I learned early on that if I didn't take care of it, it usually didn't get done."

Stephen lifted his dark brows. "So that's why you're so capable—and so good at giving orders," he said.

Brighid knew she ought to take offense, but the look in his eyes took the sting from his words. It was no longer accusing or condemning or even lustful, but somehow approving, and Brighid felt suffused with warmth in response. Dismayed, she returned her attention to her food, though she knew her fingers trembled as she broke her bread.

As if sharing her mood, Stephen said little else, but she was glad to see him eat heartily. When, finally, she had coaxed him to take the last of the platter of fruit, he rose to his feet. "I'm going to go look at the outbuildings and grounds, to get an idea of where we are and what's out there,'' he said, his casual tone belying the reason for his concern.

Obviously, he thought more brigands might appear, and although she would use a different name for those who had ransacked the manor, Brighid knew, all too well, that they might return. Nodding, she watched him go, a tall, handsome figure whose grace and power belied his mean surroundings, and then she frowned as a sudden worrisome thought struck her.

Shaking her head at her own suspicions, Brighid nonetheless hoped he wasn't going looking for wine. Without his drink, he was a different person, and as much as she hated to admit it, Brighid liked this new Stephen de Burgh very much. *Too much.*

Chapter Thirteen

Stephen had to admit that there was one benefit to be accrued from his heightened senses: everything tasted better. Even the simple meal that Brighid and her servant had prepared was composed of delightful flavors, and he had paused to savor each one with a heady pleasure more intense than he could remember. It was when he was finally sated and his thoughts turned to other, more intriguing hungers, that he rose from the table, eager to escape the lust that plagued him in Brighid's presence.

Outside, he had stalked the grounds, inspecting the area in the gathering twilight just as he knew his brothers would do, although what sort of defense he could mount with nothing but his own sword and an unreliable servant, Stephen was unsure. Swearing under his breath, he hoped that whatever forces were out there, whether rebels, thieves or murderers, would keep their distance this night, at least. And although he had been uncomfortable on the road, he would be glad to head back to Campion on the morrow.

Safety was still on his mind when Stephen returned to find the hall empty, and he was seized by a sudden, fierce fear for Brighid that defied all logic. Although he doubted anything could have happened to her while he was so close, he didn't trust Cadwy, and the ominous feeling he had known since the hollow lingered. Hand on the hilt of his sword, he hurried up the stairs, and when he found her putting fresh linens on a bed in a small chamber, he knew a rush of relief that made him shudder.

Feeling dazed and a bit foolish, Stephen sank down on a chest near the door, blew out a breath and assessed his surroundings. Brighid had righted the room somewhat, though he could see that the mattress had been slit open and the furnishings tossed about. Even the bed curtains had been slashed, he realized, as his gaze was drawn back to Brighid.

She bent over to smooth a sheet, and as he watched her in this simple task, Stephen felt a surge of something more than lust, a longing that involved more than his body. He shook his head, trying to clear away the strange sensation. He had been alone in a bedchamber with a woman countless times before, why should this be any different? Yet the feeling lingered, along with a sense of rightness that nearly made him dizzy. Startled, Stephen sucked in a harsh breath, instinctively shying away from Brighid, even as desire drove him toward her.

Deliberately, he glanced away, toward the window, where dusk had turned into night, and his heart really began thundering. In his haste to find Brighid, he had forgotten how late it was, but now with awareness came a stifling tension that was acerbated by his circumstances. He could not escape to a comfortable hall and a provision of wine, for the room below was hardly welcoming, while the bedchambers he had seen were in disarray, as well. Stephen knew he would never sleep in one of them, alone and isolated.

"I'll stay here tonight," he said, abruptly.

Brighid paused in her task to shoot him a questioning look, and he saw that her eyes held a hint of panic that matched his own, only he knew that hers sprung from a different source. She thought he wanted to take her to bed. *He did,* Stephen noted, as his body roused to the suggestion. And suddenly, the heat between them became like a living thing, pulsing and strong and undeniable. He grew hard as he held her gaze, all his will and honor and sense threatening to give way until she broke their contact and ducked her head.

"I don't think that would be wise," she said.

The devil with wisdom! Stephen thought. He was in the grip of crippling lust, one heartbeat away from diving onto the bed and tossing up her skirts, his usual finesse forgotten. Would she stop him? Stephen wasn't certain. He had seen the passion in her eyes, the wildness that she tried to suppress. But like this harsh, beautiful country, Brighid was no longer predictable, and Stephen shuddered at the thought that she might turn him away. And that, more than anything, stayed him, for even more powerful than his desire for her body was his need for her company.

He couldn't bear to be alone, not with the night upon him, and especially not now, when every sense bombarded him and no numbing wine was available to obliterate it all. With effort, Stephen wrestled his ardor into submission, laid his palms on his thighs and cleared his throat. "I meant that I would stay here, by the door," he said.

Swiftly, Stephen glanced about the room, searching for a pallet suitable for a servant or squire, until he saw one in the corner, cut open, its straw stuffing spilled upon the floor. Without waiting for Brighid's reply, he rose and strode to it, bending to stuff the missing materials inside with a nonchalance that no longer came easily to him. His back toward her, he dragged it to the door, his heart pounding apace.

Stephen's mouth twisted as he realized just how low he had sunk: the famous seducer afraid to even glance at a woman, lest she send him packing. Swallowing a snort, he tossed a fur on his makeshift bed and gathered the tattered remnants of his dignity about him before speaking once more.

"Since I'm responsible for your safety, I'll stay here, just in case the brigands who destroyed this place return," he explained, turning to bolt the door. Surely, even Brighid could not argue with that logic, he thought, until he heard her low reply.

"It wasn't brigands," she said, with a certainty that made Stephen eye her curiously. As she spoke, Brighid leaned over to straighten the blankets, and Stephen was hard-pressed to keep his mind on her words. "Whoever was here wasn't looking for coin or valuables. They were searching for my father's discovery."

Stephen finally wrested his attention from her gently curved rear up to her face. "Now, wait a minute—"

She paused to face him, with a sound of impatience that he well recognized. "If they wanted items of value, they would have taken the spices or the salt cellar or the silver cups."

"Well, maybe they aren't aware of the high price of ginger!" Stephen said, but even as he argued with her automatically, he knew that she was right. Hadn't he wondered himself about the odd manner of destruction? "Those chinks in the walls—" he began.

"Perhaps they thought to find some elixir or writings hidden behind loose stones or the like," Brighid said.

Stephen sank down upon the chest once more. "But how do we know that some strangers were behind this?" he asked, sweeping out an arm to encompass all of Rumenea. "We have only the servant's word for any of these occurrences! He could have killed your father himself and then taken his time searching for whatever he wanted, while hoarding the valuables, including the spices." Stephen felt a certain smug satisfaction at how neatly he had wrapped up the entire mystery, but Brighid, as usual, did not share in his opinion.

She shook her head as she tossed a blanket across the wide bed. "Nay, twas not Cadwy."

Stephen was unconvinced. Suspicious by nature, he knew that people were not always what they seemed. What's more, this whole hokus-pokus business didn't set well with him. He could accept that one lone servant was enamored of such nonsense, but a host of evil characters ransacking some old wreck of a manor for alchemic secrets? Not likely. "How can you be sure it wasn't the servant?" he asked.

Brighid's face was impassive. "Cadwy is an old and faithful retainer. I've known him since I was a small child."

Stephen snorted. "And you haven't seen him since! Maybe he's had a change of heart over the past few years. People do. How do you know that he hasn't gone mad or something?"

Brighid turned her head to face him, her expression implacable. "I just know."

Stephen stared at her, the conviction in her words raising the hairs on the back of his neck. She was certain all right, but he wasn't any closer to learning how, and, suddenly, the whole bizarre business began to make him uneasy, including Brighid herself, who had never denied

being involved in any of it. For all he knew, she was
some kind of witch or alchemist or whatever, though, if
so, she ought to do something to improve their situation,
he thought with a wry twist of his lips.

Rubbing his neck with a rough palm, Stephen dismissed such fancies. It was late. All this talk of murder
and mayhem was enough to set anyone's teeth on edge.
And a great howling wind had begun outside, rattling
the shutters, and adding to the unholy atmosphere of the
place. A man might believe anything…

Stephen drew in a harsh breath. All he had to do was
to get through the night. Then, on the morrow, they
could load up some stores, perhaps even find a cart and
head back to Campion, hopefully before the trouble that
seemed to be brewing in Wales erupted in earnest. Stephen let out the air he had been holding in a rush that
sounded more like a sigh. Home had never looked so
good. Leaning his head against the wall, he closed his
eyes, envisioning his own cask of wine, his own chamber and his own soft bed, preferably with an even softer
companion in it.

Unfortunately, his contemplation of the comforts he
had taken for granted was interrupted by Brighid, who
somehow always managed to banish good thoughts of
any kind. "We will know more once we talk to the
woman," she said.

"Right," Stephen mumbled, agreeing only to quiet
her. Then he realized just what she had said and opened
his eyes, narrowing them as he glanced toward Brighid.
"What woman?"

"The servant, Addfwyn, of course," she said, slipping
back into that superior tone he so detested. "The one
who arrived suddenly only to disappear after my father's
death."

Stephen dropped his lashes again, annoyed at Brigid's interruption of his fantasy. He was so weary after the day's events that he thought he actually might be able to sleep. "They all disappeared after your father's death, all except that Cadwy, which I still think is pretty suspicious," he muttered. "And she's long gone, so you can't talk to her."

"But I must. Therefore, I must find her."

That got Stephen's attention, and he jerked away from the wall to stare at Brighid's impassive countenance. "What do you mean *find* her?" he asked, all his heightened senses on alert. "We're going home tomorrow."

Having finished with the bed, Brighid sat down on the edge of it, her gaze swinging toward Stephen with alarming resolve. "I came here to find out what happened to my father, and I won't leave until I do." She paused, letting that dreadful piece of information sink in, before glancing away. "Of course, you are free to go. You have done your duty, and I will be happy to give you a message you may take back to your father, that absolves you of any further responsibility."

Stephen blinked, stunned at her words. She thought to *remain here?* He couldn't believe it. She had done some pretty senseless things since he'd known her, but this had to be the epitome. And, not only that, but she was sending him away without the slightest hesitation? *There's the door; be on your way!* Stephen felt a surge of outrage. No woman tossed him out!

And worst of all was the offer to placate Campion! Stephen grunted at the insult. He could just see himself returning to the castle, her missive in hand, to report upon his task as escort. *Why, yes, Father. I left her all alone in a tiny, falling-down manor with none but an untrustworthy old servant to protect her from brigands, murderers and the threat of war. But she said it was all right.*

That ought to finish his relationship with his sire quite nicely. He'd be lucky to be turned out on his ear. Did she think him simpleminded? Stephen shot to his feet, his weariness overcome by sudden anger that felt oddly akin to pain. Unsure of what he was going to do, he nonetheless strode forward only to feel his leg buckle, the wound throbbing sharply as he stumbled. Instantly, Brighid rushed toward him, pushing him back down onto his seat.

"Stephen, your injury!" she cried. As if she cared, he thought sourly, when she was ready to dismiss him like the lowliest servant. Still, she fell to her knees before him, and he leaned back against the wall, drawing a deep breath against the sharp pain. He had never been sick a day in his life, but he was beginning to think he wasn't invincible, and he wondered just what he would do if overcome by some fever.

"Just help me get off this mail," he said with a grunt, driving such worries way down deep.

She glanced upward, her eyes wide. "Oh, yes, of course," she said, but Stephen was too sore to savor her agreement. Bracing himself against the wall, he rose once more, ungirded his sword and lifted the heavy tunic. He missed his squire, for Brighid was of little help, her fingers fumbling uncharacteristically with the garment. Still, there was something about her touch that roused even his tired body, and when the garment was laid aside, Stephen leaned toward her.

But she only pushed him down once more, whatever momentary lapse in her own armor swiftly masked by her competency as she knelt to unwrap his bandage. However, Stephen's interest was engaged, and he studied her hands on him with anticipation. As he watched, growing harder by the minute, she pulled out a flask of something and proceeded to bathe the gash. He grunted, his jaw growing tight as other parts of him deferred to the ache in his leg.

"What's that?" he asked, rather warily. Idly, he wondered if it was some strange alchemic concoction of her father's and, if so, whether he should be worried.

"Verjuice," she said.

Stephen scowled. "Naturally, they have verjuice here but no wine," he said. Perhaps he could drink enough of the fermented sour juice to dull his senses—he gritted his teeth—or at least deaden the pain.

"Tis foul to drink and only used for cooking," Brighid commented, as if reading his mind. Why wasn't he surprised by that ability? Sometimes, it seemed to him that this slender young woman could do anything, except...

"You cannot stay here by yourself," Stephen said, glancing down at her once more. She had one hand on his knee, while the other was tending the cut. Her head was bent, and her hair flowed all around, loose and beautiful. Stephen sucked in a harsh breath. If only she would slide her palm up his thigh, he thought, his gaze settling on the swell of her breasts beneath her bodice, moving in a rhythm grown strangely rapid. Were her fingers trembling?

She dropped the cloth she was using, whispering something indelicate under her breath, and Stephen's heart began thundering in his chest. He recognized the signs, and with any other woman, he would have smiled smugly, covered her hand with his own, and let things progress from there. But this was Brighid, and he was frozen in place, uncertain what to do.

"It's not so bad. The blood washed it out well, and this should further cleanse it. I have some of the poultice left," she said reaching for her pouch. "It should have the wound healing in no time at all. I had some betony in there, which is always good, if you are aware of herb lore."

If he had not been so stunned, Stephen might have laughed. The unflappable Brighid was rattling on like an anxious bride. She dabbed some obnoxious salve on his wound, wrapping it with a fresh piece of material and tying it securely, and still he stayed where he was, hard and ready and barely daring to breathe.

"There," she said, finally, her hands still resting on his leg, and Stephen could almost imagine the brush of her fingertips in the dark hair that sprinkled his calf. She remained where she was, touching him, and then looked up, and there it was in her eyes. *Heat. Desire. For him.* Shimmering and undeniable. With a groan, Stephen reached for her face, cupped it in his hands and kissed her.

It was a revelation.

In his arrogance, Stephen had thought he knew every type of kiss, every nuance and each possible variation. He had engaged in such sport countless times with countless woman, including this one. But those early kisses had been to torment and tease, to prove something to her and to himself, while this was something else entirely.

Stephen's senses exploded in a burst of feeling. Her scent, her taste and the sound of her low gasp nearly overwhelmed him. And the feel of her! Exciting and mysterious, yet familiar and comforting, Brighid seemed the embodiment of everything he could ever want as she snaked her arms around his neck. With unseemly haste, he lowered himself over her, pressing her into the pallet that he had moved in front of the door.

Stephen groaned again when every inch of her melded against him, suffusing him with awareness, as if he had been sleepwalking all of his life until this very moment. The heightened senses that had cursed him throughout the day now seemed a blessing as he eagerly welcomed each new sensation. Unable to tear his mouth from hers, Stephen reveled in her fervent response even as his hands roamed her slender form with an urgency unrelated to his usual practiced skill.

Nudging his sex between her thighs, he knew the soft give of her and felt a heady spiral of need so intense that it left him gasping. Stephen told himself that he never gasped, that he never hurried or gave up any part of himself to his women, and yet he felt as though if he could only bury himself inside Brighid, life would be worth living again.

It scared him half to death.

The bedchamber had always been the one place where he was totally in control, confident and powerful, yet now he felt enslaved by his own need. He had honed his skills to a fine art, but to execute them he had to maintain a certain distance from his partner, which was impossible considering the frantic thundering of his blood.

With what was left of his wits, Stephen recognized that this was no typical tumble among the sheets. It had nothing to do with seduction or getting through the night or even simple lust. It was far more complex and far more necessary, as if Brighid l'Estrange had invaded every fiber of his being and only by joining with her would he be whole again.

The thought made Stephen pause, and he shuddered,

his body locked in an unheard of struggle with his mind. It grew so fierce and the pounding in his blood so loud, that he heard it thudding in his brain, like the sound of a fist against wood.

"Stephen!" Brighid broke the kiss to whisper his name with an urgency that made him open his eyes and look into her face. She was squirming beneath him, the drugged passion in her eyes fading as surely as his own. He blinked.

"The door!" she whispered. Nudging him aside, she rolled from beneath his body and struggled to stand, tugging at her gown as she did so.

"Mistress?" With a groan, Stephen recognized the voice of the servant, Cadwy, and realized that the man truly had been pounding on the door. Swinging into a sitting position, Stephen put a shaky hand to his head. What had come over him that he could mistake such? He shook his head. He had always prided himself on his performance in bed, which, by its very nature, included an attentiveness to the slightest sound, the merest gesture from his partner. Instead, he had been so consumed by need that someone could have conked him on the head, for all his awareness of anything beyond Brighid.

Drawing in a harsh breath, Stephen rose to his feet just as Brighid opened the door, then groped around wildly for his sword just in case the servant was accompanied by any unwelcome guests. It lay under the heap of his mail, and he lunged for it, though he felt like a fool when no villains rushed into the room.

"Mistress Brighid, are you all right?" Stephen heard the servant ask.

"Yes, I am fine," Brighid answered, with more certainty than Stephen could have managed. "I will not be needing you any more this evening, so you may seek your rest.''

''Have you seen the knight? I readied a chamber for him, but could find him not,'' Cadwy said, making Stephen grimace from his position behind the door.

''Lord de Burgh is here with me and will sleep in front of the door to provide protection for me since the manor is deserted,'' Brighid answered, and Stephen had to admire her aplomb. At the same time, he could well imagine the old servant's reaction to that bit of news, and he felt a surge of outrage on Brighid's behalf.

Suddenly, he realized how this would look to anyone who heard the tale: Mistress l'Estrange, an unmarried maiden, spending days and nights alone with a most notorious seducer. Stephen nearly groaned aloud. At one point during their journey, he would have liked nothing better than to ruin the good name of the woman who disdained him. But now things were different, and somehow it was important that Brighid maintain her reputation.

Stephen barely heard Cadwy's low reply and Brighid's soft good-night. But when she bolted the door, he looked up to see her leaning against the worn wood with a wary expression on her lovely face. Her shoulders sagged, and her eyes watched him, as wide and deep as the sea.

''If you are to stay, you must swear to me, Stephen, that you will remain here,'' she said, tilting her head toward the pallet. ''Alone.''

Stephen nodded numbly, his feelings an odd jumble of contradictions, for there was no way to have her and keep her chaste at the same time. At his gesture of assent, Brighid straightened and made a hurried, yet dignified, bolt for the bed.

Unable to look in that direction, Stephen pulled the pallet in front of the door once more. Unfortunately, the scent of Brighid lingered on the fur, and he drew a heady breath that nearly stole his tenuous resolve. But it was more than his vow that kept him from Brighid, more than the pleading look in those green eyes that had scored his soul. In truth, Stephen was afraid to touch her.

It was not a heartrending fright like he had felt when attacked, but more like an insidious, ominous dread. For the first time ever, he felt a connection to a woman that went beyond the physical, and even though he told himself it was all hokus-pokus nonsense, some silly effect of his surroundings, Stephen remained leery. Their recent encounter had proved that sex with Brighid wouldn't be a simple, fulfilling roll in bed. It would be a life-altering event, something that would change him forever. And he wasn't sure if he wanted his life altered.

Lowering himself to the pallet, Stephen stretched out, fully clothed. It was not exactly the sort of berth he was accustomed to, nor the way he usually dressed. He longed for a hot bath and a soft bed and the delicious freedom of nakedness that he took for granted.

But any wish for less clothing made his thoughts veer in dangerous directions and then his want for Brighid rose up, nearly a tangible thing in the darkness. Unwilling to examine his various and sundry feelings for her, Stephen nonetheless knew that nothing was settled, not what lay between them, nor even what would happen on the morrow, when he must convince her to abandon this foolish quest of hers and return to Campion.

He was not going to leave her, of that he was certain. Drawing in a long, slow breath of her lingering scent, Stephen let the essence of her seep into his awareness.

He shifted, settling into his bed, then suddenly felt something hard. With a frown, he felt around until he discovered a stone in the hem of his tunic. Its shape was oddly familiar, and Stephen realized that it was the rock Brighid had given him to hold the night before.

Hokus-pokus and nonsense, he thought, intending to toss it away, but he felt too weary. Instead, he fingered the smooth surface and closed his eyes as a strange sort of peace settled over him. And then he slept.

Chapter Fourteen

Brighid set out the cups of diluted ale, along with some bread that Cadwy had baked this morning. The servant had been up early, heating water for baths, and Brighid had washed and dressed in fresh clothing, clean for the first time in days. If only she felt rested, as well, but how could she sleep after what had happened?

Brighid was all too aware of the narrowness of her escape. If it had not been for Cadwy, she might have succumbed to the man who sat across from her blithely breaking his fast. She might even now be lying tangled in the bedsheets with him, her innocence forgotten in the heat of the moment. Brighid's heart pounded at the thought, but more in excitement than horror, a reaction that made her stand up abruptly and hurry to the kitchens.

It had been bad enough when only her body betrayed her, when Stephen's deliberate attempts to torment her had roused a passion she had never known, but now... Brighid braced her hands against an ancient hewn table and bowed her head. Now her feelings were engaged, as well. And if she had found the rogue difficult to resist before, it was nearly impossible to turn away from him when she felt a rush of emotion for him, as well as a craving for his touch. Twas a heady, but dangerous, combination akin to nothing she could recognize. *Was this love?*

Brighid jerked her head upright in panic. No, surely not, she told herself. Stephen's beauty and well-honed charm were calculated to entrance. No doubt, many a foolish woman had not only succumbed to his allure, but thought herself in love with him. And some probably deluded themselves that he felt the same, a potential for disaster that Brighid had no intention of inviting.

Turning around, Brighid leaned into the edge of the tabletop. Against her will, she had grown attached to this new Stephen, and he might very well be a help, rather than a hindrance, in her quest. Yet, she knew that she must send him away. The very thought was painful, but the ache only made her more determined to remove temptation from her path. Pushing herself away from the worn oak, Brighid straightened her shoulders and marched into the hall.

Stephen was leaning back, drinking, and for a moment he seemed much as he had been before, arrogant, lazy and graceful. Brighid told herself she would not miss him and drew a deep breath, but before she could find the words, Stephen glanced her way. Immediately, he gulped down his ale and rose to his feet, a tall, vital warrior, and all thoughts that he was as she had first seen him vanished.

He was not the man he once had been. Brighid knew it with a certainty that chilled her blood. How had this change come to pass? Before her very eyes, Stephen de Burgh, as base a being as she had ever encountered, had changed into something as fine as the most precious metal, a transmutation worthy of her father's skills. An eerie sensation washed over her, and Brigid reached out for the edge of the table, suddenly dizzy.

The images washed over her in a heated wave: Stephen lying naked upon a wide bed, his strong body bathed in the glow of firelight, his muscles gleaming with a sheen of sweat, his face intent as he reached for her....

"What is it?" The sound of that voice, deep and hoarse and seductive, made Brighid flinch, and she blinked up at the man before her, eyes wide with shock.

"Are you all right?" he asked, stepping forward, but she backed away, breathing hard. His expression reflected only concern, not the dark intensity that lingered in Brighid's mind, and so she nodded in answer, though she desperately wanted to shake her head. She was not herself, and she had a feeling she would never be right again.

That bleak realization prompted a sudden urge to throw herself into his arms, bury her face against his wide chest and surrender to whatever forces seemed to be driving them together. But Brighid struggled against the sensation, lifted her chin and told herself she didn't believe.

"If you are certain you are well," Stephen said with a hesitant look that only made her heart hurt all the more, "I would like to see if there is a cart we can use to take some supplies with us. Hopefully, the roads will be drier."

Brighid shook her head.

"There is no cart?" Stephen asked, his brows lifting slightly.

Brighid shook her head once more. "I don't know, but I think you would do better without it. Surely a man alone on horseback will be able to move faster."

Stephen's handsome face, open to her but a moment ago, abruptly shuttered, his dark eyes narrowing. "What do you mean *a man alone?* I'm not going anywhere without you."

Brighid's pulse leapt, whether in joy or horror, she wasn't quiet certain. "But you must," she said. "For I cannot leave until I uncover the facts of my father's death."

"He's dead, Brighid. There's nothing you can do to change that. And you cannot stay here alone. Come back with me to Campion, where you will be safe." The invitation was made in a low voice that teased her senses, and Brighid imagined a host of meanings in the simple statement.

"I—I can't," she mumbled, practically wringing her hands in uncharacteristic dismay. She had worked hard to cultivate her calm reserve. Why must he constantly shatter it?

"Then I guess I will remain here," Stephen said, with a stony look that brooked no opposition.

Brighid stared at him in stunned surprise, for this was a turn she had not anticipated. She had expected him to argue with her and bluster and complain, but never had she dreamed he would give up his wine and his comforts for her. Brighid firmly quelled the thrill of pleasure that shot through her, for swift on the heels of that joy was the knowledge that Stephen's continued presence meant further tests to her already strained will.

"Oh, no! Really, you mustn't," she protested, backing away from him as she recognized the threat. He was sin incarnate, and she was weakening.

His expression black, Stephen followed. "Oh? And why not?" he asked, his brows rising.

"Because, I—I'm sure you have other things to do,

other places you would rather be than here,'' Brighid said, in confusion.

The side of his mouth kicked up into a sly smile. "Oh, I'll admit Rumenea lacks the usual amenities," Stephen said, swinging out a strong arm to take in the filthy jumble of the hall. "But it boasts one very appealing feature." His rich brown eyes seemed to darken even more, as though to draw her in, and Brighid knew that if he took one more step, she might end up as she had last night, returning his kisses with unholy fervor.

With one more backward motion, Brighid bumped into the wall behind her. Jerking away from the cold stone in some confusion, she realized that she was near the entrance to the cellars. "I refuse to waste time arguing," she said, with more resolve than she felt. "You do what you must, as will I, and right now I need to examine my father's work area."

Grabbing up one of the torches that rested along the wall, Brighid quickly set it to the hearth's flame and headed down the winding stair into the blackness below, away from Stephen. It was a journey she had made many times, but now the chill air seemed especially cold, the cavernous space empty without her father. Someone had killed him here, in his most private retreat.

Drawing a deep breath, Brighid banished all such thoughts, but even as she fled Stephen, she found herself longing for his company.

His eyes narrowing, Stephen watched Brighid disappear into the gaping hole below with no little aggravation. It was bad enough that she refused to see reason and return to Campion with him, but now she was going off alone into some dreadful dungeon by herself! Spare him from willful women, he thought, with a helpless glance heavenward. Then, gripping the hilt of his sword, he followed Brighid below.

When he reached the bottom of the narrow steps, Stephen had a glimpse of a vast, vaulted space, cast deep in shadow before Brighid stepped forward, lighting a candelabra with her torch. As he watched, she moved around the room in a circle, stopping to light the tall candelabras one by one. Sometimes, she had to bend to right one, but it was obvious that the vandals who had ransacked the rest of the manor had done little here, if anything at all.

"The brigands must not have come down here," Stephen said, and as light danced upon the weird chamber, he could well understand why they stayed away.

"No brigands, but thieves," Brighid said. "They have been here, as well, but they knew enough not to destroy anything that might be of use to them."

Brows lifting, Stephen didn't see how anything down here could be of use to anyone. He had not been mistaken in thinking Brighid walked in a circle, for now he could plainly see a huge configuration upon the floor, where symbols, perhaps astrological, were carved into the tiles around a center that took up much of the area.

Beyond the carvings lay various hearths and ovens with odd means for venting the smoke from their now cold fires. And scattered about everywhere were tables upon which were the strangest assortment of objects Stephen had ever seen. He stepped toward the nearest surface, where he found flasks of every size and shape. Lifting a finger, he touched a tall piece of glass resembling a snake.

"A winding pipe," Brighid said, startling him. "And that's a three-armed still next to it." She was standing nearby, watching him with a wary expression, as though she expected him to run screaming from the room. As if he were made of such paltry stuff! Of course, it helped that he didn't believe in any of this. Or at least that was what Stephen told himself as he noticed a line of pots with such labels as Thorn Apple, Belladonna and Henbane.

"And the poisons? What are they for?" he asked, his brows inching upward.

Brighid lifted a pale hand to touch a string of drying herbs hanging above. "Not all of them are poison," she said in a remarkably matter-of-fact manner. "They are used for various tests, infusions and tonics. Would you care for a love potion?"

Stephen choked back a laugh and gave her an arrogant look. Perhaps she was not that familiar with his reputation. "I don't need love potions," he assured her.

"No, I don't suppose you do," she said rather sadly, before turning away. Her odd expression made Stephen feel that disagreeable something in his belly, but he was quickly distracted by the next table, which was strewn with more books than he had ever seen, more than even his scholarly brother Geoffrey possessed. He opened one only to blink at the illegible contents.

"Arabic," Brighid explained. "Many are in Latin, as well, or written in symbols or codes."

No doubt, she could read them all, too, Stephen thought, with a twinge of admiration. At last he found some volumes that were in English, but with titles like *The Book of Furnaces* and *Concerning Alums and Salts,* they were not exactly his idea of interesting reading. Still, the subjects seemed to lean more toward the scientific than the mystical, which was a relief.

Opening one fat tome, Stephen read aloud, "A stone but not a stone, a stone unknown and known to all." He scowled at Brighid, who was watching him with an amused expression. "What is that gibberish supposed to mean?" he asked, considerably less awed by her father's so-called work.

"'Tis the nature of the alchemist to speak in riddles," Brighid said. Her words were simple enough, but the way she smiled at him did something to his insides. For a moment, Stephen stared at her, certain he was imagining the warmth in her eyes, before he glanced away, shutting the book with a loud thump.

"Father's notes are gone," she said, as if the disturbing interlude had never occurred, and Stephen was only too eager to dismiss it.

"How can you tell?" he asked.

"He always kept them here, by his reference works."

"Well, maybe he put them away. After all, it's been a long time since you were here," Stephen said.

Brighid shook her head and roamed the chilly chamber, stopping periodically to pick up a flask or study a strange object. After a while, the silence grew oppressive, and Stephen was restless. Was she reliving old memories or planning to resume her father's art? The thought made him shift uncomfortably.

"What are you doing?" he asked.

"Looking for clues to my father's murder."

"You won't find anything here." The low, solemn pronouncement made Stephen whirl around, hand upon his sword hilt, but it was only Cadwy who stood in the dim shadows of the steps. Relaxing, Stephen nonetheless kept an eye on the servant, whom he regarded with narrowed eyes.

"And how do you know that?" Stephen asked.

Cadwy shook his head. "Little here was disturbed, except for your father's writings. Addfwyn must have stolen them, perhaps as revenge upon that which your father held most dear.''

It didn't make much sense to Stephen, but Brighid turned toward Cadwy, her gaze intent. "Do you know where she is now?"

"She came from the village," Cadwy said. "But when we tried to find her...afterward, none claimed knowledge of her," he added, his expression bitter.

Brighid paused thoughtfully. "There are too many co-incidences here, Cadwy," she mused. "If, as you say, the woman is the murderer, she must have returned later with others to look for that which she could not discover in my father's writings. The manor's destruction is not the work of brigands, but of those desperate to find something. Witness the careful, but thorough, search that has been made here," she said.

Stephen glanced around curiously, for he could see nothing amiss in the eerie chamber, except for the strangeness of the place.

"Or perhaps this Addfwyn was a spy for some other alchemist, who paid her to ferret out my father's secrets," Brighid mused.

"Then why kill him?" Stephen asked, skeptical of her elaborate theories. For someone so serious, Brighid certainly had a lot of imagination. He supposed it went with that l'Estrange heritage of hers.

"I don't know, but whether she did the deed or not, the woman knows something. I feel," Brighid began, only to hesitate and amend her words. "I *think* that she's the key."

Stephen studied her suspiciously. He still had the sense there was something she wasn't telling him, something that made the hairs on the back of his neck stand at attention. Again. He rubbed his neck and told himself the vaulted cellar and its bizarre contents were enough to make any sane person wary.

And, more and more, he was feeling like the only sane person in the room, certainly the only reasonable one. How his brothers would have laughed at that notion! Stephen shook his head. When he began this hideous journey, he had thought Brighid as stiff and sensible a woman as he would ever dread to meet. Now, she seemed full of mad ideas and a barely contained passion, fully transformed and without the aid of any magic rock!

And right now, as thrilled as he was by the appearance of that passion, Stephen would have welcomed the grim, sober woman he had first met. "Look," he said, shaking off the nagging sensation that somehow the two of them had switched places. "Whoever killed your father and whoever ransacked his manor are long gone, whether the woman from the village or someone else. There's nothing you can do about it."

Brighid lifted her chin to fix him with her sea gaze, bottomless and stormy. "Yes, the deeds are done, but I could not call myself a daughter, if I did not seek the truth. And justice."

Stephen groaned. His brothers might admire such honor and loyalty, but he didn't care to be inconvenienced by it. "Believe me, Brighid, justice is a rare and precious thing, as elusive as the Philosopher's Stone," he said, waving an arm to take in the accouterments of her father's work. Swiftly, he racked his brain to think of a way to talk her out of this nonsense.

Although Stephen didn't see any real threat in the situation, beyond that of being alone and unprotected in wild country, perhaps a warning would serve to do so. "Better to leave things be, ere you bring danger upon yourself," he said.

Unfortunately, his threat did not cause the hoped for response, because Brighid did not flinch. "You don't understand, Stephen. I'm already in danger. *We're* already in danger."

Stephen frowned. "If you're talking about the brigands who attacked us on the road, I hardly think they would follow us here."

Brighid shook her head impatiently. "Whether or not those men were connected to my father's death, I don't know, but I am in danger just by my very existence. The people who murdered my father are searching for his secrets, and where else should they find them now but with his daughter, the last legacy of the l'Estranges? And I have a feeling they won't rest until they discover what they seek."

Stephen felt a chill wash over him that had nothing to do with the temperature. At last, he could see a reason for Brighid's stubborn, single-minded purpose, but he felt frustrated, yet again. "You might have let me know about this a bit earlier, you know," he muttered.

But having made her ominous pronouncement, Brighid marched toward the stairs, leaving Stephen to stare after her. She was so certain, sometimes he wondered if she might possess some preternatural powers, after all. Or maybe she just reminded him of his father, with all that righteous confidence.

He didn't believe a word of it, of course: murdering alchemists, servant spies, hidden secrets to eternal life. Stephen shrugged, but the cold, clammy unease that clung to him remained. *What if some madman actually thought Brighid knew something?* A movement caught his attention, and Stephen swung round to find himself facing Cadwy, who still stood nearby, studying him with an intensity that renewed all his suspicions about the servant. Stephen's eyes narrowed, but before he could accuse the man of anything, Cadwy spoke.

"You'll take care of her?" the servant asked.

Stephen's brows rose at the bold question. "Of course. I got her this far, didn't I?" he countered, even though he knew full well that their arrival at Rumenea, relatively unscathed, owed more to chance than any heroics on his part. As if the servant could read his mind, Cadwy appeared unsatisfied by the answer.

"What?" Stephen asked, in annoyance.

Cadwy dropped his gaze. "We have heard of you, even here, my lord," he said. And for some reason, instead of being flattered, Stephen knew a swift outrage that Brighid's name should be linked with his own unsavory reputation.

"Now, wait a moment. I don't know what you've heard, but I am serving as your mistress's escort, nothing more," Stephen said. He stepped closer to the man, his fingers tightening into a fist in the manner of his brother Simon. "And if I hear one word of slanderous gossip attached to her name, I'll know where it came from," he growled, towering over the older servant.

Instead of cowering, Cadwy smiled, as though pleased by his answer, and Stephen wondered if everyone around him was a lunatic. "She's not like other women, you know," Cadwy said. "It's the family heritage, the power and glory of the l'Estranges."

Stephen swallowed a snort. If this neglected manor represented power and glory, then he was the king's confidant. He swung away only to hear Cadwy's low voice behind him. "Don't scoff at that which you don't understand, my lord."

Amazed at his audacity, Stephen turned upon him once more. "And just what don't I understand?"

Cadwy gave him a cryptic look. "There is more to the world than that which you can see with your eyes, my lord. You must open yourself to your other senses and what they tell you."

Stephen snorted. "Riddles! You mean this alchemy business? I think not. I've seen a lot, but I've never seen anything to make me believe you can transform one thing into another."

"Haven't you, my lord?" Cadwy asked.

He stared, unblinking, at Stephen, who shifted uncomfortably. All right, so maybe Brighid had changed a little, Stephen admitted to himself, but that wasn't the same thing as making a pile of lead turn to gold.

"Alchemy is just one of the paths toward which a l'Estrange might direct his gifts," Cadwy said. "There are other, perhaps more important, talents. Brighid's father was a fool not to see that."

Against his better judgment, Stephen leaned close, curious at the mention of Brighid's sire. "What do you mean?"

"There are those who possess abilities beyond that of most people, some who are even unaware of their skills," Cadwy said.

"What skills?" Stephen asked, still skeptical.

"The power to heal or to conjure or to see the future are some of them," the servant replied.

Stephen snorted. "You mean like those daft aunts of Brighid, whispering about destiny and such? A lot of hokus-pokus," he said in dismissal.

"And what of Mistress Brighid? Do you think her daft?" Cadwy asked.

Stephen's eyes narrowed. "She doesn't believe in any of that nonsense."

"I didn't ask you what she believed. I asked you what you believed."

Stephen let out a growl of impatience at the servant's cryptic words. He turned away, tired of wasting his time with more riddles.

"Brighid knows that which is hidden," Cadwy said.

Stephen swung back around. "What?"

"Although her father was too focused on his own work to see it, Brighid is far more gifted than the others. When she was only a child, she possessed the power to see the past, the present and the future. But her father had no use for that. Obsessed with alchemy, he rejected her gift. And so, then, did she," Cadwy said. "She has returned home, but she will not be whole until she accepts herself and comes to terms with her heritage. She is a l'Estrange, and she cannot deny it."

Stephen felt the hair on the back of his neck rise at both the tone and substance of the servant's words, and he deliberately adopted a mocking attitude. "All right," Stephen said. "So maybe she just closes her eyes and has visions. Too bad she couldn't see the attack that nearly killed us both."

"'Tis not so easily done, my lord. Nor is she willing to use her talents. But if she is to succeed at her quest, she must open herself to all possibilities," Cadwy said, watching Stephen with that unblinking gaze. "And you, my lord de Burgh, are involved somehow in her destiny."

Stephen shook his head even as he remembered the prediction of the aunts. "No. I'm just along to keep her from getting killed," he said. He turned to go, eager to escape the strangeness of the servant and the cellar, along with a nagging chill.

"Then you, too, must believe, my lord."

Snorting, Stephen climbed the steps, leaving Cadwy behind, but not before he heard one last bit of advice called to him from below. "Have her look into the water, my lord! The water!"

It was cold and overcast when they rode to the village, making the small cluster of buildings look as gloomy and forbidding as the manor itself. These were sparsely populated areas, where people survived as best they could, raising sheep and plowing a few strips of land. It was a hard life, and to his dismay, Stephen felt it keenly.

The dulled awareness that had so long characterized his life had sharpened so that he saw far more than ever before, and without the aid of any special powers, either. The wind, the smells and the sounds were all intensified, but did not seem to torment him as they once had. Stephen frowned. Maybe he was growing accustomed to this new world of his. Wrapping his cloak tightly against the chill, he urged Hades forward, following Brighid to a small croft.

The residents were so wary that Stephen wondered if he would have to storm into their crofts and drag them out bodily, but once Brighid called forth something in their native tongue, they swarmed outside to crowd about Brighid's palfrey. Alarmed, Stephen grabbed the hilt of his sword as they murmured her name, the intermingling voices gradually rising to a cry.

"Mistress l'Estrange!" they shouted again and again. Hades grew restive, and Stephen tensed. For all he knew they were preparing to burn her as a witch, but from the looks on their faces, the welcome was a friendly one. Still, these were the same people who supposedly kept as far away as Rumenea as possible, so Stephen remained on his guard, just in case the ill feelings for her father extended to Brighid.

Apparently, they did not, but when Brighid dismounted, Stephen kept Hades close by her even as he scanned the area. When she turned toward him, a grave expression on her face, his heart pounded.

"What?" he asked, urging his mount nearer, but Brighid only shook her head and swung back to the freemen and cottagers who surrounded them. Impatient, Stephen was just about to dismount himself when Brighid finally made gestures of farewell. But it was not until they were back on the track again, away from the villagers, that she finally spoke.

"Addfwyn came here from another village, northwest of here. But those who knew her said that others have been here only days ago, asking about her. Several men, hooded and mysterious."

Stephen immediately discounted the hooded and mysterious part, but even allowing for that embellishment, he had to admit that the news wasn't good.

"Perhaps her relatives came searching for her when they heard of the murder," he suggested, receiving a jaundiced look for his effort. All right, so maybe he was reaching for any excuse not to accept Brighid's outlandish theories.

"They are close upon her trail. We must hurry, if we are to find her first," Brighid said.

Stephen groaned. The last thing he wanted to do was return to the road, alone and unprotected, to chase after some serving woman. But as he watched the straight set of her back and the slender line of her shoulders, he knew that Brighid would go by herself, should he refuse her.

Swearing under his breath, Stephen paused to consider

just how all this had come to pass: how he, one of the most famous seducers in the country, had ended up playing handmaiden to a witchy, domineering female who had no more sense than to chase after murderers. And the only answer he could come up with was not at all to his liking.

Destiny.

Chapter Fifteen

Stephen was still wondering what he was doing the following morning as he trailed in Brighid's wake, up into the hills even farther away from any signs of civilization. If his brothers could see him now, they would surely have locked him away as a madman. But what else could he do? The only way to keep Brighid from going would be to tie her to her bed, and although that idea definitely had its merits, Stephen didn't think she would stand for it for long.

Not that he doubted his ability to persuade her, of course, but…knowing her, the single-minded woman would *still* take off into the hills as soon as his eyes were closed, Stephen thought. And they seemed to drift shut on a regular basis, for last night he had crawled once more onto his pallet in front of her door and slept like a baby. Two nights of real rest in a row were precious to him, and Stephen was afraid to do anything that might disturb the pattern. *All right, so maybe he was just afraid.* Period.

His lust for Brighid was still there, but it was tempered by something else, something that stayed his hand. The ominous clang of destiny? A dawning respect? A growing affection? Whatever it was, Stephen found himself shying away from his companion even as he was drawn to her. He told himself that seducing Brighid would spell trouble for both of them and tried to leave it at that.

So, here he was, watching her, desiring her and doing nothing about it. How his brothers would roar with laughter—after they cudgeled him for falling in with her foolhardy scheme. Stephen could just imagine what his father would say, and the thought of some pompous lecture made his jaw tighten. He hurried onward, keeping an eye out for wild animals, ruffians, armies and mysterious murderers.

They met none of those—only bad weather the higher they climbed, where snow and ice lingered. Stephen swore he had never faced such a winter, though nothing would surprise him anymore. Or, at least, that's what he thought until they came upon Addfwyn's village, where the residents greeted them with all the warmth and welcome due lepers or other disease carriers. Nonetheless, they pointed the way to a croft where the woman might be found, and Brighid thanked them before turning her weary palfrey toward the edge of the scattered buildings.

Stephen frowned, for he could tell that Brighid was weary, too. He could see it in the constant righting of her shoulders, in the set of her chin, in the sweep of her golden lashes, and he rued this journey even more. He felt a surge of protectiveness, along with an urge to pull her close, not for sex, but to ease her. She was a unique woman, brave and honorable and precious, and she deserved to be warm and dry and safe, not trekking through the snow to search for a murderess.

Stephen felt the weight of that knowledge, along with

his own culpability. And when they reached the hut, he made her stand aside. If the killer was inside, he didn't want Brighid walking into a knife attack. Unsheathing his sword, he swung open the door, only to stare into a dim interior that looked worse than the manor, with straw and wood and pieces of clothing scattered everywhere. It was not the usual manner of housekeeping, even for cottagers, and Stephen held Brighid back with one arm, unwilling to enter.

Peeking around him, Brighid made a low sound of dismay. "They've been here," she said. "Have they killed her?"

Stephen squinted, but he could not see anything that looked like a body among the jumble of simple furnishings: pallets, an overturned table and a broken stool, all strewn among rushes and ashes from the hearth. He sniffed, his newly sensitive nose taking in the smell of must and soot, but not the foul order of death.

"None have lived here recently," Stephen said, with some surety as he put away his weapon. "And there is no one inside."

He heard the shaky intake of Brighid's breath and could almost feel her disappointment at the servant's absence, though he was more relieved than anything else. He stepped forward, wondering if some clue might be found in the rubble, but suddenly he was aware of something else, a tingling sensation that set the hairs on his neck to rise.

"Brighid," Stephen whispered even as he put out one arm to shield her and turned, unsheathing his sword again in one swift motion. For once, he was grateful for his new awareness, for just as he thrust her behind him, they appeared over the rise, several men swinging clubs and makeshift weapons. For a moment, Stephen felt as if he had stepped back in time to some Celtic nightmare.

More likely, they had stumbled upon a pocket of over-zealous Welsh rebels, who didn't care to ask about the loyalties of an English knight. Without pausing to consider that he was well outnumbered, Stephen roared out a battle cry that would have made his brother Simon proud. Indeed, it almost seemed as though on that cold hilltop, he summoned them, his six siblings and the might of all the de Burghs, in one single shout. And should he go to his death, he knew they would avenge him.

Arm upraised, Stephen rushed forward, ready to strike down two of the approaching men at once, but Brighid called out a warning. He swung halfway round only to see her standing tall on a rocky outcropping, her hair falling down her back, her chin held high. The very image of some pagan goddess, she bore no resemblance to the staid young woman he had escorted to Wales.

"No!" she called again. And then she began speaking in Welsh, a low intonation that sent chills up his spine and appeared to have the same effect on the villagers. They backed away, lowering their weapons and muttering among themselves. Some fled outright. Others appeared fearful, and some, like Stephen himself, simply stared, awestruck by this one, slender woman.

If he didn't know better, Stephen would have thought she had summoned the weather to do her bidding, for when she lifted her arms, the wind rose to keen eerily through the hills. It whipped the hair back from her face, tore at cloaks and sent the dusting of snow on the ground up into the air to swirl menacingly.

Stephen had no idea what she was saying, but all of his senses clamored in response. Here was a woman, beyond any of the pale imitations he had known. And, just as surely as she held these poor villagers in her sway, Brighid claimed him, too, with a power that he could not begin to explain. His blood thundered in his veins, and he felt a certain pride, along with a hot surge of possession, as if she were *his*.

Then, Brighid lowered her arms, and just as swiftly as it had begun, the wind died down, cloaks fell back into place, the snow drifted to the ground, and Stephen shook his head, as if to reclaim his sanity. He turned, sword still in hand, toward the men, but most hurried away, a wary eye upon Brighid. Those few who remained stepped forward, their weapons long fallen to the ground, their attitudes now humble.

One spoke, and when Brighid answered, Stephen blinked at the sight of her. She was standing on the ground once more, and seemed nothing other than a normal woman, slender and slight. Stephen shook his head again, wondering if he had imagined the entire episode, but these men who had threatened them were deferring to her. Something must have happened; Stephen just wasn't sure what.

He watched their faces as the conversation flowed, frustrated at his inability to understand the language. "What is it? What are they saying?" he finally asked.

Brighid turned to him, her expression bleak. "They were here, the cloaked horsemen. They asked about Addfwyn, then destroyed her family's home. This man here is her uncle," Brighid explained, pointing to a short, swarthy fellow. "He says that she left years ago and has not returned, but the men who came frightened away those who lived here. They have had to take shelter with relatives. When we arrived, asking the same questions, he thought we were in league with the others and bent on more destruction of their village.''

Stephen nodded curtly at the fellow, finding it a little difficult to smile at someone who had so recently come after him with a club. And he could find no satisfaction in the fellow's tale. He had hoped that this journey into the hills would put Brighid's questions to rest, but they only seemed to raise more. Who were these men who left devastation in their wake, and why were they so interested in a lowly servant?

Although Stephen still snorted at the thought of some magic rock that worked wonders, obviously someone out there believed in it, enough to ransack homes and frighten the residents. Enough to kill? He shuddered even as Brighid concluded her speech with the villager. She turned toward Stephen, her face impassive.

''He has directed us toward his lord's manor house, just over that rise. Although they have heard that the lord himself is not in residence, his people will give us shelter.'' Her tone was even, but Stephen could see the weariness in the ocean depths of her eyes. She was disappointed by this new development, discouraged in her quest, and he knew of no way to cheer her. Perhaps a decent meal and a good bed behind safe walls would do them both good, he thought.

Nodding toward the villager, Stephen helped Brighid to mount and then took his own place upon Hades. ''Over the rise,'' he muttered, having had his fill of directions. ''Let's hope it's not fifty miles across these crags.''

But the man from the village was not exaggerating. As soon as they crested the hill, Stephen saw it, a small, well-kept building, old yet sturdy. He felt a surge of anticipation at the prospect of a hot meal and a warm bed, but the thought also made him pause. Who knew what manner of men lived here, and if the lord was not in residence during the winter months, where was he? Gone to join whatever army Llewelyn was raising? As much as he would have liked to put aside his guard and enjoy himself thoroughly, Stephen knew he could not.

And that realization was followed swiftly by another, more disturbing one: the sleeping arrangements. Stephen moved restlessly in his saddle as the thought of a bleak night alone in some strange house stretched before him. Normally, he would take the opportunity to drink and carouse into the late hours, bedding down at last with a willing woman to drive away the demons that plagued him. But he could not do that when Brighid was around.

The thought of any other woman left him cold, and even if it did not, he would not insult her. Nay, Stephen thought, with sudden fierceness, he had to be with Brighid, for her protection as well as his own ease. Who knew of these people? He, who had spent a lifetime in gregarious appreciation of everyone, now felt a sharp suspicion of all. And, for Brighid's sake he would take no chances.

"We shall tell these people that we are married," Stephen said, surprised at how easily the words he had never thought to utter sprang from his lips. Ignoring the startled look on Brighid's face, he turned his attention back to the road. "Tis safer."

Although Stephen could feel Brighid's gaze upon him, he refused to return it, staring stonily ahead, instead, even when he heard the low hiss of her sigh. "And what happens when word reaches the earl of Campion that his son is married?" she asked.

Stephen swallowed a snort, for he knew that none there would believe such a tale, most especially his disapproving father. "I'm worried about now, not later," he said. Still, the notion seized him, and for one brief, stunning moment, he wondered what the reaction would be should he truly wed. A tantalizing thought, if only to shock his siblings, which was his wont, more often than not.

Stephen glanced at Brighid's stiff back and considered what she would say to such a proposal. Any other woman would weep with gratitude, but not Brighid. No doubt she would laugh in his face or rail at him rudely. Frowning, Stephen told himself that she would do better to count her good fortune. And yet, he couldn't dismiss a sneaking suspicion that she deserved better than anything he could give her.

Brighid settled onto a bench beside Stephen and enjoyed the hearty flavor of roast boar, along with a variety of other delightful dishes. The company was small, but friendly, and after the terrors and traumas of the last few days, seemed a balm to her troubled soul. She had been glad to see the relative normalcy of the greeting: young boys running out to meet them, along with a few servants, unarmed and welcoming.

The de Burgh name gained them entrance immediately, and Brighid had been startled by the deference she had received as Stephen's bride. She could see how one could become accustomed to such treatment. It was heady, though she was grateful that none here, at least, made comment upon his reputation. Perhaps, it had not reached this far up into the hills.

When Stephen had suggested this ploy, Brighid had given no thought to his infamy. She had felt as if the ground had dropped away, launching her into thin air.

Oh, what a tempting indulgence to play his wife. To *be* his wife. Brighid scolded herself for such musings.

Never would this de Burgh marry, and if he did, his wife would have her hands full. He was no simple drunk, as she had suspected, but a very complicated man, who needed support and strength and nurturing and love in equal measure. *All that she could give him.* Brighid drew in a shaky breath and told herself that she was living a giddy dream, but nothing more.

"Wine, my lord?" The sound of the servant's casual query shook Brighid from her musings, and she stiffened as all her ease evaporated in an instant. She slanted a glance toward Stephen and saw that he, too, had tensed, his big body hard, the arm that rested on the table taut. His head was bowed, and his long, dark hair obscured her view of his face.

Brighid opened her mouth to speak, but what could she say? This was not Rumenea, where she was mistress and could order the servants to water the drink. Why hadn't she thought of this? Why had she agreed to come here? She felt a desolation far stronger than that which had filled her at the sight of Addfwyn's croft. It was a blow that went straight to her heart, and in that instant she knew the truth.

She was in love with Stephen de Burgh.

Brighid drew in a sharp breath, stunned by the realization, but she could not deny it. She loved the man beside her: knight, drunkard, arrogant lord and seducer of women, with his sarcastic wit and his dark, tormented secrets. Both charming and rude, armored yet vulnerable, blind to his strengths and all too aware of his weaknesses, he had won her heart. And now she held her breath as she awaited his answer, just as though that heart of hers stood in the balance.

Time seemed to stand still or tick by far too slowly, and Brighid imagined that every person in the room paused, listening for Stephen's response, though she was vaguely aware of conversations continuing about her. To her mind, everyone and everything came to a halt. Her blood stilled and her breathing stopped, until at last, he spoke.

"Nay. Naught but a little ale for me," Stephen said, finally, and Brighid released her air in a rush. She wanted to reach out to touch him, to throw her arms around him, but she trusted not her own composure here, before so many, and so she only looked away, blinking back sudden tears.

And all through the meal, Brighid felt wholly unlike herself, lighter somehow, as if her love for this man was a blessing and not, as she suspected, a curse. She smiled and she exchanged pleasantries with those around her. She listened when the bailiff spoke to Stephen in English, and yet she absorbed none of it, floating away in her own little bubble, as if she herself were drunk. To someone who had believed in so little for so long, the discovery of love was astounding.

It was almost like magic.

And when supper ended Brighid was rather disappointed that Stephen left to speak with the soldiers who manned the manor. He was seeking information for her, and yet, she missed him. Not a good sign, she told herself, but the knowledge did little to dampen her giddy mood. And the attendant who led her to her chamber did not help by addressing her as Lady de Burgh. *Stephen's lady.*

Although Brighid had her doubts about perpetuating this lie, she found herself trembling when she entered the room where she was to sleep with her so-called husband. Certainly, she had shared quarters with Stephen three nights now, but somehow this was different. The chamber was more spacious, a fire was burning brightly in the hearth, and the massive, carved bed took up most of the area.

With a few words, Brighid dismissed the attendant and stood alone, staring at the big bed, wondering what it would be like if the lie were true. As much as she would like to have dismissed it, the thought lingered, tapping her innermost desires, weaving fantasies that Brighid knew would prevent her from sleeping. And so she lay awake, alone in the big bed, and told herself she was not waiting for Stephen.

Yet she knew when he returned. She heard the soft closing of the door, the shooting of the bolt, and his footsteps as he walked toward the fire. She even watched under lowered lashes as he set aside his sword and mail and stood to remove his boots and hose. He stripped off his garments with masculine efficiency, lifting his tunic over his head to reveal shadowy patches of hair under his strong arms and a chest that fairly gleamed golden in the firelight. It was broad and muscular and covered with a thick mass of dark hair above a smooth stomach.

Unaware of her scrutiny, he continued, turning slightly as he drew down his braies, and Brighid sucked in a harsh breath as she saw the hard contours of his buttocks, slightly paler than his back and arms. When he stepped from the garment and laid it near the hearth, Brighid felt her heart stop in her chest.

Stephen turned around, and though Brighid thought to shut her eyes, they remained wide-open, taking in the most glorious sight she would ever hope to see: Stephen de Burgh totally naked. His arms and legs were thick with muscle, his chest wide, his belly flat and his sex massive, though it lay flaccid against a thicket of dark hair. Unable to contain herself, Brighid made a strangled noise, and he lifted his head, his eyes alert and intent in the gloom, like a predator scenting his prey.

And then he smiled.

It was the most wicked, seductive thing Brighid had ever seen. Tall, handsome, confident, the man knew no shame at his nudity, but seemed to revel in it, growing taller and stronger under her scrutiny. In fact, Brighid realized, swallowing hard, at least one part of him was definitely growing. She could only stare in amazement as that which had hung between his legs elongated and sprang upward, as if by some will of its own. And, if she had thought it large before, it was now enormous.

Brighid raised wide eyes to his face, but found no assurance there. Stephen still wore his most wicked expression, his sultry mouth moving upward in a beauteous curve, his dark brows lifting slightly as if in question, and even though Brighid shook her head in answer, he stepped forward. Her heart pounded frantically.

Now was the time to protest his obvious intentions, to tell him to sleep on a pallet, to hold him to his vow, Brighid realized, but when she opened her mouth to speak the only thing that came out was his name. *Stephen.* And she could only watch in both excitement and horror as he made his way to the bed, where he stopped before her, incredibly big and masculine and beautiful.

He paused to study her face a long moment, as if to find the truth there, and Brighid had not the strength to hide it from him. How many women had given him their hearts as well as their bodies? Although she claimed to know a man they did not, in the end, she was no different from the rest of them, succumbing to the spell he cast upon her, more potent than any in her family might weave.

And so she made no protest when Stephen lifted a hand toward the fur that covered her and slowly, so slowly, drew it away. Always before Brighid had slept in her clothes, for both warmth and her own peace of mind, but here in this elegant chamber the fire burned hot and she wore only her shift. And in Stephen's dark eyes, she saw approval as he noted the change.

As for herself, Brighid felt frozen in place, unable to move under the hot hunger of his gaze. Her skin tingled, struck by air, as the blanket slipped from her shoulders, across her breastbone and lower, to reveal her breasts, their tips growing hard and peaked.

Still, she could not move, her gaze locked with Stephen's as he gradually slipped the covering from her belly and thighs and limbs and where her shift ended, exposing her lower legs and her bare toes. Finally, his task accomplished, he pushed the fur aside, his dark eyes studying her with such intensity that Brighid trembled beneath his scrutiny.

And still, she remained prone as his hands drifted to the hem of her shift, brushing against her knees as he drew it upward just as slowly as he had removed the blanket. Inch by inch, he unveiled her body, and Brighid shivered as this man saw what no one else had ever viewed: the pale flesh of her thighs, the golden hair betwixt them, her belly, the indentation of her navel, and her breasts. And though Brighid had never thought of herself as attractive, when at last he lifted away the garment, smiling his pleasure, she felt lovelier than any other.

Perhaps that, too, was part of his skill, his charm, his allure: that he could make even a plain woman such as herself into a beauty with his attentions. But even though Brighid suspected the trick, she could not refute it. Already, he was driving any thoughts of others from her mind by reaching out a hand to stroke her body.

His fingers were rough and calloused, the hands of a warrior, yet Brighid could not contain her joy at the touch of them. When he laid his palm against her throat, she whimpered her pleasure. He brought it along her neck slowly, with exquisite patience, as if he savored every bit of her skin. He leaned over her, his hands grazing her shoulders, moving down her arms and up again, only to travel, ever so lightly, over her breasts. Brighid cried out at the sensation, and he pressed them close, drawing them together even as he dropped his head to kiss them.

Heat flooded her, languid, melting heat that made her limbs heavy and her mind hazy. This was desire, rich and exotic and unfathomable, Brighid thought, only to gasp as Stephen rubbed her nipples, his tongue tracing circles on her flesh, as he lifted his body over hers. His weight settled, heavy upon her, and she felt the startling touch of his leg between hers, nudging them open. Having no will of her own, Brighid did as he bid, then was stunned by the pleasure that washed over her when he pressed his thigh against her nether regions.

She gasped, only to swallow her own cry as his mouth covered her nipple. Sensations bombarded her, of heat and moisture, and then he drew upon it, like a suckling babe, and Brighid knew both shock and ecstasy at the motion. She lifted her hands, finally, to push him away, but instead, she buried them in his dark hair, smooth and thick and an unbearable delight to her.

Stephen surrounded her, the length of his warrior's body against her own slight counterpart, the touch of his hands, roving her skin at will, stroking, caressing, warming her flesh, and the hot sucking of his mouth upon her breast, sending a burst of pleasure-pain throughout every nerve. And there, between her legs, the hard, muscular press of his thigh, rhythmic, ceaseless, unyielding, continued until Brighid felt entirely engulfed by him, consumed by his desires.

Her heart pounded and her breath came in ragged sighs as she clung to him, discovering sensations beyond anything she had ever imagined. It grew and built, the heat and the pressure and the passion, until she was writhing and whimpering against him, begging him for she knew not what.

"Stephen!"

The sound of her own cry rang in her ears, and Brighid sat upright, bathed in sweat, gasping for air. For a long moment, her eyes were unseeing, her heart raging so violently that she thought surely she would die. But, finally, she blinked, stunned by the utter quiet around her, broken only by the crackle of the fire.

Dazed, Brighid reached out for an anchor, but her hands found nothing. And when she glanced around, her bed was empty. Indeed, the very chamber was empty, with no sign of Stephen or his clothes or the tumult that had occurred here in this bed. *Surely, it had not all been a dream?*

Brighid stared, incredulous, into the darkness. It had been far too vivid, too real, for any vision. Her mind and body rebelled against the truth, but gradually, she had to accept the fact that she had been alone and was still alone, as Stephen had not yet returned. Lifting trembling fingers to her face, Brighid realized that she must have been asleep, and yet...

She shook her head, astounded and shocked by what

had never taken place, although she knew she should be grateful that nothing had really happened. Perhaps, twas no premonition she had known this night, but a warning that she might heed in her dealings with Stephen de Burgh. Obviously, her love for him had made her all too vulnerable to his charms, and she must arm herself against them.

Brighid told herself she must be sensible, yet the dream and the surfeit of emotions it had aroused lingered. And although she tried to dismiss them, one, especially, clung to her when she leaned back against the pillows, alone: a sense of loss so acute that she nearly wept.

Chapter Sixteen

Stephen awoke slowly, with the lazy languor that followed a decent night's sleep. Reaching automatically for his bed partner, he found nothing except the worn surface of a wooden door. Blinking, he realized where he was, along with something else, far more important.

Brighid was right. He didn't need the wine.

The knowledge seeped into him like the slow heat of victory after a long battle. Although he could use a bath, he felt clean. Free. Strong. The morning rushed to meet his active senses, but he knew no panic, only a swell of greeting, clear and fine. He felt like shouting in triumph, but, conversely, longed to savor his discovery in silence.

Closing his eyes, he remembered all too well the temptation proffered to him. It would have been so easy to take the servant's offering, to lose himself in the blessedly hazy world he had missed. But he knew he could not properly protect Brighid that way, so he told himself he would simply have a sip, a taste of the flavor too long denied him. But something stopped him.

Although his desire had been great, looming even greater in his awareness was the presence of Brighid beside him. He could feel her, stiff and tense, sense her alertness as she waited for his response. Had she nagged or scolded or threatened, he might have done differently, but she said nothing, trusting in him to make the right decision, and implicit in her trust was a respect he had never before received from anyone, let alone Brighid l'Estrange.

And that, in the end, was far headier than any drink.

Drawing a deep breath, Stephen opened his eyes, taking in the hint of her scent that pervaded the room. With it came a rush of lust so powerful he struggled to contain it. He glanced toward the bed that took up most of the small chamber, and he wanted nothing more than to join her there, not particularly to seduce or even to gain his own ease, but to express somehow the feelings he had for her, feelings that were even more sharp and brilliant than everything else in his new world.

Last night he had entered the chamber after she was asleep, and it had taken all of his willpower not to climb under the covers with her. But his vow had held, and he had fallen asleep surprisingly quickly, enjoying the new-found peace that seemed to chase away the night's shadows. But now he was awake and aware of her closeness, and she was like a thunder in his blood, calling him to her.

Stephen loosed a harsh sigh, for even as he imagined the joy to be had in her bed, other considerations kept him from going to her. Not only was he constrained by his word to her, but Brighid's respect for him had inspired an answering response in himself.

She was unique, unlike anyone he had ever known, and his admiration for her had grown so much that now he wondered how he could ever take her innocence. The thought kept returning to him that *she deserved better*. She was too fine to be despoiled by the infamous seducer

known as Stephen de Burgh. No matter how heartfelt
and sincere would be the despoiling, it would still be
despoiling. And Stephen knew, with sudden, painful
clarity, that he couldn't do it.

Stephen groaned as his body painfully disputed the
conclusion of his mind, but he was determined to roll
from his pallet in front of the door and leave the room
without even glancing toward the bed, if it was at all
humanly possible. His jaw tight, he turned only to hear
a rustling among the covers not far across the room.
Stifling another groan, he closed his eyes against the
sound of Brighid's voice.

"Stephen?"

"Hmm?"

"I thought you were awake. Did you find out anything
last night?"

Just that I value you above all else in my life, he
thought wryly, certain that Brighid would be unim-
pressed by the admission. *That I can rest for the first
time in years because you are in the same room. That
you were right...I don't need the wine....* Stephen drew
in a deep breath, knowing that she was talking about the
investigating he had planned to do after she went to bed
and not the myriad revelations that had struck him during the evening.

"I did speak to some of the soldiers, but they were
loath to say much, probably because they know full well
that my family is allied to Edward. And who could
blame them, considering the rumors of war that keep
filtering into the countryside?" His tone sounded harsh
even to his ears, and he deliberately lightened it, for he
could hardly blame Brighid for the rebellion that seemed
to be brewing in their midst.

"And?" She prodded him, as was her wont, making

Stephen frown, for he liked not the news he would pass on to her.

"He said that three men were here just a few days ago asking for a woman named Addfwyn," Stephen admitted.

He could have bitten his tongue when he heard her rise from the bed. Did she have any clothes on? Knowing Brighid, she was probably fully dressed, but still he imagined every curve, every tiny glimpse of pale skin.

"And?"

Swallowing hard, Stephen turned to face the wall as he heard the sounds of more rustling. By faith, did she think him a eunuch? At Rumenea they had fled their shared chamber come morning, but here they were supposed to be married. Stephen cursed that pact even as he struggled to concentrate.

"And nothing," he muttered. "No one at this place had ever heard of her, so the horsemen left. The guard had his wits about him, though, and kept an eye on them since they were not your typical travelers. They headed back south."

When he heard her stirring the embers in the hearth, Stephen finally dared to sit up. Although she was gowned in one of those awful plain things she wore, her hair flowed down her back in erotic disarray, and he sucked in a breath as his body responded to the sight. Then, suddenly he was struck with an overpowering image: that of Brighid standing high on an outcropping, calling the winds to her bidding. At least, that's what it looked like she was doing.

He clung to the vision, thinking it might stave off his lust. After all, any man in his right mind would be scared to death of such a bizarre display of otherworldly powers. But he hadn't been in his right mind for some time

now, Stephen noted wryly, for he felt no fear, only a
surge of sexual excitement at the thought of possessing
such a woman. *Especially when she was Brighid.*

"What did you say to that woman's uncle and all
those men to send them hieing for the hills?" he asked,
leaning back against the door as he stretched out his sore
leg. It was a question that had plagued him the rest of
the day, but one he could hardly put to her in the company of others.

"What? Oh!" Brighid's voice sounded strange, with
an edge of wariness that he couldn't decipher, as she
poked at the fire. "I just warned them that it was unwise
to attack strangers."

Stephen frowned at her simplistic explanation. "It
seemed a little more significant than that." *A lot more
significant.* He rubbed his leg, where his rapidly healing
wound bore evidence of Brighid's ability to heal. What
other magic did she possess?

"Well, not really. I just mouthed some old curses and
warnings. I could see the villagers were simple people
who remember the old ways, and such are easily frightened," Brighid said. She was using a tone he recognized
from their early acquaintance, the one that told him to
be quiet and go away.

But this time he wasn't budging. "And how did you
come to know the old curses and warnings?" he asked,
casually.

She dropped the utensil she was using and turned her
face toward him. "I learned them at my grandmother's
knee! Is that what you want to hear? Or that they came
to me when I danced naked under the moon at Bel-
taine?"

Unaffected by her angry stance, Stephen grinned. "I
wish I could have seen that," he said. Although he knew

she was being sarcastic, his body reacted swiftly to the thought of Brighid clothed in naught but moonlight. Indeed, the image was more provocative than anything he could conjure, and he realized that there was something vitally appealing in such a scene: age-old powers, mystery, and a hint of darkness combined for an exotic sexuality.

Somehow it wasn't what he had associated with Brighid, but there was no denying that she was turning out to be much different from his initial impression of her. And wherever she had gleaned her arcane lore, she had done *something* and right in front of him, too. He shook his head. If he hadn't seen it with his own eyes, he would never have believed it.

"Look, I don't pretend to believe in all this business about witches and alchemy and Celtic curses, but I have to tell you, Brighid..." Stephen paused, his lips curving wryly at the admission he was about to make. "Whatever you did out there looked pretty amazing."

Dead silence met his comment, and Stephen eyed her curiously, but Brighid was staring into the fire once more. He shifted on his pallet as he tried to put visions of her dancing naked to rest. *In the moonlight yet.*

"It wasn't magic," she said, her tone surprisingly fierce.

Her vehement denial left him nonplussed, but when had he understood Brighid l'Estrange? "No, of course not," he said, keeping his expression noncommittal. But if it wasn't magic, what the devil was it?

"Magic doesn't exist," Brighid said, firmly.

All right, Stephen thought, as he saw that Brighid was back to pursed lips and grimness. Obviously, he had touched a sore spot, but even he, who didn't believe in much of anything, could see that she had done *some-*

thing, something he couldn't explain away. Nor could he accept her facile rationalization. He shut his eyes, seeking some inspiration, then opened them again with sudden insight.

"Because of your father?" he asked, gently.

"Perhaps," she answered, her reluctance evident. "He spent his whole life immersed in his work, in intangibles, while neglecting everything else. I tried to step in, but nothing mattered to him except alchemy. And when he decided I wasn't adept, he sent me away." She paused, her light laugh brittle and forced. "Believe me, if I had possessed any amazing abilities, I would have used them to be his apprentice or at least stay at the only home I ever knew."

"But would you have been any happier there than with your aunts?" Stephen asked, softly. Suddenly, he wanted nothing more than to ease her pain, whatever its source.

The silence lengthened before he heard her low reply. "I suppose not," she admitted. "I took over my aunts' household, too, by necessity, but at least they appreciated me." He watched her draw in a deep breath. "Perhaps he did the right thing, though I might have wished for some sign of approval from him, rather than to be dismissed in disgrace."

Stephen lifted his good leg and hooked his arm over the knee. "It's not easy living up to the expectations of your father. Believe me, I know better than anyone," he said, with a snort.

"But it's not as though Campion expects you to possess some indefinable ability, some impossible, nonsensical skill to transmute matter!" Brighid protested, turning toward him, with an expression of exasperation.

Stephen grunted. "No, he just expects me to be perfect! How can I live up to his standards when he's some kind of god among men?''

To his astonishment, Brighid laughed, a delightful sound that immediately eased the tension that built within him at any discussion of his father.

''Nay,'' Brighid said, sitting back on her heels to face him. ''Campion is not perfect. Nor is he a god. He is driven by the same needs and fears as any human. Did he not marry again? Why? Because he wants love and desire in his life. Yet I've heard that his new wife ran away rather than wed him at first.''

''A ploy, nothing more,'' Stephen said.

''Was it? Are you privy to their most intimate moments? I can only guess at what happened, but I know that I would not care to be married to someone who always is expected to be wise and caring and strong, to be all things to all of his people. Can you imagine the responsibilities that he bears, with the weight of his lands, his people and the fates of his sons? He has become more myth than man. Certainly, it must not be easy being his son, but, oh, how much more difficult to be him,'' Brighid said, shaking her head.

Stunned by her words, Stephen gaped at her. He always envisioned Campion as breezing through life, fully equipped to handle any crisis without blinking an eye, and yet he remembered a time when his father had been nothing but a hollow shell. While Stephen watched helplessly, Campion had suffered a long and painful grief after Anne's death.

Perhaps that was what had so disturbed him about Campion's new bride. A wife made the earl perilously vulnerable, and Stephen didn't care to see him be quite that human again. He shook his head, amazed at his own perversity, for as much as he raged against his father's godlike manner, he didn't really want Campion to be any less.

"His wife seemed strong enough to handle such a paragon, but I prefer a man who is more complicated. More interesting. For, as you have discovered, I am imperfect, myself," Brighid said.

Deep in reverie, Stephen took a moment to focus on what Brighid had said, and when he did, he was even more startled. Brighid l'Estrange imperfect? She must really be feeling wretched. Silently, Stephen cursed the father who not only had brought her low, but had brought her here, endangering his only daughter with his mad pursuit of the bizarre.

Although Stephen had agreed, albeit reluctantly, only to be Brighid's escort, now he found himself protecting her with his very life. It was a charge he accepted willingly, fiercely even, but one that he could not continue to carry out alone in the far reaches of Wales. They must return to Campion. There, surrounded by the power and might of the earldom, Brighid would be safe, at last and for always.

The thought did something to his insides, so that he nearly shuddered with relief. Or was it satisfaction? Slanting a glance at where she still knelt by the fire, Stephen felt a heady warmth. He decided he would examine those feelings later. First, he must get her there. "It's time to go home, Brighid," he said softly.

"Yes, I know," she replied, without turning to look at him.

At her words, Stephen relaxed. For once, there would be no argument. Feeling in charity with her, he sought to ease any concerns she might have. "You'll have every comfort at Campion. Whoever is after this magic rock won't follow you all the way there, and they wouldn't dare approach you on de Burgh lands,'' Stephen said, only to watch her turn to face him, her expression cryptic.

''Campion? Why would I go there?'' she asked.

The question hung in the air, as if it held some hidden meaning that only Brighid, with her witchy ways, could decipher. Stephen frowned. ''Because you'll be safe there.''

With an undignified noise that was wholly Brighid, she rose to her feet. ''You are welcome to return to your home, of course, but I have unfinished business here.''

Stephen leaned his head back against the worn wood and closed his eyes with a groan. Surely, after all that had happened, she didn't think to continue to chase after some elusive killers? Stephen felt like banging his head against the door in frustration.

''Brighid, we have no idea where your mysterious servant woman is hiding,'' he muttered. ''Faith, for all we know she could be dead!''

''She's alive.''

The words were spoken with such conviction that Stephen lifted his lashes to look at her, but she avoided his gaze and walked toward the window to stare out upon the bleak landscape. Stephen felt the hairs rise on the back of his neck. ''How do you know?'' he asked, even as he suspected the answer.

''I just know, that's all.''

Stephen blew out a harsh breath. ''All right, so she's alive, but where? How do you intend to find her?''

Dead silence met his query while Brighid stood, back stiff, shoulders straight, as if by her very will she would discover the answers she sought. And in that moment, Stephen had the giddy sensation that she could. He pushed up from the pallet and stood as she turned to face him, her hands clasped tightly before her.

"I don't know," she said simply.

She gazed at him, her green eyes bleak, and Stephen lifted his hands only to drop them, utterly helpless to provide comfort or aid her. For the first time in his life, his name and its power could serve him little. Even should he summon an army from Campion, which was impossible in this political climate, he wasn't sure if a whole host of searchers could find one woman who didn't want to be found.

Stephen knew then that if she asked him, he would turn over every rock in Wales for her and question each resident, but he sensed that it would not be enough. And then suddenly, he heard a voice in his head. *Have her look into the water.*

With a start, Stephen dismissed the echo of Cadwy's words, but they were not so far-fetched now as they had once seemed. Perhaps it was the despair in her eyes that sent him out the door, or the memory of Cadwy's insistence, or maybe just the image of Brighid standing on the outcropping yesterday, raising the winds to her command. Pushing his pallet away, Stephen stepped outside the door and called to a passing servant.

Then he closed the worn wood behind him, leaning against it as he faced her soberly. "If you are determined to find her, then perhaps you should look into the water." He spoke softly, not knowing what to expect, and was alarmed when instead of replying, Brighid paled. Hurrying forward, Stephen urged her to sit on the side of the bed.

"What are you talking about?" she asked, eyes wide. She looked so wary and accusing that Stephen began to wonder what had possessed him. With a grunt, he ran a hand through his hair and told himself he didn't believe in any of it. *Really.* All right, so maybe that business yesterday had been pretty convincing, but...but nothing. Faith, he had no idea what he believed anymore.

Yes, he did, Stephen thought with sudden clarity. He believed in *Brighid.* And, he had the sneaking suspicion that she could do anything, any blessed thing that she put her mind to do. If she could get him to stop drinking, to sleep at night, to embrace a world he had long ago turned his back upon, then she must have some powerful abilities.

A lot of people would call that magic, Stephen thought, with a wry grimace, especially his father. Even Brighid's father, were he alive, would do well to take notice, for hadn't she taken a desperate man on the brink of the void and transformed him into something whole? *Powerful magic indeed.*

Blindly, Stephen searched for some way to put into words what he was feeling, but he had spent too many years mouthing platitudes to women who meant nothing to him. And now he was bereft of speech. He stalked to the window and back and finally opened his mouth to say something—anything—when she spoke.

"I thought you didn't believe in anything that you couldn't see or hear or smell," she said.

"Well, I saw you do some pretty impressive things yesterday," Stephen hedged.

She stared at him, and his gaze faltered. "All right, so maybe, I've had this suspicion," Stephen trailed off, embarrassed to continue. "I'm not saying that I believe in all that hokus-pokus, a stone that isn't a stone and all that, or witches—the kind who are drowned, not the kind who dance naked under the moon," he added, pausing to grin wickedly at her. "But I'm willing to admit that there might be more to life than what is commonly accepted.''

He shook his head ruefully. ''Growing up with Campion as a father, it's hard not to imagine some kind of special abilities. I mean, just look at the man. I swear he knows everything, half the time before it happens.'' Stephen cleared his throat, feeling foolish for admitting something he had never told another soul, not even his brothers.

But Brighid didn't laugh, only nodded seriously. ''I thought that, too, about your father. His eyes hold so much wisdom and more.''

Stephen didn't know whether to be relieved or shocked that she so easily confirmed his own outlandish suspicions. ''Do you think that's why he sent me with you? Perhaps he knew something,'' Stephen muttered, uneasy with the notion.

When Brighid made no reply, he glanced at her only to find her studying him with a thoughtful expression, just as if he, too, might share his father's special talents. Alarmed, Stephen threw up his hands in protest. ''Don't look at me. I can barely function normally.''

Brighid smiled. ''I'm not so sure. Perhaps we were brought together for a reason.''

There was that destiny thing again. Stephen frowned. But he was saved from further comment by the entrance of a servant who carried a bowl, presumably for washing, which he set beside the bed.

''Thank you,'' Stephen said, with a nod of dismissal. He waited until the fellow was safely gone before glancing at Brighid. When he did, he was taken aback, for she looked as if she had seen a ghost. Her face was white and wan, her hands gripped together so tightly in her lap that her knuckles lost their color. She gazed down at them steadily, ignoring the vessel that sat innocently upon the tiles.

"Are you afraid?" Stephen asked, with no little concern. He knew nothing of this ability of hers. Perhaps it pained her or caused her grief.

"Nay. I fear nothing," she replied, her chin lifting. Silence stretched before them until at last she spoke in a low, halting voice. "All my life I've tried to run away from the taint of the l'Estranges. I didn't want to be burned as a witch or feared by the villagers as some kind of freak—turned upon by the very people who sought my healing arts. I just wanted to be like everyone else."

The raw confession made Stephen's chest hurt. "Well, no one's going to burn you as long as I'm alive." The words came easily, but rang as true as any he had ever spoken. He would protect this woman with his very life, if need be, and not only that, he wanted desperately to give her the normalcy she craved. He cleared his thick throat.

"And no one's going to turn on you," he said. "If that is your concern, then you are right to keep your healing skills to yourself. Faith, keep all your skills to yourself," he advised. He certainly wasn't going to push her into something she didn't want to do.

She turned her face toward him then, her green eyes questioning. "Aren't you repulsed by it all, by the l'Estrange strangeness?" she asked, her tone even, but cautious.

Stephen lifted his brows. "Actually, I'm more impressed than anything else." *And aroused*, he did not add. He was trying to forget that part himself.

Brighid remained skeptical. "Aren't you afraid that I'll put a curse on you or work some kind of spell upon you?"

Stephen laughed and ran a hand through his hair, suddenly feeling awkward, but he met her gaze as well as he could. "I think I was already cursed, and you lifted it."

She drew in a sharp breath, obviously startled by his admission, and Stephen sought to make light of it as he strode to the window. "If you were going to do anything, you would have done it long ago, like keeping me from escorting you in the first place," he said.

"And, as much as you hated me, you never lifted a finger to harm me. I don't think you're capable of hurting anyone," he added. The air through the shutters was bracing, and Stephen was relieved to turn the conversation back to safe generalities.

"I never hated you," Brighid said softly.

Safe? They were slipping into dangerous territory, and Stephen shied away from it instinctively. He reached for the bowl. "I'll just toss this away."

"No." Brighid's hand reached out to stay his arm, and Stephen shuddered beneath the light pressure of her fingers. For so long, he had desired her touch, but now it was something he didn't want, a temptation that threatened all his good intentions. Gently, he slipped from her grasp and knelt, returning the vessel to the floor.

Brighid joined him, though her expression was skeptical. "I'll try, but I doubt that I'll see anything except water," she said.

She leaned close, her gaze fixed upon the liquid, and Stephen found himself staring, too. At first, all he could see was the surface of the water, but then, it seemed to shift, stirred by some stray breeze from the window, no doubt. He stared so hard and long, his breath held, that even he imagined the shadows merging into a shape. Shaking his head to clear it, Stephen grunted at his own whimsy, and when he looked again, he saw nothing except a smooth surface, unmarred by wind or image.

''I see a chapel,'' Brighid whispered, startling him, and Stephen jerked his attention toward her bent head. ''It looks familiar, but tis hard to place in my memory. I have it! Tis an old one, not far from here,'' she cried. When she raised her face, Stephen saw her expression of astonishment and felt an echoing wonder himself, along with a surge of other heady emotions he could not name, let alone express.

''See?'' he said, when he could find his voice. ''You're a pretty amazing woman, Brighid.''

Chapter Seventeen

Brighid was still reeling from her revelations when they set out once more to find Addfwyn. It seemed that everything she'd ever believed had been proven wrong, or more accurately, that everything she'd refused to believe in had turned out to be true.

Never had she shared the dreams of other young women, of a home and family of her own, of a handsome knight to carry her off to his castle. She was far too practical, too sensible to succumb to such fancies. As a girl, her hopes had been different, fueled by her l'Estrange heritage, but even those had been ground to dust long ago. And somewhere along the line, she had quit dreaming at all, settling for a life of rigid behavior, of stark realities that left no room for magic of any kind.

But now anything seemed possible.

She had looked into the water and actually seen something helpful, not the jumbled images of her childhood or the nothingness she had told herself lay there. And once she opened herself up to the potential of her sight, everything had been so clear. Instead of fighting against the prompting of her inner senses, Brighid listened to them, and with that acceptance came a blessed peace.

Of course, her new life would not be entirely blissful; she knew that. Now that she had embraced her legacy, she could never be the plain, normal woman she had pretended. Her talents cut her off from others and carried an inherent danger. But somehow that prospect was not as frightening as it once had been, when Stephen de Burgh, the loudest scoffer, not only accepted her skills, but had urged her to use them.

Brighid took a moment to savor the lightness that came from loving him, the warm glow that reached clear down to her toes. To her, it was a magic far more amazing than any mysticism. And there was more to it than her own burgeoning emotions; something had changed between them, as well. Brighid had suspected it for some time now, but worried that her own feelings were coloring her perceptions.

Now, she could not dismiss the notion that Stephen's attitude toward her had altered. Not since that night in the croft had he teased or tormented her or spoken cruelly. Although they might not always agree, their disputes had taken on a different aspect. Stephen harbored some affection for her, Brighid was certain, and she hugged the knowledge to her tightly.

Oh, she still had enough sense to know that the notorious seducer wouldn't suddenly be seized by undying love for her. Stephen's fancies were fleeting, and he certainly was not the type of man to commit to a lifetime of marriage. Anyone who tried to cage him would only find herself miserable when he returned to his usual ways.

Brighid knew that, and so she simply enjoyed the pleasure of his company, the beautiful sight of him and the wondrous bond that seemed to grow between them. She held no expectations and made no demands, for she might have begun to believe in magic, but not in miracles.

"Is this chapel a pagan place?" The sound of Stephen's deep, gravelly voice, roused Brighid from her thoughts, and she glanced at his face, hard and set. Although he claimed to be undisturbed by Celtic curses, he didn't look very comfortable, and Brighid suppressed a smile.

"Nay. Tis one of the old Christian churches that were abandoned when the pope introduced his sanctioned form of the religion," she answered.

"Perhaps she seeks sanctuary, then, if this is a consecrated building," Stephen mused.

"I doubt it, for there is no one to whom she could confess her misdeeds, no bells to ring, no Mass to attend. Tis more a ruin than anything else," Brighid answered. "Perhaps she is simply hiding, driven away by the true murderers."

"Or maybe she was working for them and decided to strike out on her own. I wonder what kind of deal she could make for this rock of your father's," Stephen said.

Brighid laughed, without humor. "Should she truly have a means to turn base metals into gold, then I would say she could name her price for such information."

Stephen grunted, his skepticism still apparent, and Brighid smiled. "I take it you won't be bidding on it," she said, enjoying the banter with him that she had once so disdained. Despite the bleakness of her quest, she felt lighthearted and whole, eager to meet with Addfwyn, so that she might put her father's death behind her finally and move on. *To what?* she wondered, even as she avoided the question.

"There," Stephen said, pointing toward a shadow upon the snow, and Brighid recognized the chapel she had seen in the water, tucked into the side of a hill, small and isolated.

"It looks deserted," Stephen said, but Brighid shook her head.

"She's here," she said, accepting the certainty of her knowledge, and Stephen did not argue. He urged Hades behind a stand of withered trees and dismounted, unsheathing his sword with a grace and majesty that made Brighid's heart pound. She, who had always refused anything from others, now found herself welcoming his protection. Those long years of standing alone, denying her heritage while remaining apart from everyone else, seemed foolish, a self-imposed exile that had ended with this man's arrival.

As had become his habit, Stephen helped her to the ground, then placed himself between her and the chapel. Although Brighid did not sense any immediate threat, she let him push aside the remnants of the door and step inside ahead of her. Immediately, she smelled smoke, as if a fire had been doused swiftly, and she peeked inside but saw nothing except Stephen prowling the gloomy interior.

"Addfwyn," Brighid called, as she joined him. "'Tis Brighid l'Estrange. We mean you no harm, but would speak with you, if you will." Silence met her words, and she glanced toward Stephen, grim-faced and dangerous looking. Who would willingly approach them while he was brandishing his weapon?

"Put away your sword," she whispered. Stephen's dark brows rose, but where he would have argued with her only days ago, he simply sent her a skeptical look and did her bidding. Still, he kept his hand ready on the hilt and stayed so close to her that Brighid could feel the heady heat emanating from his warrior's body. She smiled at him, so caught up in her love for the man that she momentarily forgot her quest.

"I am here." The sound of the soft voice brought Brighid's attention back to the matter at hand and made Stephen tense behind her, ready for battle. Brighid laid a staying hand on his arm and stepped toward the shadowy corner. There, crouched by a smothered fire, was a woman, wrapped in several cloaks.

"Addfwyn?" Brighid asked, though she knew the answer.

The woman nodded, her pale face drawn, and Brighid studied her with interest. She was not young, as Brighid had expected. Yet she was lovely, with high cheekbones and the regal bearing of royalty, not of servitude, and the wisdom of years etched in her elegant features.

"Are you well? Let us light the fire again. Stephen?" Brighid asked, turning toward him. He wore a disgruntled expression, as though he didn't approve of treating with a woman who might knife them at the first opportunity. But Brighid knew better. This frightened creature was no killer.

"What happened?" Brighid asked, kneeling in front of her.

"You came back," Addfwyn said softly, watching Brighid with pale-blue eyes. "Your father would have been so pleased. You have the look of him."

Brighid's expression must have given away her dismay, for Addfwyn reached out to place a hand upon her knee. "He regretted much, you know, but most of all he regretted losing you."

Brighid rose to her feet, unable to accept this woman's sympathy for past hurts. "I find that a bit hard to believe, but I imagine he was angry when I didn't rush to answer his summons." Brighid's momentary outrage faded at the knowledge of what came after, and she turned to face Addfwyn.

"I am sorry for that," Brighid murmured. "Perhaps, if I had been here…" Finally, she forced out the thought that had been torturing her ever since she had received word of her father's death. She was no alchemist and no doting daughter, but maybe she could have prevented this tragedy, if she had come sooner.

Even as Stephen grunted his denial from his place by the growing fire, Addfwyn shook her head. "Nay. You might have been killed, as well," she said.

Although some lingering doubts remained, Brighid drank in their absolution with relief, relishing the warmth and strength of Stephen when he moved to stand beside her. "But the missive was so urgent, that he wanted to pass something on to me, some great discovery, perhaps?" Brighid asked.

Addfwyn nodded sadly. "Yes. He made a great discovery, and one which he wanted very much to tell you about, but I think, perhaps, you have already found it," she said, with a cryptic glance toward Stephen. "He wanted you to search your heart," she added with a gentle smile.

For forgiveness? Brighid wondered. She gazed curiously at Stephen, but he simply shrugged, and she returned her attention to Addfwyn, who continued to speak.

"I lost my husband and son to sickness that swept through our village several years ago," she said. "My family was concerned for me. Thinking that a new situation would be good for me, they sent me to relatives near Rumenea, and it wasn't long before I was working at the manor."

Addfwyn paused to smile wistfully. "Your father was

so caught up in his work that he didn't even notice me at first, but eventually, he did, and…'' Her words trailed away as she stared down at her clasped hands. ''We were happy together, for a brief time, and that is what he wanted to let you know, Brighid, the knowledge that some things are more important than alchemy.'' She sighed, her gaze, clear and direct, meeting Brighid's own startled one.

''And when he learned that, he was so sorry that he sent you away, that he had never taken the time to know you, to watch you grow. He realized, then, just how much he had lost by letting his work rule his life. And though he knew he could not change the past, he wanted so much to see you again, to make amends.''

Brighid felt her initial incredulity and denial fade away in the face of the woman's sincerity. Addfwyn spoke the truth, and Brighid sagged against Stephen, overcome with reaction. She felt a myriad of emotions: shock, wonder, guilt and finally, a kind of peace, as Stephen's arm closed around her.

''An interesting tale, to be sure, but what of his murder?'' Stephen asked.

Addfwyn shook her head, her thin, pale hair falling over her face. ''Perhaps, rumors about his newfound happiness became garbled, drawing the attention of rival alchemists or the kind of men who lust only for the gold they hope to create. All I know is that one evening your father asked me to marry him, and that night, when I went to look for him, he was dead, all his writings gone.''

''Had anyone been to see him recently?'' Brighid asked.

Addfwyn shook her head again. ''If your father met with a fellow alchemist, I was not aware of it, but from what I know most of them are very peculiar and secretive. Although I helped your father in the cellar sometimes, he kept me away from visitors.''

No doubt to salvage her reputation, Brighid thought. Cadwy had made his own disapproval of the relationship apparent, so she could imagine what outsiders might think. Brighid frowned as she recalled more of Cadwy's words. ''They said father was especially distant that night, as if preparing for something.''

Addfwyn nodded. ''I thought he was working on some surprise for the wedding.'' Her voice broke.

''When I saw the body, I didn't think, I just ran. There were some in the household who did not approve of me, some who jealously guarded their master's secrets, and I was afraid the murderer was still there, waiting for me.''

Although unaccustomed to reaching out to others, Brighid placed a hand upon the woman's shoulder. ''You were right to go, for I think that whoever killed Father did not find what they were looking for in his books. Someone returned to ransack the manor, and we have heard reports of several men, ahead of us, asking for you.''

Addfwyn's eyes widened with panic, but Brighid squeezed her shoulder in comfort. ''Whoever they are, they do not know you are here, but I fear you cannot elude them forever. Come with us, back to Rumenea,'' she said.

''Nay, I can never return,'' Addfwyn said, and Brighid glanced helplessly at Stephen.

His brows slightly lifted, he appeared skeptical, as usual, but Brighid knew the woman spoke the truth. ''I understand. However, you cannot stay here, and they have already sought out your relatives,'' she protested.

"I am sorry for that, but I haven't the heart to return. I am weary of life's trials, yet too cowardly to evade them," Addfwyn said softly. "I wish only for peace, which ever eludes me."

Brighid's gaze again met Stephen's, and she felt as if they both had the same idea even as he spoke. "What of a convent?" he asked, softly.

"There is one nearby, dedicated to Saint Mary," Brighid answered. She turned to Addfwyn. "Would you like to go there?"

The servant's eyes grew round with hope before her face fell. "They would never accept a mere servant, and I have no money."

"I'll take care of it," Stephen said, before Brighid could reply, and for the first time, the bleak woman seemed to rouse to life.

Rising up immediately, Addfwyn beamed and bowed before him, her gratitude evident in her every movement. "Oh, thank you, sir," she cried.

"My lord," Brighid corrected with a smile, granting him the title he well deserved. "My lord de Burgh."

The abbess at the local convent had been only too happy to accept Addfwyn after Stephen made a hefty contribution to the order from the de Burghs. He paid extra for safeguards to ensure that the servant, whose name they changed, would be protected from any outside threats. And he suggested privately to the abbess that she advise him of any complications. Although Brighid seemed convinced of the woman's innocence, Stephen still wasn't too sure.

Her story had been full of a lot of romantic nonsense, he thought, but it had seemed to comfort Brighid, so Stephen had made little comment. Although he had expected his companion to argue over his payment to the convent, for once Brighid only smiled, a sweetly mysterious curve of her lips that made him wonder if she knew something Stephen didn't. Considering her curious abilities, he had no doubt that she did.

But she couldn't name the murderer, and so Stephen had kept a close watch all the way back to Rumenea. Now, he was weary and cold and none too pleased to return to the defenseless manor. Nor was he thrilled to see Cadwy, whom he still regarded with some suspicion. Although Stephen cautioned Brighid against telling the servant too much, she ignored him, as usual, and relayed most of their experiences to the man during their hasty supper. Only Stephen's black look of warning prevented her from revealing the woman's whereabouts.

After that, Brighid had retreated to her chamber, leaving Stephen to glare at the servant, who was slowly gathering up the remnants of their meal. Stephen was just about to threaten the old man, if he so much as looked wrongly at Brighid, when Cadwy looked up from his work and fixed Stephen with a probing stare.

"You'll do right by her, won't you, my lord?" the servant asked, studying Stephen shrewdly.

"Do right by her?" Stephen echoed, his eyes narrowing. How dare this man question him, especially concerning Brighid? And especially when he *was* doing right by her, though it was killing him. "Of course," he grunted.

Cadwy let out an audible sigh of relief. "When?" he asked, his gaze fraught with speculation.

"When, what?" Stephen replied in irritation. He saw no need to explain himself to a servant, and a rather dubious one at that. Who was to say that this conveniently lone resident of Rumenea had not betrayed his master to some band of rogue mystics? And now planned to do the same to Brighid?

"When, what? Why, the wedding! When will it be?" Cadwy asked, bringing him out of his dark thoughts with confusion.

"Wedding? What wedding?" Stephen was truly exasperated now. Did everyone in Wales speak in riddles or were they all simply mad?

"Your wedding, my lord," Cadwy said, as if bewildered by his attitude. "You've been alone with her for long days and nights and, well, your reputation being as it is, her fair name would be ruined." He sent Stephen an accusing glare. "You said you'd do right by her."

Stephen stared in stunned disbelief. Surely none but his own sire, the earl himself, had ever had the audacity to suggest that he marry, and now this Welsh servant was trying to tell him his business. It was laughable.

Except Stephen wasn't laughing. Nor did he recoil, as was his wont, whenever he heard the word mentioned. Idly, he rolled the notion around in his mind, feeling none of the usual panic, disgust or boredom. Instead, a sense of rightness flooded his entire being. Gingerly, he took the idea one step further and let himself imagine it for a moment, and still he felt no abhorrence. Rather, he was filled with peace, as if at last he had found his place in the world.

No more days spent drinking himself into a numbing haze. No more nights spent running from his own demons. No more waking up with strange women and playing the gallant, when he was not inclined. No more playing at all. Stephen sucked in a harsh breath. He could be himself. *With Brighid.*

Suddenly, all the aching want that he harbored for her rose to the fore, nearly bringing him to his knees with its strength. *No more sleeping on a pallet.* Finally, he would have Brighid in his bed, where she belonged. It was a heady, compelling thought, and in the old days, he might have acted on his first impulse, selfishly seizing any opportunity for his gratification. But now he hesitated.

He would have what he most desired, but what of Brighid? Stephen loosed the breath he had been holding in a low hiss at the realization that she would gain precious little. Brighid cared nothing for her reputation, else she would never have pushed on to Wales. And none outside of this country knew they had been traveling together. His men would not know or care should he invent some nonexistent companion for the time since they had parted.

Such things meant little to Brighid, who was concerned with larger issues of truth and loyalty and honor. The knowledge made him shift uncomfortably, and Stephen frowned as his earlier suspicion returned with greater force. *Brighid deserved better.* She was a woman of unique strength and power and beauty, a combination of hardheaded capabilities and erotic mysteries. She was entitled to more than a broken-down man taking his first toddling steps toward standing on his own, a man who could offer her nothing more than a famous name and his skills in the bedchamber.

Stephen blinked at the painful truth, but faced it as he never had before. Despite all his delusions of power and lineage and knighthood, he had little money and no prospects to provide a wife. *And then there was the other.* Stephen flinched, unable to summon enough strength to confront it, the worst of the realities of being Stephen de Burgh.

Suddenly, he was aware of Cadwy, still watching him

intently, awaiting his answer. With a harsh grunt, Stephen swung toward the servant. "I'll do right by her," he said, his jaw tight. "Which means I won't marry her." Turning on his heel, he strode away, leaving Cadwy to draw his own conclusions.

Brighid lay in bed, letting herself relax against the soft mattress beneath her back. Where once she would have ignored such comforts, now she felt more aware of herself and her own pleasure. Or perhaps, the burden of her past having lifted, she was simply free to enjoy herself more thoroughly. Whatever the reason, she was at ease, the battle that had been raging inside her all these years over, each side making peace with the other.

With the wisdom of maturity, Brighid knew now that magic was neither good nor bad in itself, but took on the characteristics of those who wielded it. She knew, too, that she could still run a household and listen to the prompting of her gift, that one skill did not preclude the other, and that exercising her abilities would not make her lose herself in the manner of her father's single-minded drive or her aunts' whimsy.

She was herself, and finally, she was reconciled to it. Thanks to her conversation with Addfwyn, the last vestiges of bitterness toward her heritage had been swept away. But that was not the only result of her speech with the woman. Brighid had been thinking, too, about her father's discovery, and she knew that Addfwyn spoke the truth.

Search your heart, and Brighid had been doing so. *Maybe it was too late for you, Father, but tis not too late for me,* she whispered into the night lit only by the glow of the firelight. *I will accept your legacy.*

Yet even as she spoke the words, Brighid felt a twinge

of trepidation. What if Stephen did not share the depth of her feelings? What if the emotions she attributed to him consisted only of lust and a mild accord? Did she really want to be nothing except one in a long line of his women? Brighid shook her head.

She could be sure of just one thing: if she ignored the magic in life, then she would only be living half measure.

Stephen had worked out some of his frustrations by prowling the grounds, but he had been loath to leave Brighid alone too long. He told himself that Cadwy's officious concern for his mistress might very well mask a more sinister plan. Was it just coincidence that l'Estrange was killed the very day he proposed to his lover? Stephen frowned. He knew that jealousies, especially female jealousies, ran deep. But who among the missing servants could be to blame? And what of the mysterious men who sought Addfwyn?

Stephen shook his head, still unable to make any more sense of the murder than he ever had. But concern for Brighid drove him inside, and he hurried back to their chamber only to hesitate, worried that she might still be awake. Finally, as quietly as possible, Stephen entered the room and bolted the door. He struggled with his mail, then sucked in a harsh breath when he felt another set of hands upon him.

Brighid. She was awake and helping him remove his garments. And clad only in a thin shift. His sword clattered to the floor. "I can do it myself," he snapped, immediately regretting his harshness. "The leg's all better, see?" he added, stretching out his right limb even as he tried to stop another part of his body from expanding, too.

"Let me check under the bandage," Brighid said, and Stephen backed away toward his pallet.

"No. It's fine. Really," he said.

"I just want to make sure it's healing properly," Brighid explained, giving him an odd look.

Although he felt foolish, just the thought of her touching him frightened Stephen to death. How much could one man take before his will broke? Beads of sweat erupted on his forehead, and he knew that he could not stand the temptation.

"I'm too tired," he protested, but Brighid was already pushing him toward the bed. Swiftly, he veered for the chest and sat down hard, refusing to meet her quizzical gaze.

Leaning his head back against the wall, Stephen closed his eyes, unwilling to watch her fall to her knees in front of him, but he could not block out the soft brush of her hair against his thigh or the gentle caress of her fingers as she untied the bandage and stroked his skin experimentally. His muscles went rigid and his jaw clamped tight as he tried not to react.

"It looks good," she said in a sultry voice that made him think of everything but his wound. Then, while he remained tense and stiff, she rebound the injury, an achingly slow process that had him ready to shout in an agony that had nothing to do with his leg. When at last she tied the knot, Stephen was certain his torture was over.

He took a deep breath only to feel the slide of her fingers against the bare flesh of his calf. The breath caught and held as her palm rode the muscle, then roved higher to graze the sensitive skin behind his knee. She halted there, and Stephen was thankful for the barrier of his braies, which could be pushed no higher without some effort. His relief was brief, however, for she only moved to the outside of his garment, her hand gliding along the inside of his thigh, while his groin reacted painfully in response.

Through the mind-numbing pounding of his blood, Stephen was aware that she had moved between his thighs and was running both hands toward the part of him that was hard and eager. The breath he had held was released in a rush as he jerked upright and surged to his feet, knocking her backward onto the floor.

"What the hell are you doing?" he growled, both outraged and enraged at the liberties she had taken. Had this woman no sense of self-preservation? Stephen glared down at her, only to shudder at the sight of her sprawled before him, her shift hiked up to reveal small, bare feet, slender ankles and pale skin to her knees. His body jerking in response, Stephen tore his gaze away and turned toward the door.

"Clothe yourself and return to your bed," he said, even as the words stuck in his throat. Surely, he had never uttered anything like them in his life. He felt in the grip of some nightmare, hot and sweating and unbearably aroused, yet unable to act upon his desire.

"I've been thinking about that," Brighid said, as he heard her stand. "And I don't think that you can be comfortable on the remnants of that pallet. Why don't you share the bed with me?"

For a full minute, Stephen wondered if Cadwy had drugged him with one of those herbs in the cellar. How else could he be hearing such speech from the lips of Brighid l'Estrange, who had so long been his enemy? His pulse pounding, his blood thundering, Stephen nearly fled the room, but the night loomed outside, and so he croaked out a denial.

"No. Tis perfectly fine here. Truly," he said. And, as if to demonstrate, he found the pallet with his foot, dragged it in front of the door and stretched out on it. Pulling the fur up over his head, he turned his back to Brighid and pretended indifference.

It was the most difficult thing he had ever done.

"You mean to tell me that the most famous seducer in the whole country is *refusing* to come to my bed?" Brighid asked, putting her invitation in no uncertain terms. Stephen flinched. Against all odds, the woman he lusted after above all others was trying to seduce him, and he had to refuse. Was this some kind of cosmic irony or punishment for his conquests?

"Yes. Go away," he muttered.

"Why?" she asked.

"I'm not attracted to you in the least," Stephen lied. "You're domineering, obstinate, rigid and too smart for your own good—all the things I hate in a woman."

Brighid laughed. "But what about all those times you tried to kiss me and paw me?"

Stephen drew back the fur enough to stick out his head and glare at her. "I don't paw."

"Well?" she challenged, and what a challenge it was. The woman who had consistently garbed herself in drab garments from the top of her head to the tip of her toes now stood before him revealing more skin that he had ever hoped to see, and all of it gilded golden by the firelight's glow.

Jerking the fur back over his head, Stephen turned to the door. "That was just to taunt you, to prove that you weren't as stiff and uninterested as you pretended to be," he muttered.

"And you felt nothing at all?" Brighid persisted.

Faith, what would it take for her to leave him alone? "Nothing," he grunted.

"Would you care to put it to the test?" she said, causing every nerve in his body to heat and expand in assent. Had he done this to her? Had he somehow turned her into some sultry siren bent on losing her maidenhead? Stephen groaned. But even through the haze of his desire, he kept to his vow. He had seen her in all her guises: prim and cold, passionate and giving, mysterious and erotic, and he knew he was unworthy of this woman.

Brighid deserved a decent husband who could provide her with the finest comforts and unstinting devotion unhindered by cowardice or lechery or drink. But most of all, she deserved a husband who could give her sons. And daughters. Children of her own to pass on her gift, to carry on the wondrous legacy of the l'Estrange blood. And even if he discounted all else, that was something that Stephen could never give her.

That horrible truth made him grunt his denial in the face of hellish temptation, but Brighid was not through with him yet. Just when he thought she might give up and return to her bed, she whispered something else, soft and low.

"I love you, Stephen."

Stephen groaned as the sudden pressure on his throat and behind his eyes rivaled that of his nether regions. His chest expanded, his heart thundering in protest at her words. He had heard them often enough, from the cherry lips of his ladies, young maidens or ripe women alike, but never in his life had he expected to hear such a declaration from the one woman from whom it would actually mean something.

"No, you don't," Stephen said hoarsely. "You've just been fooled by my practiced charms."

It was enough to insult and hurt any woman, but Brighid only laughed, and the sound tore at his heart. "I don't think so. Actually, it was the times that you weren't charming, the times that I saw the real you, the part of you no one else sees, that drew me. I'm in love with *you*, Stephen, not some girlish image of you."

Her avowal tore at his insides, and although Stephen wanted nothing more than to turn and pull her down to him, to crush her to him and never let her go, he could not. He desperately tried to think of some way to turn her aside, but he was usually on the other end of the pursuit, and his emotions were rolling and pitching, his gut churning painfully as he clung to his good intentions with the last thread of his being. Finally, he pretended to snore, hoping against hope that she would storm away and leave him be.

But Brighid only laughed again, softly. "I've seen the future, Stephen," she said. "I saw it right after we left Campion. I denied it then, and you may deny it now, but I have seen us together. Whatever lies between us, tis inevitable."

Stephen swallowed a groan as she turned on her heel and went back to her bed. *Destiny again.* And it was up to him to save Brighid from it.

Chapter Eighteen

The next morning, Brighid found that Stephen had noticeably absented himself from their chamber and the hall. Cadwy claimed he was out checking the defenses, but since the manor could hardly have any, Brighid was skeptical. He was avoiding her after last night, and if she wasn't so certain of her own visions, she would probably have died of embarrassment.

How often did Stephen de Burgh refuse an invitation from a woman? Surely, she was one of only a handful who knew that unique humiliation. And, for all her special sight, Brighid couldn't figure out why. His excuses had been feeble, at best, especially when she had felt the passion rage between them more than once. He had to be attracted to her, and she was sure he felt some affection toward her, too. Then, why would he turn his back to her, making a mockery of her laughable efforts at seduction?

Apparently, she was so inept that she had killed whatever desire he once had for her in one fell swoop, Brighid thought with depressing logic. The notion dogged her through the day until she even began to doubt her premonitions. After all, the future was flexible. Perhaps, her images of the two of them together had been altered, and by her own actions!

Finally, exasperated by such thoughts, Brighid decided to go down to the cellar and look for any clues she might have missed among her father's things. Now that she knew there was no Philosopher's Stone or hidden writings, she could search from a fresh perspective. And perhaps, if she opened her senses, she would be able to see something new.

Below, in the quiet of the vaulted chamber, Brighid wandered the area where her father had spent most of his time, at least until Addfwyn arrived. The thought sent Brighid's thoughts twisting down other paths, and she wondered if all that talk about love yesterday had disturbed Stephen. Mayhap he worried that she would try to snare him, she thought suddenly, remembering all too well how she had offered him a love potion.

Brighid cringed, wishing now that she had made no such jest, for she could understand how almost anyone would shy away from a connection with the l'Estranges. Although Stephen had scoffed at such things often enough, he might think she had cast some spell upon him. Brighid sighed, tempted to look into the water for answers, but she knew that was more likely to confuse her further. Besides, the visions she had of herself and Stephen had occurred without any divination aid, more often than not. If only she could see something other than their lovemaking!

Frowning, Brighid walked toward a table piled with books and manuscripts. She knew her father's habits, and someone had rifled these materials. Lifting a translation of *The Emerald Tablet,* she leafed through it, lost in thought, drifting between her memories of the old lore and her present problems. So absorbed was she that she didn't hear anyone approach until a soft voice spoke.

"Mistress l'Estrange?"

Startled, Brighid glanced up, expecting to see Cadwy, but it was a stranger who stood before her, clad in colorful robes. "I was looking for your father, but the manor is deserted...." His words trailed off, and he held out his hands, long and elegant. *The hands of an alchemist.*

"He's dead," Brighid said.

The man, lean and sporting a dark beard, evinced an expression of shock. "I'm sorry. I had no idea! When did this happen? But I have journeyed so far to treat with him!" he said, pausing suddenly to bow. "My humble apologies. I am Maximus Proffitt, a colleague of your father's."

"How do you know me?" Brighid asked.

Proffitt appeared taken aback. "Why, I remember you, of course. Perhaps you remember me, as well?" When Brighid said nothing, he sighed. "Ah, but I was a young man then, an adept serving a greater master."

The words flowed from his tongue eloquently, and he held himself with a certain grace that bespoke his sincerity, yet something about Maximus Proffitt did not ring true. News traveled slowly, so he could be as ignorant of events here as he claimed, but Brighid felt uncomfortable alone with him in the cellar. And, instead of fighting it as she would have in the past, she gave in to the prompting, opening up all of her senses, seeking...

But Brighid had not yet learned how to control her gift, and she swayed as unease washed through her, making her wish for Stephen's calming presence. Discord flooded her in a black wave, emanating from the man in front of her, and she reached for the edge of the table to steady herself. Blinking, Brighid stared at this man and knew he was not what he seemed. Was he one of those who had ransacked the manor, ruthlessly seeking some imagined secret?

"Are you all right?" he asked, solicitously. "I beg your pardon for bringing up such an unpleasant subject when you must be racked with grief." He stepped closer to the table as if to approach her, but Brighid backed away.

His black eyes narrowed, his polite manner more abrupt as he eyed her with dark intent. "What is it, girl? Do you fear me?" he asked, sharply. "I assure you that I came here with the noblest of intentions, to share my work with your father," he explained, more graciously.

But Brighid could see through his smile, and she saw evil: greed and hunger for glory and a reckless arrogance that knew no boundaries, moral or otherwise. "You are wasting your time," she said. "My father made no great discovery other than that of the heart."

"I see," he said, his expression no longer cordial, but cruel. "I have underestimated you, just as I underestimated your father. He has kept his secrets well hidden." Proffitt sighed. "Indeed, I had nearly despaired of my goal, when I heard a rumor that his daughter had returned. Imagine my pleasure and surprise, for I had forgotten your very existence." He paused to study her. "'Twas most unwise of you to come back here, Brighid. Bad for you, but good for me, for now I would have the information I seek."

And suddenly, Brighid was aware of her own danger. So intent had she been upon this stranger and the revelations that came with his arrival, that she had forgotten her own precarious position here alone with him. Where was Cadwy? And Stephen? She sent out a silent plea to him even as she lifted her chin and faced her father's murderer.

"As I said, you are wasting your time, for my father didn't make any great discovery," Brighid said, inching along the edge of the table. But Proffitt stood between her and the stairs. Slowly, Brighid moved behind the next table, where some empty flasks and beakers stood.

"Surely, you don't believe I'm that stupid?" Proffitt asked, ominously. "I am not some fanciful peasant, but a masterful alchemist, far more powerful than your pitiful father! When I heard he had made some momentous discovery, I came here, curious to learn of it, but he was not very accommodating, so I was forced to do away with him."

Brighid flinched at the words, which Proffitt uttered without the slightest remorse. He stepped closer to the table that separated them. "Unfortunately, I found nothing in his tedious writings, and so I returned, thinking he had hidden them away. I even sought out his leman." He paused, to shake his head. "But it appears that you know all this, Brighid dear. So why don't you just give me what I want and avoid any further unpleasantness?"

And in that instant, Brighid knew there would be no reasoning with him, no convincing him that he had done murder and destruction for naught. Her only chance lay in escape, and Brighid calculated it on one level even as she tried to distract him on another, while beneath both, down deep, she thought of Stephen. She had always considered herself sensible and cautious, but how many times had he claimed her reckless? Again, she had proven him right. *I'm sorry, Stephen....*

"Well, I..." Brighid began, hesitantly, as she fingered an empty flask. Lifting it slowly, she appeared to examine it only to bring it down suddenly against the edge of the wood, shattering the top. The bottom remained in her hand, a weapon of sharp glass, which she brandished before her as she slipped from behind the table.

"Do you think to dispatch me with that puny weapon?" Proffitt asked, laughing as she moved along the wall.

"*Perhaps this is more your size.*"

The sound of Stephen's low challenge made Brighid's heart leap, and her senses flooded with his presence, even before she saw him standing behind Proffitt, unsheathing his sword. He had come for her, whether through coincidence or design, and she had the feeling that whatever bound them reached beyond the tangible world.

But Brighid had no time to dwell on such possibilities, for they still faced a murderer. Over Proffitt's shoulder, she saw Stephen incline his head toward her in a gesture for her to move away, lest the villain try to snatch her, and she slipped toward the stairs even as Proffitt slowly turned.

"Who *are* you?" he asked, staring at Stephen with an expression of annoyance.

"I am Stephen de Burgh, and you are a dead man."

"I think not," Proffitt said with a sneer, and he reached into his cloak. Brighid shouted out a warning even as he tossed some kind of dust in Stephen's face, an alchemist's trick. Brighid frantically wondered if she might have to use some tricks of her own, but at the very last moment, Stephen turned his head away, avoiding the blinding mixture, and lunged forward.

"It appears I have underestimated you, a failing of mine of late," Proffitt said. "No mere oafish knight are you. Where do you get your power? Whatever its source, I assure you that we need not be enemies. We can work together. I am a master alchemist. If only I have the stone, I can create as much gold as you will, or perhaps even greater discoveries await us. Just persuade l'Estrange's daughter to give me the information I seek.''

Proffitt was backing around the room toward where Brighid stood on the stairs, but Stephen followed, his face hard and intent, his sword moving in tight circles. ''Brighid doesn't need any rock to transform,'' he said.

His words made Proffitt gape. ''What?'' he asked in a strangled voice.

''Brighid has transformed me, and without the aid of any object whatsoever,'' Stephen said, seriously.

Well, there was that piece of amethyst, Brighid thought wildly, but she wasn't about to argue. Although Stephen prowled the room with a lethal grace, she didn't need special abilities to see that something had happened to him. His perfect hair was mussed and clinging to his neck, and there were marks on his elegant tunic, dark streaks that looked like dirt and maybe even blood.

Although he showed no weakness in his step, Brighid felt fear for him, sharp and piercing, and she glanced around the room, searching for something, anything, she could use against the man who threatened them. In her mind, she catalogued the herbs and plants and elixirs at hand even as she kept one eye on Proffitt.

Having recovered from his surprise, he studied Stephen with a jaundiced look. ''And just what has she changed you into? Funny, but you don't look immortal,'' he said. Then, as if to prove his words, he pulled a dagger, seemingly from nowhere and leapt at Stephen.

Setting aside her own meager weapon, Brighid ran to a nearby table and sorted through the flasks even as she searched her memory. Finally, she grabbed up a distinctive fat-bellied container and lifted it high, letting out a low hiss of relief to see the liquid it held. Grasping the glass tightly in front of her, Brighid whirled around to face the two men, struggling in a death match.

While she frantically tried to see what was happening between the two men, her fingers gripped the stopper, ready to release the contents, but there was no need. Already, Proffitt was slowly sinking to the floor as Stephen rose above him, looking weary and shaky, but victorious.

"Are you all right?" Brighid asked. The words came out in a breathless rush, and she trembled, staring at him for a long moment as if to assure herself of his continued existence.

Stephen nodded. "What is that?" he asked, inclining his head toward the flask she still clutched in an iron grip.

Brighid looked down at the container she had momentarily forgotten. "Oh! Aqua Fortis. I used to make it for my father from a recipe in Jabir's *The Chest of Wisdom.*" At Stephen's blank look, she set the flask aside. "Tis a corrosive mixture," she added. And if she had thought Stephen endangered, she would have tossed it in Proffitt's face without hesitation.

When she turned to Stephen again, Brighid's last desperate efforts at composure gave way. She wanted nothing more than to fling herself against his broad chest, and this time she gave in to her desire. With a strangled sob, she went to him, and his strong arms closed around her. He gathered her to him so tightly that Brighid could feel his thundering heartbeat and knew his own agitation. "I'm sorry. Twas my fault," she whispered.

"Nay, I should have never left you alone. A fine protector I am," Stephen said, his voice rough. He lifted his head to look down at her, his expression thoughtful. "But I knew you were in danger. I knew when, and I knew where, Brighid. I just *knew*."

"Yes," she answered, meeting his serious gaze with her own. "Thank you." He had saved her life thrice over now. Was it any wonder they were bound together?

But such ruminations could wait, for Brighid sensed that Stephen was not quite as well as he would have her believe. Even as he held her, he swayed on his feet, and she steadied him as best she could. "You're hurt! Did he cut you? Where?" Brighid asked, searching his warrior's body for wounds.

"Nay, he did not, but I have a few more scrapes for you to tend," Stephen said. "Three ruffians, his henchmen, I assume, came after me in the bailey."

Brighid drew in a harsh breath. "Where is Cadwy?"

"Nursing his own wounds, I suspect," Stephen said. "When I was attacked, the old fool came running out of the barns, screaming like a lunatic, with some villagers behind him, all of them armed with farm implements." He paused, then burst out with a laugh that ended in a wheeze.

Brighid felt her chest constrict with worry. "Come along then. Let's have a look at you," she said, and for once, Stephen did not argue as she helped him up the stairs and out of the cellar.

Stephen sank down on the edge of the bed with a sigh, weariness washing over him, along with a relief so strong it nearly stole his breath. Brighid was all right. They were alive, and the villains had been vanquished. Yet he remembered too well his alarm when he was attacked and his ensuing fear for Brighid, acerbated later when he sensed she was in danger. It was a feeling he never hoped to know again.

Reason told him that he had imagined that sharp, clear foreboding. After all, any fool would suspect foul doings afoot when faced with three ruffians. But Stephen recalled things long buried, memories of his childhood, and a time when Anne had asked him if he was aware of things like his father. *If he knew whether she would die....*

Stephen closed his eyes against the recollection, and when he opened them again, Brighid was there, alive and well and making him forget all else. He let her help him off with his mail even as he wondered why he had ever needed a squire. But when she lifted his tunic over his head, as well, he blustered in protest.

"I need to tend your wounds," Brighid said, tossing the garment aside with a determined look.

Stephen might be tired and sore, but he was not incapacitated, and he knew that sitting there on the edge of the bed in nothing but his braies was not a good idea. Although Brighid barely glanced at his naked chest, warmth rushed through him that had nothing to do with the nearby fire. His blood raced and his body stiffened.

"See? Nothing except a few bruises," Stephen said, attempting to rise, but Brighid halted him with a hand upon his chest. Startled at the sudden caress, Stephen sucked in a breath. It was a casual gesture, not one of seduction, and yet her fingers touched his skin, the tips resting against his nipple. Normally, he could call up some glib comment to relieve the tension, but his tongue cleaved to the roof of his mouth.

As he sat there, unmoving, Brighid leaned down and reached for something. She had a pail of water she had warmed over the fire and to his astonishment, she brought up a cloth and laid it against his neck. He blinked, stunned, as he, the master of all things sexual, had never known anything so erotic. Women had washed him before many times, but never like this, never so selflessly, and never had the woman been *Brighid*.

With an effort, Stephen found his power of speech. "This really isn't necessary," he mumbled.

"I have to cleanse away the dirt to find out where you've been hurt," Brighid said. But it was his tunic that was soiled, not his skin. All she was doing was washing away the sweat, or causing more of it, Stephen thought, as he felt a bead erupt on his forehead.

Pausing to wet the cloth again, she brought it down across his chest in one smooth, exotic stroke, and Stephen shuddered, his body reacting painfully to her ministrations, whether medicinal or something else. And in that moment, he knew he had to act, lest his will be overcome. Lifting a hand, he snared her wrist. "Don't, Brighid. *Please,*" he murmured.

Her gaze flew to his, her startlement obvious, along with a hurt that it pained him to see, especially when he was the cause. "Why?" she asked, her head still held high.

"Because you deserve better," Stephen answered. He spit out the words, hating them, hating the truth, but determined not to let her settle for anything less.

"There is no one better than you," she answered, her green gaze as strong and as deep as the sea, and Stephen closed his eyes against what he saw there. Surely, no wound could make him feel this agony, as if his very heart was being torn from his body. Even the feel of her pulse beneath his fingers made him ache, so he released her wrist and drew a shaky breath, forcing himself to look at her once more.

"I have nothing except a fancy name—little money, no property, and hardly any honor. You know that," Stephen said. When she would have argued, he lifted a hand, trying to hold on to what little composure he had left. "I am selfish enough that I would marry you despite all that, but there is something else," he said, his voice dipping precariously. He looked her directly in the eye and spoke. "I cannot give you children."

Her beautiful face reflected her surprise, and then a gentle admonishment. "And how do you know that?"

Stephen turned his head away and ran a hand through his hair in frustration. "Faith, Brighid, do you know how many women I have bedded? And not one of them—*not one of them*—has ever conceived."

Brighid didn't even flinch at the bald declaration. "Perhaps you just needed to find the right person for that, as well as for your unusual communication," she said.

Stephen snorted. He could easily convince himself that he had imagined that whole business about Brighid being in danger in the cellar, old memories notwithstanding. But, as if reading his mind, she gave him a quizzical look. "Unless you are denying that, too, now?"

Stephen frowned, uneasy. "All right, so maybe there's some kind of special thing between us, but don't expect me to start dousing," he said, with a sharp glance toward the pail of water.

Brighid laughed, and Stephen felt something in his chest expand at the sound, so incongruous considering that their conversation was desperate, their situation hopeless. How ironic that after his surfeit of women, he would find the one he could love, only to be denied her. And, at last, when he had a reason to live, he must refuse it.

"Perhaps I should have you gaze into the water, for that might ease your mind," Brighid said softly. But Stephen could not even look at her, knowing as he did that nothing would ever give him ease. Unheeding of his silence, Brighid stepped closer. "One can see many things there. For instance, do you know what I saw when I fetched this pail?" she asked.

"It doesn't matter," Stephen said, too lost in his own despair to care about any hokus-pokus.

"So you speak now, but what would you say if I told you I had seen our children?"

At her words, Stephen felt as if his heart stopped beating. He jerked toward her, his gaze questioning, but she only smiled, that sweet, *knowing* smile he had come to recognize. His breath caught and held as he stared at her, not daring to believe, and yet, when he looked into her eyes, he knew she spoke the truth.

Stephen released his pent-up air in a rush. "Then, I could hardly object, could I?" he asked, not realizing what he said, only aware that the last barrier that stood between him and Brighid had fallen by the wayside.

"Unless you're wary of marrying a l'Estrange?" she asked, suddenly cautious.

Stephen put his hands on her waist and urged her between his knees. "Actually, I find it very appealing. Your power arouses me," he whispered, stopping her gasp of surprise with his mouth. His lips covered hers and he gained entry, seeking and taking, even though he would never have his fill of her, no matter should he live forever.

They kissed, a deep, endless communion that heated his blood and flooded his soul. Emotions coursed through him, wave after wave, but instead of running from them, Stephen embraced them—kinship and love and lust long held in check. That desire no longer need be contained, and Stephen gave it full rein, falling back onto the bed and taking her with him. He had removed his boots before, and she kicked off her slippers, her slender limbs entwining with his as she lay full upon him.

Sensations bombarded him: the sight of her above him, her beauteous hair falling all around; the light press of her breasts against his bare chest; the texture of her drab clothing as he stroked her supple curves; and the sound of her breath, soft and erratic, between kisses. Burying his face in her hair, Stephen drew in the sweet scent of her, filling his lungs, his very being, with the essence of Brighid.

His need knew no boundaries, no more denials, and his body shuddered in urgency. Impatient, he turned on his side, so she lay facing him, and drew away her gown. His hands were trembling, and Stephen stared at them in wonder, for they were not those of the notorious seducer. He had not fumbled like this since his youth, Stephen thought, only to shake his head ruefully as he realized he had *never* fumbled like this. Because he had never felt like this.

From his first bout of lovemaking to his last, he had been detached, skilled at giving physical pleasure and taking a certain amount as well, but never sharing of himself. Now, for the first time, his whole being was involved, mind, body and soul aware and interconnected. And hungry for Brighid.

It was a force so strong that even though he told himself to slow down, Stephen could not stay the thundering of his blood. Ordinarily, he would have teased and aroused his partner through her clothing, but this was *Brighid,* and he had to see her. *Now.* And so he drew up her shift as well, drinking in the sight of her like one parched.

She was beautiful, her skin flawless and her breasts gently curved, with pale pink tips. Her waist was narrow, her legs slender, and between them lay a nest of soft, blond curls. With trembling fingers, Stephen slipped off her hose, then slid to the floor to remove his own, along with his braies.

She was lying across the width of the bed, unheeding of her nakedness, staring at him, and when Stephen saw her gaze dip and hold, he reminded himself she was a maiden. But, instead of restraining him, the knowledge only aroused him further. She was made for him in all ways, and he would make her his, for always.

"Brighid." Stephen called out her name, a hoarse cry as he moved over her, pressing her down into the blankets and cupping her face in his hands. "I take you to be my wife," he said, his voice rough with emotion. She nodded, as if too overcome to speak, but Stephen saw her answer in her sea green eyes before he covered her mouth with his own.

Stephen had never said the words in his life, and now he couldn't stop them. "I love you," he chanted as he discovered each freckle across her nose. "I love you," he whispered against her breast. "I love you," he mouthed against her belly. Every sensation was as new...a wondrous, aching pleasure beyond any he had ever known, building with a reckless abandon he had never allowed.

And Brighid urged him on, running her hands over his back and flanks, placing tender kisses on his throat and his shoulder and his chest. When he parted her legs, she gave no protest, and, at last, Stephen could do what he had wanted on that morning in the croft when he had awakened in her lap.

He tasted her, and she was so soft and slick and sweet that he felt dizzy, drunk upon her essence. Gripping her pale thighs, he lifted her to his eager mouth until she writhed and whimpered within his grasp, clinging to him even as she begged him to release her.

Stephen smiled wickedly against her, for hadn't he once predicted such a fate for her? But he had never imagined his own frantic response. He felt out of control, and when, at last, she fell back, spent, upon the bed, Stephen knew he could not wait much longer. *Now*, he thought, lest he embarrass himself, but he paused, loath to cause Brighid even the slightest pain.

"I don't want to hurt you," he said, the words a hoarse, broken whisper. He had initiated maidens before, and knew well the ways in which to ease them, but this was no nameless female. Even as need drove him, emotion stayed him, for this act was beyond all his forgettable past experience. This was his wife, and for the first time in his life, Stephen was going to make love.

Brighid watched him, her sea eyes hazy with repletion and a certain witchy eroticism. Then she lifted a leg to graze his side. "I won't let you hurt me," she said. "Do your worst, my lord de Burgh."

Groaning at her challenge, Stephen raised himself above her, intent upon going slowly, but at the first warm, welcoming touch of Brighid's body, he lost all mastery over himself. He had never felt so *much*, and he could not hold back. A harsh cry erupting from his throat, Stephen thrust heavily, burying himself inside her as far as he could go. And when she closed around him, he could only cry out again while his body jerked, driving deep, his seed spilling forth as shudders racked him.

Dazed, Stephen collapsed on top of her, his heart thundering, his breath a ragged rumble. He was vaguely aware of his own failing and knew that he should be shamed by this unheard-of performance, but he was so consumed with bliss that he could not rouse himself to feel anything else. And this was Brighid, after all. She murmured sweet words in his ear, and with a sigh, Stephen gave himself into her keeping.

For a long while he lay with her, unwilling to sever the connection of their bodies, but finally, afraid he was crushing her with his weight, Stephen rolled to the side, taking her with him. Feelings, hot and fresh and new, welled up in him until he felt he might weep like a babe, his joy was so great.

What would Brighid say to that, Stephen wondered ruefully, even as she stirred in his arms. Her fingers, splayed against his chest, stroked the hair there, stopping to linger over nipples that grew hard at her urging. Startled, Stephen caught his breath and held it. "And what do you think you're doing?" he asked.

"Exploring," she whispered as she dipped her head to press inexpert kisses along his ribs, her hair gliding over his skin like the brush of an angel's wings. Stephen shuddered. He had never felt anything so erotic in all his life. "Very well. Work your l'Estrange witchery on me," he said, falling onto his back and spreading his arms in invitation.

Brighid's hand slid lower, to where a certain part of his body was ready and eager for more. "I think something's already been transformed," she teased. And Stephen laughed, enjoying this new playfulness in his love. *His wife.* The knowledge filled him with satisfaction beyond anything he had ever known, but roused his pro-

tective instincts, as well, especially since her fingers
were drifting perilously close to his sex.

"Are you all right?" he asked. "I was rough, heed-
less. I—"

Brighid stopped his speech with her slender fingers.
"Twas wonderful, and besides, I know well your skills,
for I have had enough visions to learn that your reputation is not undeserved."

Accepting the business about the visions without a
qualm, Stephen frowned at the mention of his past, so
distant and bleak now that he didn't want to examine it
at all. But he needed to do so, to explain himself as best
he could, and to give Brighid his vow. He drew her
close.

"About all that," he said, slowly. "The things I
did...I don't want you to think that I pursued women
for the sake of conquest, for I did not. I sought the pleasure to be had with them, yes, but also the comfort they
gave me when the night was dark and lonely and I had
only my demons for company," Stephen said, admitting
what he had never before dared to voice.

"I felt no love for these women, but I gave them
pleasure. And though I appreciate what they did for me,
that part of my life is over," Stephen said, with purpose
and promise.

"I know of none of them, nor care," Brighid replied.
"Except perhaps Gaenor."

The name meant nothing to Stephen, and he tensed,
searching his mind in vain until Brighid prompted him.
"The widow at Glenerron."

Stephen relaxed as he let his palm slide over Brighid's
slender back. "Nay. She was not one of them."

"Really?" Brighid asked. "Twas much talk of you
together." She had resumed her exploration of his chest,

and he closed his eyes at the sweet pleasure it engendered.

"I found her in my bed that night, but tossed her from it. Perhaps, she, too, possessed some special insight, for she accused me of lusting after you most inappropriately," Stephen said, lifting his lashes to grin at Brighid, but his smile faded as he met her gaze, his emotions still running high. "Twas you I wanted that night and each night since and every night to be. There is no one else for me now, nor will there ever be."

Her sea eyes turned misty, and Brighid laid her face against his chest. "Surely, there will be great gnashing of teeth and mourning when the world learns of your vow," she said.

Stephen laughed, envisioning his family's shock at the news, then paused, thoughtfully. "I consider us married already, but I suspect my father would have other wishes in the matter."

"Hmm?" Brighid murmured, snuggling closer.

"Well, Dunstan married in haste away from home, and my father was not able to travel all the way to see Geoff or Simon wed. So..."

"So you think he would like to have a ceremony and celebration at Campion," Brighid said.

Stephen nodded, though why he should care about pleasing his father in any manner, he didn't know. But he supposed he owed the man something for sending him to escort Brighid. *His wife.*

And, in the end, it was she who provided the explanation. "He'll be so proud of you," Brighid said simply, proving once again that she knew Stephen better than he knew himself.

Epilogue

Brighid carefully emptied a flask and placed it into a nearby chest. She had told Stephen she wanted to put away her father's things before they returned to Campion, just in case anyone else should come seeking his secrets, so she was back in the cellar, deeply immersed in alchemy once more.

Setting aside some of the herbs and plants for healing, Brighid had tossed away the rest and was now packing up the implements that had once loomed so large in her life. Lest she become too lost in the past, Stephen prowled the room, poking at things and making caustic comments that quickly delivered her from any unpleasant memories.

"Perhaps we can donate all these instruments to a priory," Brighid said, wondering what to do with all the containers. "I've heard that some monks study the elements, as well as making various elixirs and wines."

Stephen snorted. "I don't think even I would drink anything brewed in these," he said, holding up a piece of glasswork that resembled two bulbous wombs.

Brighid laughed, pausing to enjoy the sight of him here in her old home, his tall, strong body seeming to ward away any sadness or ill. He was such a complex man, literal-minded and sharp-tongued, but at the same time so deeply sensitive that he accepted all that she was and loved her for it. Brighid shook her head, still amazed at what had happened between them.

"Do you think we could come back here, someday?" she asked. Although she effected a casual tone, Stephen was already too attuned to her moods to be fooled. He turned away from a fat vessel to eye her curiously.

"You mean you don't want to live at Campion?"

"Oh, Campion! It's beautiful and luxurious and all, but…" Brighid let her words trail away, hesitant to continue, lest she insult her husband's home.

Stephen lifted his brows slightly before taking pity on her. "Yes, it is all those things, *but* it belongs to my father," he said. "I wonder if I shall ever get used to you knowing my mind better than I do," he muttered, flashing her a rueful grin, which Brighid acknowledged with one of her own.

"I know this isn't much," she said, nodding toward the once-proud manor above their heads. "But it is mine. And, of course, I shall someday inherit my aunts'—"

Stephen cut her off with raised palm and a look of alarm. "I am *not* living with your aunts, even if my father should toss me from the castle!" Brighid bit back a smile as she carefully set a vial on the floor.

"I suppose we could spend part of the year here, once I am assured that there is no chance of war," Stephen said, thoughtfully. "But we would need servants and villeins to serve the place and plow, and sheep, for the land won't support many crops."

Implicit in his tone was the need for money, which it didn't appear they possessed. If her father had left her any, it had no doubt been stolen by Proffitt and his men,

unless Cadwy knew of something. Brighid resolved to
speak with him before they left.

As if reading her thoughts, Stephen glanced around
the vaulted room. "I'm surprised that they didn't do
more damage down here," he said.

"I'm not," Brighid answered, following his gaze.
"An alchemist would have a certain reverence for another's tools. Plus, he didn't want to disturb what might
end up being the secret he sought," she said, pointing
to various liquids that remained untouched in their containers. "I'm guessing that he let his ruffians look up-
stairs, while he conducted a more careful search here."

Stephen nodded, moving to one of the sooty walls. "I
guess he did try to chisel into the stones. I'm surprised
he didn't bring the whole manor down on our heads."
Glancing up at the supports, Stephen stalked around the
room and into the center, where a huge sign of the zodiac
was carved into the floor. Halting there, he bent over.
"He even tried to pry these up," Stephen said, reaching
out to touch one of the tiles.

"Oh, I doubt that. Such deliberate mutilation might
invoke powerful forces," Brighid said. Setting aside a
bolt-head, she walked around the table to see what had
attracted Stephen's attention. Naturally, he was crouched
over one astrological sign in particular, Virgo the Virgin,
whose chest he was examining with interest.

"Oh, that's just my heart," Brighid said, with a smile,
when she saw what he was fingering. "When I was
small, I thought Virgo, being the only female, must be
me."

The look Stephen gave her under thick lashes was so
sultry and seductive that Brighid shivered from the heat,
the memory of the loss of her maidenhood implicit in
his dark eyes. She swallowed, tempted to go to him right

here and now, so strong was the allure of this man she loved.

"Your heart?" he prompted, dark brows lifted as if in query, while the curve of his erotic mouth told he knew full well what plagued her.

Later, in bed, Brighid promised herself, she would do her best to make the master of seduction lose every shred of his arrogance, a feat which she had accomplished aplenty in the last few days. Meanwhile, she drew in a shaky breath and tried to concentrate on her answer.

"However, the lady, Virgo, that is, looked so sad that once I tried to draw a smile on her face and a heart upon her breast," Brighid explained. "Father was *not* pleased. I think I was banished from the cellar for a month."

Stephen didn't laugh at the tale as she had expected. Instead, his expression grew pensive as he stared down at the crude etching, his beautiful masculine hands tracing the lines. "Search your heart," he murmured.

Brighid recognized the advice Addfwyn had given her, but she did not see how it applied to a childish drawing. She stepped closer, uttering a soft cry of dismay when Stephen began to pull at what appeared to be a loose corner of tile. The dire warnings of her father, ingrained after her youthful indiscretion, returned only to be usurped by a fresher memory.

Search your heart. Brighid drew in a sharp breath. The words had also been in her father's missive, but she thought he had been beguiling her with guilt. Never had she imagined some message there beyond his wish for her to return home. Now, however, it looked as though Stephen had discovered what she, for all her l'Estrange abilities, had not seen.

Reaching for a sharp tool, he slid it into the small crevice and pushed, and suddenly the floor erupted.

Brighid stepped back as Stephen lifted the top of a trap-
door cleverly concealed in the tiles. It had been hidden
in plain sight, so to speak, but were the contents undisturbed? "I wonder if Proffitt found this," Brighid whispered, leaning forward, but her voice died away as she
caught her breath.

"Obviously not," Stephen said, dryly.

There, secreted tightly in the narrow opening, lay bars
of what looked like gold, gleaming brightly in the torch-
light, a surfeit of the perfect, unblemished metal so
sought by alchemists. Astonished, Brighid stared at Stephen, who stared right back, his brows lifting halfway
up his forehead.

Brighid swallowed hard. "Perhaps he used it for his
study, if it is, in fact, gold," Brighid said, expressing
her doubts.

"Oh, I'm pretty sure it's gold," Stephen said, a bemused expression on his face. "And more than enough
to set your manor to rights and keep us in comforts for
the rest of our lives."

"There's an old Roman mine nearby," Brighid said,
searching for an explanation. "Perhaps he found it and
eked out the last of the ore."

Stephen shrugged. "He probably was just hiding his
wealth from the threat of the crown."

Brighid knew all were reasonable possibilities, yet
when she stared down at the gold, it was hard not to
wonder about its source.

"You don't think he actually found a way to…?"
Stephen murmured, as if reading her thoughts.

"No," Brighid answered, shaking her head vehemently.

"No," Stephen echoed, even more firmly as he met
her gaze. And yet, when she looked into the deep brown

eyes of this man she had come to love against all odds, Brighid realized that anything was possible.

Even magic.

*   *   *   *   *